A Taste For
Money

A Taste For
Money

A novel based on the true story of a dirty Boston cop

Peter Mars

Commonwealth Publishing
Boston, Massachusetts

Manufactured in the United States of America

Library of Congress Catalog Card Number: 99-74333

ISBN: 0-9664475-1-4

Book design and production by Tabby House

Cover design: Pearl and Associates

Cover photo: Michael Glover

Commonwealth Publishing
P. O. Box 1234
Hyannis, MA 02601

DEDICATION

This book is dedicated to Frank Hackett, former Sheriff of Kennebec County, Maine, the best chief law enforcement officer that this county has ever had. Frank was devoted to upholding the law and to initiating new and innovative programs designed to keep young people out of jail.

He was a former city police officer who developed his innate abilities to take small ideas into great manifestations. His overwhelming support of the Boys and Girls Clubs allowed for significant progress as a way to keep kids off the streets and out of the penal system.

His creativity and charisma provided the means by which Maine's newest correctional facility was constructed—a model of modern incarceration that removed the stigma of an antiquated dungeon.

ACKNOWLEDGMENTS

I take this opportunity to thank the following people for their help recalling incidents that were integral in the composition of this book.

Francesco Gianni for his candid facts concerning his years operating a gambling parlor; Renee Lafayette for her very graphic details, which made my face turn crimson as she related them to me; John Cologgi for his recollection of the early years at Old Orchard Beach; *Seamus O'Neill* who refused to answer my questions but whose facial expressions told me more than he would ever have admitted; Nathan Berkowitz for his openness as he still believes marijuana should be legalized for medicinal purposes; *Tony Marcello* for his input on the Patriarca years; Frank Devlin for his recollections about *Joseph O'Fallon* and *Roger Gallagher*, and *Gloria Petrillo* for her memory of some sensitive issues.

Some names are in italics for reasons of protection, they are not the actual names of the people involved. As famed writer, Harold Robbins, stated in some of his works, "All my characters are real. They are written as fiction to protect the guilty."

FOR DAVID E. MARS

A professional in every sense of the word. A believer in all the things that are good, right and morally correct. Recruited off the campus of Northeastern University to work for the CIA and later to take a position with the City of New York Parks Police as he continued his education at Columbia University—changes that opened up his perspectives to a world filled with corruption and illegal activities—the real world.

Appreciation

There are many people to whom I am sincerely grateful for their assistance in the mechanical areas for putting together this book. First, to photographer Michael Glover for his contribution to the cover and for helping to organize the pictures in the book. Second, to Jesse and Judy Cook for the use of their home in the gathering of information and the reconstruction of events. Third, to Gary Hauger whose assitance in photography was invaluable. Fourth, to Mike Poulin, chief of security at the Osceola County Courthouse in Kissimmee, Florida for all his help when he was a part of the Kennebec Sheriff's Office in Maine and for the availability of his computer (once again) while I was in Florida.

I also express my most sincere thanks to several members of the Boston Police Department: Bruce Blake from the office of the commissioner, Kevin Foley from fleet services administration and John Dow, also in fleet services administration, but who ought to be in public relations.

And last, most important of all, to my wife, Margery, for accompanying me on so many interviews of the characters in this book, and who helped me keep my perspective during times of discouragement.

Foreword

The following is written by Mike Burns, a man who has a fierce passion for young people and who has an equally fierce disdain for that which destroys young lives—drug abuse.

Mike lost a youngster to drugs years ago. His son's death caused him to join forces with his close friend, Frank Hackett, and together they put on a program to educate school children and young adults as to the overwhelming negative influence of drug experimentation and the subsequent losses that can result from drug use and abuse.

"My dad was a policeman in the city of Augusta, the capital of Maine, so I knew what a policeman's life was like. I understood the stress and the anxiety he suffered on many occasions. I think it was through what I saw that I had the greatest respect for policemen. And, because they were like my dad, I placed all my trust in policemen.

"When I see that some of the people in law enforcement have gone bad, I find a very sour taste in my soul—something I cannot explain other than the hurt one realizes when something that should be so right can go so wrong. When I couple that hurt with something very personal, I wonder what has happened to our world. My own son was lost to an addiction to drugs. Some people know the pain of the death of a youngster because of the influence of this terrible power. There is no feeling on earth any worse than this. Then, when I hear that a policeman, who has gone bad, gets involved with selling drugs, it is like a two-edged sword. The sinking depression from one aspect is awful enough; the total loss caused by such complete malfeasance destroys one's faith in a system that should be close to perfection.

"My dad, were he still alive, would be devastated to see what corruption has taken place in positions that should command the utmost in confidence. I am only glad that in his day there was a higher degree of morality and not the great enticement to succumb to such temptations."

PROLOGUE

What makes a good man go bad? This is not a new phenomenon. The thought has haunted many people for centuries.

Is it worse when a person who has changed so drastically is a police officer, a keeper of the peace, a person charged with upholding the law, a person who above all others should be trustworthy?

Over the years, there have been stories written about rogue cops who have taken bribes, stolen money or goods, performed indecent and lewd sexual acts, dealt in drugs or used them, have been guilty of assault and battery, or have gone so far as to commit murder. In general, these were cops who were bad from the beginning. They never should have gone on the job. But what about the ones whose chemical make-up, whose psyche, has undergone a change while on the job? Is there a legitimate reason for this metamorphosis, one that can not be foretold? If that is the case, what can be done to reverse this action? What can be done to prevent someone who begins with the best of intentions from entering a life of corruption?

The following story is true. It encompasses the life of one such man whose goodness turned a complete opposite and, through the taste for money, made him the worst example of police presence.

What made him think he could get away with such contempt for the law he was sworn to uphold? Who was he to think he would not get caught? After all, everyone knows "crime doesn't pay"

. . . or does it?

INTRODUCTION

Kennebec County Sheriff's Office
Augusta, Maine

August 16

Michelle St. Clair, "Mimi" to all of us at work, came rushing into my office. She was the communications sergeant at the sheriff's department.

"Pete," she said, "Mike's off at a shooting at Great Pond in Belgrade. One subject is deceased. Mike's requesting someone from administration to go out there."

Sgt. Michael Poulin was a patrol supervisor and a senior deputy sheriff in our organization.

"Give me some details and directions and, while you're getting those, I'll advise the sheriff," I responded.

As Mimi left my office, I entered the office of Sheriff Frank Hackett and told him what we had and that Mimi was coming back with some information.

"We'll take my car," Sheriff Hackett said.

As he headed down to his vehicle I grabbed the computer print-out from Mimi who had just reentered my office. I told her to get on the radio and let Mike know that we were en route.

****

As the sheriff and I headed toward Belgrade Lakes, I observed two things: first, the increase in radio traffic as more of our deputies were responding to the location; and second, how quickly the news media picked up on our activity—we passed several television station vans going in our same direction.

The blue lights and siren on the sheriff's unmarked car gave us swift passage through the mid-morning traffic.

I was surprised, as we approached the yellow barrier tape emblazoned with the words, SHERIFF'S LINE—DO NOT CROSS, that there were news people already setting up their camera equipment. As we entered the "protected zone," Sergeant Poulin came up and, speaking quickly, told us that he had secured the area and that we could enter the house through the side door which had been left open by the wife of the deceased. He said that the body was on the first landing going up the stairs to the second floor. He also said that the wife of the deceased had admitted shooting her husband even before Mike had an opportunity to advise her of her constitutional rights. She was presently in her neighbor's back yard. Another deputy was standing near her. Technically, she was in his custody at this point in time but this would not appear evident to her nor to anyone else who might observe them. Sometimes, subtlety works to the advantage of an investigation.

The body was slumped over in the corner of the landing. There were five obvious bullet wounds. One was just beneath the right eye. The second had penetrated the neck and exited through the back near the spine just above the left shoulder blade. The cartridge was embedded in the wall. The third bullet was to the right of the heart. The fourth one had gone right through the belly button and the fifth one had removed his right testicle. A sixth bullet missed the body completely and was also buried in the wall. It is possible that the order in which the bullets entered the body was the reverse of this as the recoil of a large-caliber gun will elevate the weapon as each shot explodes. Also, the fact that the deceased was sitting in a large pool of blood would indicate that the heart had still been pumping and caused the blood to flow freely from the lower extremity. Where there was not much blood exiting from the point of entry in each of the upper parts of the body, it must be assumed that the heart stopped shortly after the bullet nearest to that organ had expanded upon impact. A great deal of trauma had taken place as the heavy caliber bullet ripped a significant section of the heart and had blown it out through the back of the body along with a large chunk of the lower skull from the bullet which pierced the area beneath the right eye. There was an enormous pool of blood in which the victim sat. No doubt it was as a result of the flow which was released from the area of his groin. The blood had begun to take on a thickening texture; such viscosity not unusual with prolonged exposure to the air.

Next to the body was a kitchen knife, the type used for carving meat. It was clean. Odd, I thought, where so much blood had been spilled from the bullet wounds and which formed a spatter both in front of and beyond where the knife lay. Even more odd when the knife was later moved and blood droplets had been discovered underneath where the knife had been.

I went outside to see the wife who was seated on a log next to her neighbor. It was fairly clear which one was the wife as she had her hands up to her face and was crying as the other female comforted her.

I introduced myself and reiterated the Miranda warning, which I was sure Mike had given to her—even after she had blurted out her admission. I asked her what had happened. She raised her head just a bit and moved her hands down so that they covered only her nostrils and mouth. She inhaled deeply through her nose and mumbled, almost in a whisper at first, between her hands, "Oh, god, how could this have happened? He came after me with that knife . . . I was so scared . . . I ran upstairs. I knew he kept that gun in the night table. It . . . it's just that . . . oh, I don't *know*. . . ." She pushed the last word out with a loud emphasis.

"Why did he come after you with the knife?" I asked.

"We had a fight." She uttered the words abruptly. Then she made a somewhat guttural sound. "Uchhhh . . ." she said and then continued. "His *eyes* . . . that look in his eyes. I've never seen him that way before. His whole face was red and his eyes were like dark black holes. I told him to stop but he kept coming toward me. It was like he wasn't even hearing me and . . . and . . . I was screaming at him to stop!"

I asked her where he had gotten the knife and what they were fighting about. She said that she knew about an affair he was having with a young girl who worked for him.

She dropped her hands. "At first he denied it but I told him I knew." The expression on her face changed and she became intense. "I saw them together last weekend. I saw what they did! That's when he walked away toward the kitchen and returned with that knife." Again, there was a transformation in her demeanor. She raised one hand to her forehead as she lowered her head downward. Once more her voice had softened to a whisper. "I . . . I couldn't believe he was coming after me with that knife. I was so scared."

As I continued with my preliminary inquiry, she suddenly became more aware of her situation. Her neighbor had excused herself from where we were standing as Lt. Kevin Cookson, chief investigator for the sheriff's office, approached us. Once the neighbor was out of earshot, Kevin began his examination of her story. He is very skilled as a detective and before long he had gained her confidence. Then, without any warning, he fired questions at her, which were almost accusatory in their content. She stammered as she tried to take a moment before answering them but Kevin was not allowing her time to concoct something other than the truth.

As he pressed for immediate responses, she became frustrated and started to cry. It was a defensive response, which soon became amplified with stories about her husband being involved with gun-running and drug trafficking. She was desperately trying to take the onus off of herself while rationalizing her extreme action against the man she married.

It was at this point that she started to involve her next door neighbor, an ex-cop from Boston, as a conspirator in her husband's activities. As she spoke, I made notes that would lead into the story that follows.

PETER J. MARS
Chief of Administrative Services

CHAPTER 1

Richard Cardinal Cushing had just been elevated from archbishop of Boston to the second highest position in the Catholic Church; only the pope held the ultimate rank next to God himself.

With this most respected of ecclesiastical standings, the power the cardinal wielded became enormous in a city whose population was largely Irish and Italian and, as such, belonged to that particular faith.

During this era, it was on orders of the priesthood that churches of other faiths were off-limits to anyone who wanted to avoid the scourge of hell. So intimidating was this restriction that Catholic children would automatically cross the street in order not to pass in front of any Protestant house of worship. Parents were urged not to allow their youngsters access to activities held at the local YMCA or any other non-Catholic youth organization. The differences between Protestants and Catholics had become as widespread in Boston as they had become in Northern Ireland, and many of the Boston Irish had their roots in Eire, the Irish Free State. There was a bitterness that existed over many centuries, the cause of which was long ago lost in history.

Cardinal Cushing tried to accomplish two things during his tenure. The first was to continue building up the Roman Catholic Church in Massachusetts as a powerful religious institution, and the second, to erase some of the tension created over the years between Protestants and Catholics.

Cardinal Cushing also worked wondrous feats for those deemed to be the hard-working faithful within the church. With his penchant for publicity and his many established connections to a very influential and effective radio, television and newspaper media, his charisma opened doors for up-and-coming politicians as well as wealthy businessmen, whose desire was beyond their present experience. Not all of those whom he helped were Catholic, either. Many a Brookline or Newton Jew or Beacon Hill Brahmin Protestant received the graciousness of the cardinal's favors in exchange for some later-to-be-cashed-in "chips." And his connections to the Kennedys were a definite plus; a plus which brought his name to the nation and the world when he was asked to deliver the invocation at President John Kennedy's inauguration in 1960.

Joseph O'Fallon had been an altar boy in the church where Cushing had previously served as pastor. When he had reached the age of twenty-one, he applied to the Boston Police Department for a job as a patrolman. He had taken the Massachusetts Civil Service exam and had scored high. His next step was an interview before representatives of the department and several city officials. What made for his immediate placement, above anything else he might have said or done, was a letter of recommendation written and signed by none other than Richard Cardinal Cushing.

* * *

Joseph began his career as a cadet trainee along with a number of other young men who were mostly of Irish and Italian descent—all practicing Catholics. The latter was almost an unwritten requirement for anyone who wanted to become a part of this department, which nearly two-hundred years earlier was almost exclusively Protestant and very anti-Catholic.

When his class graduated from training, the rookies received their assignments and reported to their specific posts. They were prepared as best they could be for nothing more than the proper filling out of paperwork and how to use their .38 caliber firearm, handcuffs and brute force. The real training came out on the streets where no books or teachers could ever truly explain or accurately mimic the events of actual experience. Every new cop walked a beat and practiced community policing—a concept that was not to be formalized for another twenty-five years.

Joseph's training officer was Ignatius "Red" Halloran, an Irish cop who had been on the job some twenty years and was called "Red" because of a crop of brilliant red hair in his youth, which over the years, had become pure white. He was still called "Red" as he despised the name Ignatius, first of all, because in his growing up years the neighborhood kids all referred to him as "Iggy," a nickname he hated, and secondly, because Red was the name he had been known by ever since he joined the force. There was a time in his life he even considered changing his name officially to Red Halloran, but his mother had loved the saintly name she had given him after her Dublin-born grandfather and would have surely suffered emotionally had he changed it in any way.

Red knew the streets like the back of his hand. Over the years he had seen a number of changes take place in his beloved Dorchester, once predominantly Irish but now becoming exclusively black. He opted to make a transfer to West Roxbury where there were more of his "own people" as he called them, but because of a conflict between himself and his commanding officer, Captain Edmund Doherty, he never got the change he so desired. No one knew the real story behind the conflict, but rumors had passed through the station house over the years that they had been in competition for a promotion to sergeant when Red discovered that Doherty was receiving payoffs for allowing gambling in their district. Red's biggest mistake was threatening to blow the whistle on Doherty.

Red mentioned his concerns to a detective he had often confided in when something was on his mind and he needed advice. Bill McInerney had that kind of face with a beguiling smile that almost said "trust me, I'm on your side," was soft spoken, and was a good listener. He was an effective cop. Through the years, his countenance gave perpetrators a feeling that they could open up to him and admit things they would never have said had they been in an interview room with any other investigator. He had been responsible for solving more cases than any other detective in the division; a feat, which he was very proud of but never allowed his pride to show in front of those with whom he worked. That was, perhaps, another reason Red placed his trust in Bill.

What Red did not know was that Edmund Doherty was the reason Bill had been promoted to detective some years before Red ever had become a cop.

* * *

Back then, Edmund was a rookie who had stumbled across a burglary in progress while checking doors on a warehouse in Boston's South End. Being alone, he knew not to try anything on his own, but ran to the nearest call-box and rang the station for assistance. Portable radios had not yet become one of the policeman's vital pieces of equipment.

Bill was the first officer on the scene. Having been a street cop for awhile, he recognized two of the men who were entering and exiting the building with crated television sets. Both had been involved in petty crimes of theft and minor assault. Their rap sheets were quite lengthy but the actual incarceration time served was minimal. They obviously had not learned a lesson, as crime continued to be a way of life for them.

Rather than converge on the activity, Bill convinced the other officers who had responded, rapidly but silently, to hold off. In making some quick observations, he had noticed that the alarm system, which operated over telephone lines to a central receiving station, had been bypassed with a plastic box with two wires coming from a hole in its side and terminating in two alligator clips.

On the face of the box was a voltmeter, which read the outgoing voltage and polarity from the alarm system and transmitted over the telephone lines. Next to it was a toggle switch with the handwritten words "On" and "Off" scratched above and below the two settings. This was accompanied by a rotary switch with a pointer on it, similar to those used on old-time, tube-type, AM radios, which pointed to "Off," "On," or "Stand-by." In this case, the pointer had a choice of voltages: six, twelve or eighteen. It was currently set at six volts, with the alligator clips attached to the telephone line. The line leaving the building was severed. Now the black, plastic box was providing the signal that told the central station that all was normal at the warehouse.

Bill's instincts told him that these guys had to have an outlet for the items they were taking. Even though he recognized these small time hoods, the complex equipment convinced him that this had to be part of a bigger, more professional, operation. And, based upon the amount of goods they were hoisting from the warehouse, they had to be delivering it to someone who had space available to receive it and to rapidly sell it.

He advised the cops who were standing by to move their cruisers out of the area and to station themselves on streets close to the warehouse. He then radioed headquarters to open the channel so that he could have contact with the other cars positioned to assist.

Ordinarily, radio cars could only communicate with headquarters. However, when a major incident was taking place, headquarters could flip a switch on the radio control remote that would allow officers in cars to talk to one another through the base station.

Quickly, and without a lot of noticeable movement or headlights, the radio cars took their places on a variety of streets. Bill took Edmund in his car with him and they moved to the only location where the big truck, still being filled with stolen goods, could leave the warehouse yard. Finding a spot between some fifty-five-gallon drums and a wall of wooden pallets, they had the advantage of monitoring the driveway while hidden from anyone driving past.

It took nearly twenty minutes before they felt the rumbling of the truck as it drove toward them. Bill picked up the radio microphone and advised the other cars that the truck was leaving the yard. They paid close attention as the truck went by and turned onto the deserted street. Again, Bill radioed the truck's direction of travel and requested that other radio cars watch for any change in direction. Bill then began moving, headlights out, following the same path as the truck.

One of the radio cars watched from an alleyway as the truck, with its lights now on, drove by. The officer managed to read the license plate number and gave the information to Bill. As there was no computer system in these early years, it would be morning before the number could be run through the police station teletype to the Registry of Motor Vehicles.

Radioing the various locations through which the truck passed, Bill was able to follow it to another warehouse off Massachusetts Avenue behind Boston City Hospital. Once there, he parked his cruiser and called for all available cars to meet by the hospital. When they arrived, the cops surrounded the warehouse on foot. Bill was quick to note that there were several newer model cars parked in the warehouse parking lot, including two luxury Cadillacs. It was obvious that the people inside did not realize anything had gone amiss in their plans. No one even stood guard outside when the big truck backed in through the large overhead door.

One of the responding cars had a sergeant who had brought with him a Thompson submachine gun from the station house. Otherwise, the officers were not heavily armed as they carried only their assigned sidearms. Once everyone was in position, based upon a prearranged time and synchronized wristwatches, they burst into the building and ordered everyone to raise their hands and stand firm.

There could not have been a more perfect arrest. Although the officers were, not one of the perpetrators was armed. Not only were the thieves arrested, but also two well-known and somewhat-respected businessmen, who had been found carrying a large sum of cash with which to pay off the burglars. A police wagon was called in and the men were taken to the district headquarters for processing and interrogation.

Caught red-handed, the burglars admitted to everything and implicated the two men who were making the payoff. This was the first time that Bill used his charismatic character to lure confessions out of the perpetrators. According to Edmund, who had witnessed the interaction between the thieves and the senior officer, Bill's interrogation was a work of art. He had observed investigative techniques before—some of which were ruthless—as suspects were forced to own up to criminal events or actions that they may or may not have actually committed. Admitting to them, however, at that moment, seemed much less severe than the continued beatings which would leave them physically injured.

In this case, Bill had been smooth. He had the facts. After all, they *were* caught in the act. There was no recourse. No denial. He almost congratulated them on their method of operation. He fed their egos and played advocate in their behalf. And, confused by this, they boasted of their near-success to the officers they recognized, having dealt with them on many previous occasions. Thus, they implicated the men who originated the scheme. Once in possession of their sworn testimonies, Bill used their statements as a lever in opening up the men who concocted the theft.

When the interrogation was complete, the prisoners were transported to the Charles Street Jail, the finest facility of its kind in the city. Each cell had a cement floor, an iron bed and two pails: one for

fresh water, and the other for any waste products the prisoner might produce during his stay awaiting arraignment or trial. The odor from the jail permeated the walls, or so it seemed, until the stench of the less-than-human population incarcerated within could be detected anywhere in close proximity to its doors.

Bill credited Edmund with the promotion he soon received as a reward for a job well done. Since that time, Bill has maintained a kinship to the man who made this possible. So when Red told Bill about his problem with Edmund, Bill

felt obligated to let his friend know what was being said, even though he did not believe he was "on the take." Or, perhaps it was that he refused to listen to any such accusation. After all, Bill owed Edmund for his change in status and he would not jeopardize their alliance.

Edmund Doherty thanked his friend and feigned understanding why Officer Halloran would make up such a story about a fellow officer, while neither confirming nor denying the insinuation. Not wanting to explore the issue any further, Bill simply offered that maybe it was because the two of them were in the race for the position of sergeant. That sounded plausible and satisfied both men. Before parting, however, Edmund made one final comment: "Jealousy can be a terrible thing. I just hope that Halloran doesn't want this rank so badly that he resorts to some foolish actions. It could be embarrassing for all concerned."

* * *

Doherty's gambling connections included some of the best-placed Italian politicians in the city, which helped him enormously.

Al "Big Eyes" Giardella, so named because of bulging eyes— which sat in wide hollow sockets and made him look like a Boston toy terrier—arranged for a reverse sting in which Doherty, instead of being caught for an illegal activity, would put Red in a compromising position.

It all took place one evening inside the Casa Mia Restaurant on Hanover Street in the North End of the city. It began with a phone call to Edmund at the station just before the on-going shift of men was to hit the streets. Edmund positioned himself in such a way as to let Red hear what he was saying, but not being so obvious as to look like a setup. What Red definitely knew was that Edmund needed to be at the Casa Mia around suppertime.

Red disappeared around the corner of the room and placed a quick call to Bill McInerney, letting him know what was going down.

Bill said he would have undercover men stationed at the restaurant but that he needed Red there as a witness, to keep everything flowing and connected, since it was his word against a fellow policeman.

Red felt a cramping in his stomach. "Why do you need *me* there? Can't you just do a surveillance and, once you have the proof of what I'm telling you, handle the situation?"

"It's not as easy as that, Red. This involves an indictment against another officer. We need to witness Doherty's reaction to your presence there."

Red was now very uncomfortable but agreed to do what he had to do. Before leaving the station he ran into the men's room and emptied his bowels. It was a nervous diarrhea, not unlike that which he experienced when he suffered from the flu or from eating a heavy meal, especially one with fatty meat.

Arriving at the restaurant minutes after hearing Edmund Doherty sign off on the radio for supper there, Red spotted Bill's unmarked car down the street. Red went into the restaurant and looked around for the plainclothes detectives and Doherty. Not seeing anyone he recognized, he walked over to a waiter and asked if Edmund Doherty was around. The waiter told him the meeting was in the back office.

"Meeting?" Red asked himself as he walked toward the direction in which the waiter had pointed. Going through the swinging door that separated the restaurant's dining area from the kitchen and office, he saw Edmund turn in his direction. He sat at a small table and was eating some kind of a stuffed pasta with a man Red did not recognize—"Big Eyes" Giardella.

As Red entered the room, "Big Eyes" turned and flashed a huge smile, greeting him with, "My old friend, Red Halloran, I thought you were going to be late. I have your envelope right here."

"What?" Red asked emphatically, at the same time observing a smile cross Edmund Doherty's face.

"You know," Giardella continued, "you made it difficult for me to get such a large sum so quickly."

"What the fuck're you talking about?" Halloran asked.

"Hey, c'mon, you're among friends," Big Eyes responded.

"I don't even fucking know you!" Halloran replied.

"Oh, I understand," said Giardella, "you're concerned about doing business in front of Ed. No sweat, he's got no interest in our dealings."

With that statement, Bill McInerney stepped into the kitchen from the back door of the building.

"What's the story, Red?" he asked. "I came here based on what you told me and I've been standing, listening, outside the rear door of the restaurant and now I'm hearing something different from what you said?"

"Bill, I don't know what's going on here, but someone is fucking me bad."

"Look, Red," said McInerney, "I think we ought to drop this whole foolishness. I've known Ed Doherty for a long time. I also know that he's not the type person to do what you suggested. And more than that, I know how easy it is to try and set someone up when two guys are in a competitive position."

"But, Bill. . . ."

"Listen . . . carefully . . . to what I am saying!" McInerney demanded as he spoke in slow, well-defined words. "We are going to drop this now! You're a good cop and Ed's a good cop. You're both vying for the same job. You cannot use unfair tactics to get ahead; this is all based on merit. I don't want to hear any more shit. You understand?" It was more an order than a question.

"Yeah, I understand all right."

Red left the restaurant without another word. It was not long afterwards that the announcement was made that Edmund Doherty was promoted to the rank of sergeant.

Red always kept to himself following that experience, keeping friendships to only a few people and being very cautious about whom he trusted. Never again would he have contact with Bill McInerney, except on the most professional basis.

The final blow, that divided Red Halloran from Edmund Doherty, came when Red discovered that Sgt. Doherty's family's background originated in Northern Ireland and that he had been in support of the Separatists. He wasn't even a Catholic, but one of those damned Protestants.

In those years, simplicity, non-sophistication and a kind of naiveté were the dominant factors in police work.

Years later, Joseph O'Fallon's training was influenced, although the influence was somewhat cunning, by the bitterness Red Halloran had for the man who had risen in the ranks from sergeant to captain. Capping this, although not quite so subtle, was the hatred Red displayed toward the rest of those who were Northern Irish Protestant.

When the more pronounced battles broke out in Northern Ireland and were relayed by the news media, Red was very vocal in his support of the Irish Republican Army (IRA).

Until his retirement Red impressed upon Joseph at every opportunity, the enmity that rightfully existed between England and Eire, between Catholic and Protestant. Having spent a significant amount of time with Red, Joseph was likewise affected by his negativism.

CHAPTER 2

The first several years on the job in Boston gave Joseph the opportunity to prove himself as an effective and competent police officer. Walking the beat during his tenure as a rookie, he often fell upon illegal activities and turned all the significant arrests over to the detectives.

This was the way things were done in big cities. If you wanted to stay a beat cop all during your career, you took credit for all arrests and gave nothing to the detectives. By doing this you also ended up on their "shit list." However, if you were progress-minded and had hopes of moving up in the department, you called the detectives in when you had a good case and an imminent arrest, giving all the information and suspects over to them to effect the final disposition. Then you and the detectives recorded who did what for whom and, when the need arose for you to advance, you called upon the help of those you helped in the past.

Joseph learned how the game was played early on, and adhered to the rules without wavering. It did not take long before he earned his upgrade to that of detective.

* * *

The world of the detective is different from that of the patrolman. Detectives depend on shared information from the patrolman, who is on the street. The patrolman is not privy to information held by the detective unless the detective deems a benefit to be derived from such a discourse.

In his early years as a detective, Joseph was involved in a number of cases. What impressed his commander most was that many of those cases assigned to him did not remain unsolved. Joseph's acumen made him successful in arresting scores of individuals and closing out burglaries, thefts, robberies and homicides at a rate in excess of those more experienced detectives who had made this division their career.

Keeping his mouth shut and ignoring the jealousies often voiced by those with whom he worked (albeit as asides meant for him to hear), it wasn't long before Joseph again made a move in the department, and was promoted to sergeant in the detective division.

This was a good position for him. Those co-workers who gave him the most crap now had to answer to him, and he saw to it that the ones who had persisted in being the most negatively vocal received the worst assignments. It was also good because Sgt. Joseph O'Fallon was still involved in dealing with people on the street as he conducted his investigations. He didn't like being removed from the people he served—nor from those who came to serve him.

As sergeant, Joseph took assignments that gave him a challenge, yet allowed him some freedom of movement. He enjoyed working either in a suit or in coveralls. Depending upon the situation, he often went alone out into neighborhoods, getting to know residents by visiting local bars and pubs, massage parlors and newsstands, restaurants and stores, without tipping his hand that he was a cop. It is amazing what one can learn just by being friendly and mingling with those who frequent such establishments.

Because he wasn't married, he could spend endless hours at this task. He was so smooth in his demeanor that people responded to his casual inquiries without question. He was, therefore, able to determine what illegal activities were taking place in his district and many times had been invited to participate.

So when he discovered a rather large off-track betting ring being operated out of a bar near Dudley Station, the MBTA public transportation stop, he was not surprised. He had made the bar one of his regular stops, and watched as the owner would take fifty-cent and dollar bets (or more) in person and by telephone. The owner would then feed them through to the back room of the bar, where his partner would be in touch with friends who stationed themselves at Suffolk Downs or Wonderland Park—the local horse and dog tracks—and with some of the larger similar entertainment facilities on the east coast. It was a small operation, but one that netted several hundred thousand dollars a year for both of these men and their cronies. Licensed off-track betting parlors were still a few years from becoming a reality.

Francesco Gianni, the back-room man, established dependable communications with the men in the field by using the telephone and a community repeater radio system. The men at the local racetracks carried small, concealed portable two-way radios and spoke in code, giving numbers only, as each race was completed. The numbers reflected the race sequence, the number of the horse or dog that won, placed or showed, and the corresponding payouts for each position. The low-power portables would gain their strength from the repeater transmitter antenna located on top of a tower on a nearby high hill or building. The signal would then be carried to the back room of the bar where the race results were posted and winners and losers were notified when they came to check the outcome of their bets.

Once knowing the routine and seeing the amount of the cold cash that flowed between gamblers and the bar owners, Joseph began to collect evidence that could shut down this procedure and lock away the perpetrators. It would take some time to have everything in place, but this was a "given." He knew he had a good case.

* * *

In the meantime, as summer was approaching, Joseph gave some thought to making his annual trek to Old Orchard Beach in Maine. His folks had gone there every year for as far back as he could remember. They had often spoken about going down to Cape Cod, but that idea was always put to rest once they saw the traffic jams that made Route 3 look like a parking lot on Fridays and Sundays— and when they discovered just how expensive the beach-front rentals were.

Always, they stayed at the same cottage colony, The Alouette, located at the intersection of East Grand Avenue and Mullen Street. Originally, it had been LaVoie's Beach Front Motel and Cottages but with age and the stress of dealing with a more demanding public, Laurent LaVoie had sold out to his neighbors.

Entering Mullen Street from East Grand Avenue, there were two cottages on the right, situated before a driveway that led to a parking area at the back of the buildings. Farther down Mullen Street, past the driveway, was the cottage in which Joseph and his family stayed, followed by another cottage and a small strip of motel rooms. Beyond that was the beach.

At the entrance of the motel, across the street, was the office and restaurant, a driveway leading to the rear units, a long strip of motel rooms and two more cottages before the beach. Separating the beach from the cottages was a walkway with perhaps ten or twelve wooden beach chairs with wide slats. The chairs were designed for bathers to use as they dried off after swimming or simply to catch the rays of the sun, while watching people enjoy their vacation time on the sand or in the water. The beach was accessible by a set of stairs that went down, just a few feet from the walkway, to the sand. Adjacent to the stairs, heading to the beach, was an area designated for refreshments with a table and benches.

Only two and a half hours from Boston, even in the heavy summer traffic, it was a place where one could feel free and easy. The weather usually cooperated; of course, as everyone knows the old saying about Maine, "just wait an hour and the weather will change." If bad weather came in, it was only a matter of time before it would clear. The only drawback was the intensely cold ocean water. Maine's southern coast is protected by the "arm" of Cape Cod, Massachusetts. Therefore, the warmer south Atlantic water would reach Canada long before it could swirl around and inside the arm toward Old Orchard and the beaches north of Boston. But this still was a pleasant and very clean beach.

For nearly a century, early in the morning, the beach cleaners were out with horses and wagons to patrol the sand—scooping up seaweed that had rolled in off the ocean during the night. The horses all had been affixed with a bag, which caught their droppings as they pulled the wagons.

In August, when Joseph and his folks took possession of their cottage for the month, hundreds of people, mostly from Montreal, Quebec, would swarm the beach. French became the most prominent language in the area during this time of the year.

Joseph would refrain from any thoughts of his job while he was on vacation. Only if someone asked him where he was from or what his occupation was, would he mention in very few words that he had an interest in law enforcement.

This was to be a different kind of summer. He met, for the first time, a girl who did not fall in love with his uniform, as had several others during the early years of his career.

Renee Lafayette was on vacation with some friends from Quebec City. Co-workers at La Banque Royale du Canada, they had just arrived at the motel and Renee was eager to get to the beach. They quickly hauled their luggage out of their Honda station wagon and dropped the bags inside their room, which was diagonally across from Joseph's cottage. After changing into their newly acquired bathing suits, the friends rushed outside toward the three steps that led from the parking area, past the walkway, to the beach.

Renee was in a hurry to be the first one onto the sand. Giggling with excitement and looking behind her to see how close her friends were, she rushed down the steps, lost her balance and fell right on top of Joseph, who was lying on a blanket just to the right of the pathway.

"Je le regret, Monsieur. . . ." she began to sputter, apologizing for her error.

"It's OK. Are you all right?" he asked.

"Oh, you are from the States. I am so sorry to have fallen on top of you. I was not paying attention as I run to the beach," she replied. "Yes, I am fine, thank you."

"You are from Quebec?" he asked, more a statement than a question, noting the obviously French accent as she spoke.

"Yes, I am from *La Ville de Quebec* . . . Quebec City," she answered. "And you are from Maine?"

"No, I'm from Boston. I'm here on vacation with my family."

"Oh, your family. They are not here on the beach with you?"

"No, my father usually walks down toward the pier and visits with people as he goes along. My mother stays close to the cottage because she can only take the sun for a little while."

"Oh," Renee laughed, "when you said family, I thought you meant your wife and children."

"No, I am not married," Joseph said with a smile. "I guess I have not found anyone who can stand the pace of my work."

"What is it that you do?" Renee asked.

36

For the first time in many years he did not give his traditional glib response. Instead he said, "I am a policeman."

"Ohhh, how exciting! Have you been this for a long time? Have you ever been hurt? Is Boston a dangerous place to be a policeman?" The questions came so fast, Joseph was not sure which to answer first.

Before he had an opportunity, Renee interjected, "I am again sorry. I did not mean to ask so many questions. I have just never met a policeman from the States before."

As Joseph began to reply, he noticed for the first time the other two girls who had been standing behind Renee. Both were very pretty: one had long, dark brown hair reaching halfway down her back and wearing a two-piece, yellow bathing suit that left very little to the imagination; the other had shoulder-length, dirty-blond hair and wore a one-piece, brilliant red, thong bathing suit that left absolutely nothing to the imagination. Both had been whispering and smiling as they listened and commented and giggled to one another about Renee's convenient fall and the tall, handsome, red-headed man.

For the first time, also, Joseph really noticed Renee. She, too, was a dirty blond, but with short hair. She wore a two-piece bathing suit, more conservative than those of her compatriots. As he looked at her, he realized what a beautiful girl she was. Her voice was as soft as her facial features. She had blue eyes that were warm and sparkled as she spoke. Even though her suit did not expose as much of her body as did the ones her friends were wearing, he could see that she filled it out in all the right places. His interest in her started to arouse, as did a part of his anatomy.

As Joseph continued their conversation, he finally introduced himself formally to her and she to him. By this time, the other girls moved on toward the surf and set out their beach blanket. They positioned themselves so they could watch the two "accident vic-tims" and still get the most sunshine possible on their very white bodies.

It was obvious that the chemistry was right for both Joseph and Renee; everything they said seemed to connect one with the other, including their religious background. Renee had been the prod-uct of a very strict Catholic family. She had attended L'Ecole de Sainte Marie, a parochial school in her neighborhood, and was present at early mass every Sunday.

When she heard that Joseph had been an altar boy and had known, actually had known, Richard Cardinal Cushing, she could not wait to telephone her parents and tell them.

They spent the entire day on the beach together. Of course, Renee introduced Joseph to her co-workers, Giselle and Helene. Because English was their second language, communications were very easy. And those things that the girls wanted to say, without including Joseph, they said in French, a language with which he was not familiar. He was only slightly irritated when they did that, because when they moved into French it was always to say some-thing that made the others laugh. Renee would only say, "They are teasing me."

That afternoon, Joseph introduced the girls to his parents. They seemed glad that he had made their acquaintance, to help occupy his ordinarily quiet days and nights. His mother's only comment, made later, was that she wished he had met an Irish girl—not that she had anything against the French, after all they were, thank good-ness, Catholic—but she just preferred Irish.

That night, the three girls accompanied Joseph to Palace Playland, the amusement park at the pier. In their shorts, the girls invited looks from men, young and old, all along the sidewalk and walkway to the pier. Joseph felt a kind of euphoria he had never experienced before in his life. It was almost as if he were a celebrity as he watched people turn and look at him and his entourage.

They participated in every ride and amusement in the park and, as crowded as it was, they had no problem taking part in each form of entertainment afforded in this honky-tonk arena. Joseph won a number of stuffed animals and trinkets for them, never complaining that the expenditure outlayed for tickets far exceeded the worth of any of the prizes. Before leaving the park for the night, they stopped for a few drinks at a bar that catered to motorcyclists. They had no qualms concerning their environment, and the girls, especially, had no fears being among bikers. After all, they had a big policeman to protect them.

By the time they returned to the motel, it was well after midnight. Joseph asked Renee if she would like to take a walk along the beach. She said she was tired and asked if he would mind, instead, making it tomorrow. A bit disappointed, he decided not to push the issue and thanked her for a very pleasant evening. Renee lifted up on her toes and gave him a quick kiss good night.

Early the next morning, Joseph decided not to wake the girls but wandered down onto the beach alone. There were only a few people already there and most had on some kind of light covering, as the sun had not yet heated the air. It was promising to be another brilliant day of comfortable warmth and sunshine.

Walking and thinking, Joseph felt that he had met someone he wanted to know better. He wanted to know her as fully as he could because he wondered if this might be the woman for him.

As he stood near the pathway leading from the sand to the parking area, he heard someone calling his name. He turned and saw Giselle by the motel door. She asked him if he would like something to eat. She had walked down to the little market on East Grand Avenue and had picked up doughnuts and milk. He entered their motel room and, noticing that the chairs were strewn with a variety of clothes, he sat down on the edge of one of the beds. The girls offered him a choice of the doughnuts and a plastic cup full of milk.

As he looked around the motel room, Joseph took in the details—a habit from being a policeman. He noted that it was rather spacious, with two queen size beds separated by a large, square night table upon which had been placed an inexpensive and gaudy lamp, with a melange of colors on the base. A remote control for the twenty-one inch color television sat just to the left of the lamp and a telephone with a card depicting a variety of instructions in both English and French was at the right.

The television took up most of the space on an elongated bureau, three feet beyond the end of both beds and set against one of the motel room walls. The girls' suitcases occupied the remaining expanse of the bureau. The room also had a dining table, and two chairs that appeared to be comfortably padded, but were in reality as hard as though the cloth material covering them had been fitted directly to the wooden frame. Two equally uncomfortable easy chairs completed the furniture appointed to fill the room. Beyond the sleeping area was a small refrigerator and a vanity with a single sink and to the right of that was the bathroom.

Helene was coming out of the bathroom; she was the only one not dressed. She had just taken a shower and was wearing only a flimsy robe that barely covered her nakedness. She brushed her long brown hair and shortly thereafter, without any hesitation, reached into her suitcase and removed a bathing suit, different from the one she wore the day before, and took off her robe—changing in front of Joseph as though he were not there. Joseph nearly choked on the doughnut he was eating and quickly swallowed half of the cup of milk, turning away from the sight in front of him and blushing at the same time.

Helene just looked up and laughed as though to say, "What? You've never seen a naked woman before?"

Renee was seething. Her face turned red and she walked out of the motel and down toward the beach; the motel room door almost coming off its hinges with the anger, which radiated through her entire body. The spring on the door caused it to close with nearly the same amount of force by which it had been opened.

Joseph immediately got up and ran after her, nearly spilling his remaining milk as he tried to balance everything in one hand while pushing the partially closed door open with the other. "Don't be upset!" he called out, "She's just trying to tease you. I'm not interested in her."

"She is a bitch. I knew she would do something to try and attract you. She spoke about you half the night."

"But I am not interested in her. Do you understand?"

"Do not tell her that. She will try even harder to attract you if she thinks that."

"Let her do whatever she wants and pay no mind to her. She will be wasting her time. Today all of us will spend time together and tonight you and I will spend time alone," Joseph said. "Pretend it did not happen and just let it pass. Show her that you are a stronger person than she is by not letting it bother you."

* * *

Soaking up the sunlight, swimming in the water and sitting under a large umbrella to avoid the height of the ultraviolet rays, the day passed quickly because of their conversation. They each had so much to say in so few hours as they tried to find out more about one another.

When nighttime arrived, the girls were invited into Joseph's folks' cottage for supper. The great advantage to the cottage was that it had a full kitchen. Joseph's mother was a wonderful cook.

For more than a dozen years Joseph and his family had rented the same odd-shaped cottage. Next to the front door was an enclosed porch, circular in shape. On the second floor, above the porch, was the master bedroom, square on three sides and rounded on the fourth side.

The second floor had three additional bedrooms and a full bathroom with a tub. The best part of the bedrooms situated above the street and facing towards the water was the fact that as the cottage's residents prepared to sleep at night, with the windows open for the fresh sea air, the sounds of the waves and the ocean breeze would lull them off to dreamland almost immediately.

The first floor of the cottage had a living room with a television, two couches and an odd assortment of chairs. The dining room had a very long, old table and six metal-framed chairs. Everything had been designed for practicality and not necessarily for comfort. Much of what filled these old places was the result of shopping at auctions or of items transported from other family's hand-me-downs. Against the center wall, which separated the dining room from the kitchen was a fireplace for those nights during the summer and fall when cooler weather would sneak in. The kitchen had a table and three chairs along with a gas stove, a double sink—circa 1930—and a refrigerator. There was also a closet that served as a pantry. The bathroom on this first floor was very accessible to those coming in from the beach, with the basic necessities of a toilet, a sink and a metal stall shower.

The cottage was very pleasant and a great getaway from the city. And, as a cottage, it required no apologies for its amenities or furnishings.

An old upright piano also sat in the living room almost beneath a hanging three-globe, turn-of-the-century, chandelier, which Joseph continuously bumped with his head whenever he crossed from the dining room to the porch. His favorite place in the old cottage was the porch. He could sit there for hours almost unnoticed in a rocking chair, watching people walking to and from the beach.

One of his fondest memories was from when he was but a youngster. On his first trip to Old Orchard Beach, he was sitting on the porch when he saw a strikingly beautiful young woman wearing a bikini—the first one he had ever seen in the flesh. The bikini was shiny white and reflected the sunlight as the woman walked toward the sand. He never forgot how smooth her strides were and how beautiful she appeared to him. She was obviously French-Canadian, as they were the only people who dared to wear such revealing bathing suits in an era that was just beginning to relax its styles. He saw her several times during her week stay at LaVoie's, and was disappointed the day she and her husband, driving a Pontiac Parisienne with Quebec license plates, left on their return trip to Canada. He would never forget her.

* * *

After dining and sitting for a while, the girls wanted to go back down to the pier, where all the action was. They knew that Renee would not be interested as it was obvious she was enamored with her new-found friend.

Renee said to Joseph, "Do you want to take that walk on the beach now?"

"I'd love to," he responded, and they excused themselves from his folks, thanking them for their sumptuous meal of roast chicken and cranberry sauce, mashed potatoes with gravy, asparagus with hollandaise sauce, and German chocolate cake for dessert.

They walked down to the beach and headed toward Black Point, the opposite direction from the pier, where her friends had headed. There were few people on the beach; most had already retired for the night or were down at the amusement park.

As the two walked in the shadows, they reflected on the topics discussed since they had met. They stopped and looked up at the sliver of moon, barely visible since a new moon was in the offing. Turning toward one another, but saying nothing, they looked into each other's eyes and drew closer together. Renee reached up and put her arm around Joseph's neck, kissing him. They did not move apart for the longest time, enjoying the passion that had come to fruition between them. He tasted her lips and liked the softness and the moistness she imparted. She, too, welled up inside with a love she had never felt before; she could have cried the feeling was so good. Over the next half hour, they could not stop sharing the physical side of their emotions.

They moved closer to a retaining wall separating the sand from the older homes, which sat above and back from the ocean side. Lying down on the sand, their fingers began to explore one another, soon groping at each other's buttocks, feeling the perfectly rounded firmness of one another's buns, soon progressing to those areas reserved for the fullness of love-making. Had anyone been walking along the beach at that time, they would have wondered what kind of night animal made the sounds that emitted from the throats of the lovers as they moaned in pleasure. Only once did Renee stop suddenly; it was when she discovered just how much masculinity Joseph possessed below his flat, muscular stomach.

As they made love, Renee found that she wanted to see this device that was giving her so much internal pleasure. After relaxing, following a climax, she moved her head down to that region and began to massage this bodily extension and to watch it grow once again to its towering height. Her petite fingers seemed even smaller as they encircled the circumference of his penis and continued the gentle up and down stroking that stimulated its growth. Fascinated, she moved her lips toward it and began to kiss it as though thanking it for giving her the ultimate in physical excitement. Joseph, watching this, could not move. He was in ecstasy. He had received blow jobs before but never with such caring and loving.

Renee finally put her mouth over the end, which was oozing moistness, and tried to bring it all the way down her throat. It was impossible, but she did not give up trying. She moved her tongue around it and began to moan in harmony to the moaning being made by Joseph. The result was a humming not unlike that heard at meditation seminars. The greater result was a vibration to Joseph's penis that made it explode with love juices. Renee could hardly swallow as fast as the liquid poured down her throat.

Joseph had never in his life had an experience like this. If ever he knew that he wanted to have this woman as his love partner, it was now. In fact, as far as every other aspect in their developing relationship was concerned, he knew that this was the frosting on the cake.

For the next two weeks, they made plans to see each other. She was anxious for her parents to meet this man she had fallen in love with and about whom she spoke incessantly on the phone every time she called home.

Joseph was lost when Renee finally had to return to Quebec. He knew they would be getting together soon, but soon was not quick enough. It was then he realized that this had to be true love.

* * *

A second life-altering thing happened that summer. Joseph's father, with whom he was very close, suffered a heart attack. It happened while Joseph was walking to the grocery store to pick up some items for the cottage. As he was heading back he heard sirens and soon an ambulance and police car drove past him and pulled into Mullen Street. All of a sudden he had a sickening feeling in the pit of his stomach and he began to run toward the motel.

As he turned the corner onto Mullen Street, he saw what he dreaded, the ambulance was parked in front of their cottage. A group of vacationers had gathered outside, and the attendants were already inside the house. He threw down the bags he was carrying and ran inside. There was his father, lying motionless on the floor, with his mother kneeling between two of the attendants, leaning over her husband holding his hand. She looked up and saw her son coming through the door and just shook her head. Her husband was gone. There were tears in her eyes but she was not crying. All she could say was, "I think it's time for us to go home now."

The funeral mass was well attended. The O'Fallons had been lifelong residents in their neighborhood and they were well liked. Father James Flanagan did a remarkable eulogy as he recalled things about the senior O'Fallon that people had long forgotten. He had tears in his eyes as he spoke kind words about his friend of so many years—often having shared a drink or two in the rectory when day was done. He told the people who had gathered there how Sean O'Fallon had given his heart to the church and had helped to build, with his own hands, an addition to the church. He did not have the money to give at the time, not that he ever had any real money, but he was a talented carpenter and that was worth more than anything money could buy. Why? Because he put his entire self into the woodwork and wasn't doing it as if he were being paid for doing a job.

Father Flanagan did not have any notes, yet he spoke for a half hour and, probably, could have gone on for days. As the family left the church, there were motorcycle cops and mounted horse cops to lead the procession to the cemetery. More than a hundred cars followed to the Mount Hope Cemetery where Sean was laid to rest.

Eileen O'Fallon, who had been the strong one in the family over the years, could not cope with the passing of her husband. She refused to eat, could be heard at night speaking to her departed husband as she cried to Jesus, Mary and Joseph to take her to be home with him in heaven.

It is not surprising that within three months of his death, just a few weeks before Thanksgiving, her wish was granted. She, too, was accorded a funeral mass similar in scope as that of Sean. Father Flanagan asked some of the ladies who were closest to her to come forward and speak.

The priest was a human being and not just a clergyman. His connection to the people was something few others possessed. He was loved more than any other who had ever served in the parish church.

Renee came for both solemn occasions. She offered her condolences—and herself—to Joseph, in an effort to help him cope with these major changes in his life.

But something had changed in Joseph. It was not something Renee could determine because she had not known him very long. But those who worked with him saw him in a different light.

Perhaps it was the expense of two funeral services from Moran's that prompted the change. After all, the bills came to nearly $20,000—for caskets, burial permits, cemetery lots and a dozen other items associated with funerals. Or, maybe it was the mortgage on their house, which had been rewritten recently without the benefit of an insurance policy to cover death. The mortgage was guaranteed by Joseph as he took responsibility where he still lived in his parents' home. Or, perhaps it was a number of his parents' bills still outstanding and due for things they had bought and had anticipated paying for with their monthly Social Security checks.

Whatever it was, Joseph found himself in debt.

* * *

Despite all his troubles, Joseph returned to work soon after his mother's funeral. He concentrated once again on the off-track betting case, and quickly gathered enough information to move forward with the crackdown.

As he sat in the bar that he was about to close, he had a few more drinks than he would usually imbibe when doing his investigation. Finally, he said to Francesco Gianni, the owner-partner, that he wanted to have some words with him.

"What's up?" Francesco asked.

"Not here, Frannie—some place quiet."

"OK. Come inta my office," Francesco replied, waving to Joe to follow him.

Joe got up off the stool and walked the length of the bar to the opening at the end. He stood there as Francesco pulled a set of keys from his pocket and unlocked a door located next to the wall mirror, which reflected the faces of patrons seated at the bar.

The office was a small, converted storage closet with no windows. Most of the space was taken up by a gigantic wooden desk, the remnant of a much earlier era. It so overpowered the tiny room that Joseph wondered how it was ever brought in.

The room had two chairs, an executive-style swivel model behind the desk, and a metal folding chair in front of it. Francesco offered Joseph the metal chair as he maneuvered himself along the side of the desk to the larger, more comfortable piece of furniture.

"Now," inquired Francesco, "what is it?"

"Frannie, I like you and I have ever since I came into this place for a drink. But, I've got a problem," Joseph said.

"What's that, Joe?" Francesco asked.

"Frannie, you do a good bar business here and you do a great betting business here. Up until now, no one has bothered you about the off-track betting, have they?"

"What're you gettin' at?" Francesco asked, looking Joseph directly in the eye as he spoke.

"Frannie, the people I work for have been watching you for quite some time. They know you operate alone—I mean, you aren't part of any syndicate. This is a small-time operation."

"Yeah, so what? What is it you want, anyway?"

"Frannie, the cops have enough on you to shut you down and send you to jail."

"Aw bullshit! The cops don't even know I'm here. And what the fuck are you gettin' at anyway. Are you gonna tell me you're part of the Mafia and you're gonna muscle in on my business? You're as Italian as the moon, ya Irish Mick."

"No," said Joseph, "What I am gonna tell ya is that I'm a cop and I'm gonna shut you down, ya Guinea Wop."

"Cut the crap! Tell me what you're up to," Francesco replied.

Joseph took out his identification wallet and showed it to him. Francesco just stared at it without saying a word.

"All this time, you been comin' in here and actin' like you're a friend, and you're a cop?" Francesco stated, holding back the anger that was evident in his voice.

"Frannie, you're takin' advantage of people who have nothing. They come in here and spend what little they have drinking away their troubles and thinking they have a chance at winning big bucks through the race track. No, I'm not your friend, as much as I like you, because that's not helping people, that's hurting them."

"Look, Joe, whether or not I serve them booze or sell them chances on a race, they're gonna do it anyway. What else have they got going for them? And if I don't do it, someone else in this city's gonna do it. So, it may as well be me. The one thing I offer them is hope; they got a better chance here than they do with the Mass. State Lottery and it don't cost as much. A few of them use their cigarette money. The way I look at it, it may be a disease, but it's better than cancer.

"I tell you what; I'll make you a deal. You obviously got a handle on this where your ID tells me you're a sergeant. I don't know what you got on me but you wouldn't a told me you're gonna close me down if it was nothin'. I don't know how far you've gone with this thing with your people but I can make this worth your while if you let me stay in business. You got the upper hand. I don't wanna go ta jail and I can't run because I can't leave everything I got here. So you tell me, whataya say?"

"Frannie, I can't afford to lose my job. I mean, I've got all the evidence and if I don't bust ya and anyone knows I'm letting you continue, my job is on the line," Joseph said.

"Joe . . . who knows? Who would have any idea that you're lettin' me operate if they don't know themselves that I'm here. You just said you're the one with the evidence. If you got it in a safe place then no one knows but you and me; if it's well-known at your department then I've gotta get outta here. Look, I'll give ya a grand a week ta help me out; it's worth that to me," Francesco responded.

"A grand a week?" Joseph repeated, stunned.

"A grand a week. You want it, I'll start right now in good faith that you'll watch out for me," Francesco continued as he opened a drawer in the bottom of his desk and took out a wad of money and counted out a thousand dollars. He handed the money over to Joseph before he could say another word.

Joseph took the money, looked at it and shoved it in his pocket.

"OK," was all he could say. He turned and left the bar.

All the way home, he kept thinking, "What am I doing?" But he also knew a thousand bucks was a thousand bucks.

* * *

Never in his life had Joseph even considered taking something that was not rightfully his. He had been raised to respect the property of others. If he wanted something badly enough, he would work for it

— after all, that is how he was taught by his father and mother. Besides, if he had ever taken anything that did not belong to him, his father was not averse to a heavy hand of corporal punishment.

His parents had been the epitome of ethical conduct; they had been reared with family values that had been passed down for generations. All through the potato famine, which had almost devastated Ireland, their families maintained strong, moral principles. As poor as they were, they never would have contemplated doing anything inappropriate or of taking anything without offering some sort of barter in exchange.

Sleep did not come easily for Joseph that night. He had taken the money from his pocket, counted it several times, finally folded it and put it beneath his wallet next to the clock-radio on his bureau.

Before getting into bed, he paced the bedroom floor, his hands clasped behind his head as he walked. It was as though he was sorting things out in his brain but his mind would not let go of the guilt implied by his actions. He was very confused. He looked at himself in the mirror, which hung on the wall directly above his bureau. He tried to see into the image that was reflected in the glass. He stared at his eyes, the lids half-closed. For what seemed no reason at all, tears welled up and then dropped onto his cheeks. He began to feel dizzy. He felt like he did when he got lost as a six-year old at the Franklin Park Zoo. He had wandered off while intrigued by the animals and could not find his father or mother. Terror encompassed his whole body. He began to shiver with fright as his head quickly turned and his eyes darted in every direction and he realized he was alone. He remembered his father telling him that if he should ever get separated from them just to stay where he was and they would find him. He remembered the words, but he was not comforted; he was scared. Suddenly, a huge hand was on his shoulder and he slowly turned and looked up. He was met with his father's big smile.

Turning away from the mirror, he glanced about the room and spoke as though to no one, "Where are you now, Dad, when I need you?"

He shut off the light and climbed into bed, raising the covers over his shoulders. He closed his eyes in the pitch-black bedroom and he tried to clear his mind of the activity that had taken place earlier at the bar. No matter how he might change his focus to other subjects, his concentration reverted to the money that now sat on his bureau. Again the dizziness came and soon he lost all concept of reality. What went through his mind no one will ever know but it was obvious from the condition of his bed that his subconscious wrestled with his conscience throughout the night.

The change, which manifested after the death of his parents, and as witnessed by those with whom Joseph worked, would now govern him for the rest of his life.

CR

Once a week, Joseph stopped at the bar to pick up his "retainer." Other than that, he avoided that particular location and began watching for other operations. There was no doubt that the thousand a week helped cover the expenses his parents unwittingly left him.

His next venture was the Irish Pub on Adams Street in Dorchester. Most of Boston's bars came in one of two categories: seedy or classy. The Irish Pub was an anomaly. It was truly a drinking establishment reminiscent of those still found in Ireland, with its dimly lighted, dark-wood interior set off by rectangular booths along the walls. The pub had rounded tables accompanied by wide wooden armchairs in the center of the room and heavy, wooden four-legged stools surrounding a well-worn yet polished bar. The bar itself was separated from the back wall only by the runway, which allowed the bartender access to the numerous bottles of liquor on the shelf attached to the wall. Two sets of three long, wooden arms provided for the flowing of draft lager beer from large kegs in the cellar into the frosted mugs and steins of the patrons. The mirror on the wall was almost totally covered with autographed photos of famous Irish politicians and celebrities who had made stops at the bar. Numerous wood carvings, reflecting such passages as the Gaelic greeting CEAD MILE FAILTE—A HUNDRED THOUSAND WELCOMES—and the old Irish blessing that begins with the words "May the road rise to meet you and may the wind be always at your back....," adorned the walls of the pub. Likewise, there were pictures of Dublin's Clontarf Castle, pastoral field scenes of shepherds tending their flocks, and great hills overlooking the North Sea.

The outside of the pub aptly denoted what it was—the sign on the building had green shamrocks bordering the pub's name written in bright gold lettering and set upon an orange background. The building's facade appeared more like something from the Tudor period. Wooden beams were separated by wide swaths of stucco and windows made of leaded glass, not unlike the stained glass found in many churches.

Here Joseph found a camaraderie unlike anything he had ever before known. Here was a bar filled with Irish men just like himself. Men who were hearty drinkers, full of stories to be shared and laughs to spread around. Again, he did not identify himself as a cop. He came here dressed in the work clothes of a laborer and sat and drank rounds as he listened to the talk of the men.

One of the prime subjects was that of Northern Ireland. There was a hatred that permeated the evening sessions at the Irish Pub whenever a certain group arrived. These men always sat in a corner away from the more boisterous and jovial patrons who were part of the usual clientele.

Joseph had come to enjoy this bar. He found no indication of criminal activity that would warrant an investigation, so he made this a stopping-off place where he could relax and listen to the patrons tell their stories.

Many times Joseph would sit up at the bar and engage in conversation with whomever happened to light beside him. At other times, he would sit at a small table near the greatest crowd of people, nodding in their direction if someone happened to recognize him as a regular.

This time, however, he sat close to a group of men who were discussing the "war" in Northern Ireland. He casually looked in their direction when one of the men's voices elevated in pitch as he was making a point. The man, Seamus O'Neill, saw Joseph look and immediately asked him, "Don't ya think that's so?"

"I'm sorry, I didn't mean to listen in" Joseph said, "but, I didn't hear the whole question."

"Today's paper said that the Brits fired on our people and that two were killed. They claimed to use rubber bullets. Well, rubber bullets don't kill, do they?" It was more a statement than a question.

"And I just said," Seamus continued, "that if the people were properly armed, Ireland could take back its northern territory. Don't ya think that's so?"

"I really don't know. I mean the Brits have a large army," Joseph responded, "and . . ." Before he could complete his thought, however, Seamus broke in.

"Aw, the Brits have jack-shit. It ain't the size of their army that's a worry. If you're armed with the right equipment, there's no army gonna be able to hold back the people!"

"Maybe," said Joseph, "but aren't the people armed with sophisticated guns now?"

"For a redheaded, obviously Irish lad, you don't know a hell of a lot," Seamus said and the men with him began to snicker. "Most of them are still throwin' rocks and bottles filled with gasoline—Molotov cocktails. Come on over here and get a proper education."

Joseph took hold of his chair and pulled it with him as the men separated enough to give him room to join them.

The course of the discussion was a one-sided history; the history of Ireland according to Seamus O'Neill. Joseph enjoyed Seamus's magnetic personality. He drew Joseph into the conversation and managed to fill him with the pro-IRA propaganda that had continued to fuel the strife in Northern Ireland. Amazingly, Joseph found himself agreeing with the men.

That night, after Joseph returned home, much of what he had heard seemed to make sense to him. Perhaps it was the excess of liquor, which made him more susceptible, or maybe it was Seamus's voice of knowledgeable authority. Maybe it was the feeling of jumping on the bandwagon with the rest of the group, or maybe it was something of what he remembered from years ago when Red Halloran spoke so vehemently against the Irish Protestants of the North. Whatever it was, it kept Joseph awake most of the night as his mind went over and over the conversation at the Irish Pub.

CHAPTER 4

Renee had traveled to Boston some eight times since the summer and Joseph had been to Quebec City twice. She made herself more convenient to him than he to her, yet it had nothing to do with anything but the demands of his job. It was again time for him to visit there. Finally, he took a long weekend and drove the six hours to her hometown.

She had made arrangements for them to stay at the Manoir Victoria in the old city, which was the drawing card for Quebec.

She had told her parents that she was staying with a friend for the weekend. On the two occasions that Joseph had visited before, he stayed at Renee's house. But the lovers had to keep a proper separation during the night. This time, their passionate desires needed satisfaction, and there was no way that could be accomplished at her parents' home.

Renee met Joseph at the hotel late Friday night. Leaving his car for the valet to park in the garage, he made his way up the long flight of stairs that led to the lobby. He carried only his overstuffed overnight bag and walked past the reception area to the elevators, just past the hotel restaurant. Renee had called him on his cellular phone about five-thirty that evening and told him that she would be in room 317. He did not have to ask any questions at the desk, but just go directly upstairs where she would be waiting for him.

Joseph knocked at the door to the room and within seconds it glided open. Renee was standing behind the door, out of sight. When she closed the door, Joseph was treated to a view that enhanced his already excited libido. Renee was wearing a very short, see-through negligee under which she had on satin white, very brief panties. Her breasts pushed against the negligee so that the pinkness of her nipples could easily be seen.

Joseph tossed down his suitcase, threw off his jacket, and, with Renee's help, managed to get out of his clothes, even his underwear in a record-breaking eighteen seconds.

Throughout the night, they made love, catching up on the time that had passed while they had been away from one another.

When they awoke in the morning, they had "one for the road" before they went down to La Creperie Restaurant for breakfast.

Wanting to show Joseph more of her "old city," Renee guided him past the Frontenac Hotel, the most famous resort there, to the Funiculaire, an enclosed, outside elevator that led from the upper city in Old Quebec to the lower city, close to the St. Lawrence River. Because the city is built on a hill, this is the quickest method for traversing the height of the hill, which could be more appropriately called a mountain.

They wandered the city for hours, returning to their room only to grab a "quickie," freshen up and change for supper. They visited the museums and the artists' alley—a cobblestone walkway between buildings leading away from the upper city square with its monument and statue of Samuel de Champlain. Here Renee bought a print of Old Quebec for Joseph to remember her by when he returned home. They watched the changing of the guards at the fortress called the Plains of Abraham, which gave a resplendent view of the St. Lawrence River and proved to be an advantageous and strategic position during the battles fought in earlier centuries in order to protect the old city. The couple also toured the city by horse and carriage, even though Renee knew every area perhaps better than the fellow who was conducting the tour. But it felt more romantic as the driver, dressed in his colorful longcoat and top hat, guided them along the rugged streets. He made playful, mildly suggestive comments regarding this small section of the city known for catering to those who were in love. Fortunately, because the old city is such a tourist attraction, Renee's parents were not likely to pass beyond the city wall and catch them in their secret romance.

On Sunday morning, they went to the Frontenac Hotel for its well-renowned brunch. The hotel had been built in the last century and had become a center of attraction for the well-to-do in both the United States and Canada. Its massive peaks, which look more like spires with solid copper sheeting to protect them from the rain and snow were, in fact, individual roofs for the various rooms that comprised the hotel. Perched high above the lower city, the hotel resembled a fortress or a castle. Hundreds of employees were dressed in brightly colored period-costumes. Were it not for the Frontenac's expense, and Renee's frugality, the couple would probably have changed hotels.

They continued their Sunday outing with a drive just north of the city to Montmorency Falls, a higher waterfall than Niagara, but not nearly so powerful. Here they traversed a walking path that led close to the thunderous down-pouring of water and implored another tourist to take their picture in front of the cascading water. They also visited the nearby Shrine of St. Anne de Beaupre where, it is said, hundreds of people had been cured of illnesses and handicaps. Many had left their canes and crutches and wheelchairs and walked away without any assistance.

As they passed through the large wooden doors leading into an enormous sanctuary surrounded by a variety of bluish tints that dominate the stained glass windows, they were treated to an organ concert by a visiting artist. For nearly an hour they enjoyed beautiful music and both hesitated to leave these serene and contemplative surroundings, even after the music had stopped.

One great thing evolved out of their weekend together. Joseph asked Renee to marry him and they spent the remainder of the day making plans. They stopped at a jewelry store in La Baie, a large mall outside Quebec City, and picked out a diamond ring to seal their commitment. Renee was so excited that she wept while trying on the ring. As much as she wanted to wear it, she did not dare tip her folks to Joseph's presence in Quebec. They agreed to have Joseph come to Quebec City two weeks later so that he could formally ask for her hand in marriage at the home of her parents.

Monday was a difficult day as they had to say good-bye for a little while. The long weekends were not long enough. Renee returned to her home by way of her girlfriend's house so that she could coordinate their stories and make sure that no one had called looking for her. She really had nothing to worry about, however, because her friend said she would call and leave a message at the · hotel if anyone was trying to track her down.

It was a long drive back to Boston for Joseph. The one thing he could revel in was his memory of the magnificent weekend he had spent.

* * *

It was business as usual at the station. Joseph made case assignments to his people as he looked over the complaints that needed investigation. As he scanned through the incidents, he noticed one in particular involving a similar method of operation as a theft ring that had been working in a section of Roslindale. He contacted the detectives in that division and asked to have more information faxed to his attention.

Tom Martin, a detective for the past three years, had been watching a character by the name of Ahmed Amir. A naturalized American citizen, Amir had entered this country from Iran at about the same time as Tom was promoted to detective. He spoke English well and had applied himself at a number of menial jobs since his arrival in the States. His primary objective, or so he told his employers, was to bring his family to America. His family, evidently, consisted of all males near his age who had managed to escape the justice system in their homeland. Had they been caught and charged with theft, they would have relinquished their right hand for the first offense and the left hand for the second. Had they raped any female in their country, there would be a like removal of the offending appendage. Their true purpose was to steal anything and everything in order to make money and live like Americans.

Tom had been called in on a theft from a Radio Shack store. Three, dark-skinned men had walked in and engaged the sales clerk in conversation about a computer. It was during the lunch hour when most of the sales people were either at a local fast-food restaurant or enjoying a break away from the shopping plaza. As with every Radio Shack store, an electronic annunciator at the front door indicated the entry or exit of customers. Upon entering, however, one of the three men quickly and discreetly disabled the unit. While the clerk's back was turned, two more men, who had been inside the store looking at another computer, evidently walked out carrying their arms full of electronic equipment, including computers.

When the clerk realized what had happened, all of the men had already left the store and had disappeared. The only clues were their style of clothing, their physical description, and several fingerprints, which had been lifted off of other items in the store.

When Tom heard that the men spoke with a Mediterranean accent, he sent the fingerprints to the Department of Immigration and Naturalization. It was from there that he learned the identity of two of them. Both were known to have entered the country in New York and were sponsored by a third man, claiming to be a relative, in Boston.

The address was a dead end. The landlord stated that he had evicted the men when their rent became three months overdue. He had no leads as to their whereabouts. He was only interested in getting the money owed to him if they were found.

When Joseph read the details and compared them to the latest theft, he knew the same guys were operating in his district. He sent an informational bulletin to all radio cars in the hopes that someone might spot these men. In the meantime, he requested notification of all the electronics stores in the area to be aware of the *modus operandi* of these characters.

Many times in police work, an investigation of one incident can lead to the discovery of other illegal activities, perhaps being perpetrated by the person being investigated, and *sometimes* being perpetrated by the person who is the victim. This turned out to be one such case.

Nathan's Computers, located at Upham's Corner, was also visited by three dark-skinned men who spoke with an accent. Nathan Berkowitz, the owner, had heard about thefts that had taken place at Radio Shack so he was prepared. He hit the holdup button that sent a silent signal to the alarm company's monitoring board. The company, in turn, notified the police.

A Dorchester radio car less than two blocks from the store received the call. Responding quickly and quietly, the cops approached the store just as two men were walking out to a van, their arms loaded with computer equipment. When they saw the cops, they froze in place, still holding the computers. The officers directed them back into the store by pointing their Glock handguns.

Carefully surveilling the store before walking in, the cops saw Nathan, back-to, nervously talking with the three men who had been keeping his attention. It was not until the three spotted their two buddies coming back into the store that they realized something had gone wrong. With only the rear of the store available as a place for escape, they stopped their talking and began to run. It was at this point that Nathan turned around and, with a great sigh of relief, said, "Thank God you made it in time."

There was a loud crash as the three men tried to move things out of their way in an effort to leave through the back door. "They can't get out—the back of the store has steel bars and huge locks," Nathan stated. One of the officers, Charlie Canning, went to the back of the store and hustled the men out front once again.

Andy Wright was the second uniformed officer. While keeping the other two men in custody, he called in on his portable radio for the detectives to come to his location giving headquarters a heads-up on what they had.

Joseph was the first detective to arrive. Upon entering the computer store he was approached by Officer Wright, along with Nathan Berkowitz. As Andy gave details, Nathan interrupted him and interjected his own comments. Joseph said nothing but listened intently to the officer and the chattering of the nervous victim. Nathan's stature, features and mannerisms resembled the classic example of one of the characters in a typical "nerd" movie. The only noticeable difference was his age, which was somewhere mid-thirties rather than that of a college student.

Joseph called Tom Martin and asked him to respond to the electronics shop. Tom was the principal detective, based upon the original theft case, so he took over the investigation and the subsequent arrests. However, while they were in the store, Charlie Canning whispered to Joseph that when he was bringing the men from the back of the store to the front, he observed something interesting. He had spotted what appeared to be a very large quantity of marijuana in plastic bags in an unsealed computer carton, knocked over when the men tried to escape.

Joseph thanked him and said to Nathan that he needed to see if the men who had run in the back of the store might have dropped anything that would serve as additional evidence. Without any hesitation, Nathan said to go ahead. He obviously had no worries that the detective was interested solely in the case at hand and would not discover his hidden treasure.

As Joseph walked through the open doorway, he could immediately smell the odor of the marijuana. He located it easily and realized there had to be several kilos sorted into plastic bags. The bags had been secreted in four large cartons that had been used for shipping computers. On a shelf next to one of the cartons was a spiral notebook with the date, a set of initials written on every line and numbers placed next to each one—a log book of sales and when they occurred. It looked as though Nathan was doing a brisk business.

Joseph returned to the front of the store and advised Tom that he also would be doing an investigation. However, this one involved the victim. While they were talking, a patrol wagon arrived at the store to transport the prisoners, who had been placed under arrest by Detective Tom Martin.

Once the store was emptied except for Joseph and Nathan, Joseph told Nathan to handwrite a statement concerning what had taken place at the store. "Just make it brief. Detective Martin will be calling you in for a more detailed report later."

Nathan sat down at one of the empty computer tables and took a pen from his pocket and a pad of paper from beneath the adjacent counter. He began to compose a quick description. When he finished, Joseph took the note, looked at it carefully, and then asked Nathan to accompany him into the back room.

For the first time, Nathan appeared shaken. As Joseph followed Nathan into the room, he asked Nathan what he was doing with all the marijuana. Nathan took a deep swallow and considered whether he should just play dumb.

Joseph advised Nathan of his rights and said, "You don't have to say anything. I found your notebook and, guess what? Your handwriting in the description of the attempted theft matches the handwriting in the notebook. Is there anything you'd like to tell me?"

Nathan said nothing for almost two minutes. Droplets of sweat began to form on his forehead. Then he spoke; his voice somewhat jittery. "I . . . I . . . have been supplying some people with marijuana who have cancer. It's the only thing that relieves the pain. I know it's wrong but it is also legal in California for just that purpose. My best friend died a couple of weeks ago from lung cancer and this was the only thing that helped him during his suffering."

"Well," said Joseph, "first of all, we are not in California. I saw the television news program where it was being sold over the counter as medicine—even before it was made legal. The fact of the matter is that we are in Massachusetts and not California. I know there is legislation in the state to legalize it, and it may happen someday. But until it does, it is not legal. Second, I'm sorry for your friend. Third, I don't know if it takes away pain or not. Maybe it does. It appears that you are doing a significant business here and I would venture to say that *all* of your customers are not suffering from cancer. If that were the case, you have more 'patients' than the Dana Farber Cancer Clinic."

Nathan paused before speaking again.

"Well, maybe I have some who claim to have cancer. I don't know for sure. All I can tell you is that since I opened my shop and offered to help out a few friends, I have had an increase in the number of people who say they need it for pain," Nathan finally responded.

"Nathan, how much money are you bringing in a week here? And where are you getting all your weed?" Joseph asked.

This time Nathan remained quiet.

"You may as well answer my questions because I *will* get a search warrant based on my discovery here and the testimony of the detectives who are, also, aware of its presence. I will destroy your house in an effort to find what I am looking for and then I will destroy you by putting you away. Trust me. I mean what I say," Joseph said.

"All right, all right. . . ." Nathan said, nodding his head and motioning with his hands as though to calm down a gathering of people. "I raise the stuff myself. And it's quality grass. I have grow lamps in my cellar and I have enough plants to take care of my customers," he said, almost proudly. "As far as what I am making weekly . . . ," Nathan continued, shaking his head and pursing his lips as though in contemplation. "It's probably somewhere around two, maybe three-hundred dollars."

"Nathan, I'm gonna arrest your ass. Don't try to bullshit me. I know numbers and I know what I saw in that logbook. Now you better give me the right answer or we're gonna walk outta here like a bride and groom, but we'll be connected at the wrists."

Nathan paused.

"You're not gonna arrest me? You said 'or.' That means you're not gonna arrest me?" Nathan paused momentarily then said, "OK. I do three-thousand a week here. That's all I can handle." He again paused for a moment and then continued. "Ahhh . . . now I get it, you want a deal. I split the take with you and I can continue with your protection. . . . OK."

"No, you don't get it. I'm not gonna give you protection. If you get caught, I will not help you. The only thing I'm gonna do for you in return for a piece of the pie is shut my eyes. You're gonna leave off a package for me once a week at a place I designate, and that's all the contact we will have. If you don't, you will go to jail. If you try to involve me, your family and friends will be sitting *shiva* for you and you will know before you die that you fucked up."

"How much?" asked Nathan.

"I think a third is fair," Joseph replied, the taste for money beginning to form in his palate.

"What choice do I have?" Nathan asked.

"Jail," Joseph answered matter-of-factly.

CHAPTER

The bar at the Irish Pub was just beginning to fill up when Joseph walked in and spotted his newly befriended Irish buddies at a table near the back. They quickly waved him over and offered him a seat and a glass of stout. He accepted and they passed pleasantries for a few minutes.

Seamus seemed to be the ringleader. He, no doubt, had influence over the rest of his companions. When he spoke, just like the old E. F. Hutton stockbroker ad on television, everyone listened. He was also the best-dressed of the group. He was in real estate and once in a while bragged about his success. Usually it was when he was well-oiled and felt the need to express himself, as though he had just kissed the Blarney stone.

That night, Seamus had a proposition to make. He had located a piece of property that was eventually going to be taken over by the city for the construction of a new building. A friend of his on the local government planning board had tipped him off. What he wanted to do now was to give his pub friends an opportunity to make some good money.

He looked directly at Joseph and said, "This is where you can make a killin', kid. If you have a few bucks put away, you can get more 'interest' here than with any bank. And that goes for the rest of you as well."

Joseph knew he had money coming in. What could he lose? He asked, "Where is this property? What makes it so valuable?"

"It's located in East Boston by the airport. It's an old tenement house near the access road to the maintenance buildings and the people who provide the catering to the airlines—Sky Chefs I think they call themselves. When my friend told me that the city was goin' ta take by eminent domain three of the buildings there, I quickly made offers to the owners and scooped them up. This fourth building wasn't gonna be needed, or so they thought at the time. Now, all of a sudden, they decide they want the fourth building, the tenement house. I made a fair profit on the three that I bought and then sold to the airport commission. That was consummated three months ago. So, now that I have this illustrious group of friends, I thought I might invite them to join me in a sure thing."

Joseph said, "I'll go in with ya. How much do you need and how soon?"

"That depends on who else wants to take a chance," Seamus said. "If these boys are willin' to make a commitment then you won't need to put in as much. Of course, it means you won't make as much either."

Only Joseph agreed to buy in. For some reason the other men stayed quiet. Seamus said to Joseph, "Why don't you dig up ten grand and we'll call it a deal?"

"It'll take me a couple of weeks to collect on an investment I have," said Joseph, "but I will have it." This would allow Joseph enough time to do some research into Seamus's background and also to collect enough from his "business partners."

"Done!" said Seamus.

As always, the topic of the conversation focused on Northern Ireland once again. This time, however, Seamus turned the attention over to Michael Meara, one of the others at the table.

Michael spoke in a low voice. He told them of his knowledge of a variety of weapons and how they could be obtained without interference from the Bureau of Alcohol, Tobacco and Firearms.

It was at this time that Joseph realized these guys were very serious about becoming involved in the war in Northern Ireland. And Joseph also realized that he was now being included as one of the "boys." Evidently, he had somehow gained their trust from the first time he interacted with Seamus and his history lesson.

When Michael stopped talking, Seamus invited Arthur Boyle to take "center stage."

Arthur said that he had spoken with several sympathizers to the cause who had fishing trawlers available to use for transportation of large and small weapons and destructive devices. He then explained the procedure that would insure the mission's success.

When he ended his speech, Seamus again became the moderator and turned to Edward Clancy for his input.

Edward said that he had made contact with the IRA and that they had whatever money was required. Many people of Irish descent in the United States had donated funds to support their effort. All the money would be transferred electronically to an account on the Cayman Islands and from there to a bank in New York.

"All that we're waiting for is the right timing to pull this together," said Seamus.

* * *

Joseph knew he could not sit idly by. Over the next several weeks, he ran computer checks on Seamus O'Neill, first by running a "page" on his name through the Registry of Motor Vehicles computer-link in order to determine his date of birth, exact physical address and automobile ownership. Following this, he went through the department's records and identification as well as the National Crime Information Center. He also spoke with neighbors of Seamus under the guise of getting involved in some real estate transactions with him. He told them he needed to know more about the man with whom he would be dealing. He was not too concerned if word got back to Seamus, because he knew he would not know who was asking the questions. Dressed in a business suit and a short-brimmed hat, sporting a mustache and plain lens glasses—borrowed from a disguise kit kept in his office at the station—Seamus would not recognize any description his neighbors might offer. All of the people with whom he spoke, who knew Seamus, gave Joseph positive feedback on their neighbor and friend.

Seamus had been a Dorchester native and had never moved out of the area. He spoke with a slight Irish accent, no doubt the result of the great influence had upon him by both of his parents who were born across the sea. At forty-six years of age, having enjoyed some successes in the real estate business, he had become a respected supporter, both financially and vocally, of the Democratic Party. Although never running for any political office himself, he made his mark through his outspoken stand concerning Irish affairs in Boston; a stand that gained for him new and greater influence among many politicos of like descent.

His close associations and limited allegiances also found him in favor with the Catholic Diocese of Boston. He became a representative of the Knights of Columbus and was always seen at their various charity drives. He refused an office there, however, on more than one occasion, stating that was for younger men who needed community exposure. He preferred to remain humble and, to a degree, innocuous.

Being a tough businessman, with charisma and numerous connections in the city and in the church, he was afforded an invitation to become a board member of the First New England National Bank. This was one of the rebel banks not "owned and operated" by the

Protestant faction, which had held control of so many other financial institutions in the metropolitan area since their founding in the eighteenth or nineteenth centuries.

Seamus had been married as a teenager but his work ethic was such that the marriage did not last. On only two occasions did he ever mention his estranged wife. And both times he expressed his feelings toward women in general as weak, both physically and mentally, and as purposeful only to serve man. Careful where he spoke and what he said, it was only in the company of his closest bar buddies that he would let loose with a flood of expletives used as adjectives to describe all the women he knew.

To the outsider, he was a prince. In every way, in everything he did, Seamus portrayed himself as the epitome of the American businessman. He did well in his work; he shared out of his wealth; he practiced what he preached to others. What remained hidden was his intense negativity encompassing those things that he feared or did not understand .

Only in his marriage had he failed; perhaps therein lay the key to all he rejected. Perhaps it was in the fact that his mother had sided with his wife during the conflict that led to their divorce. His mother who had been born in Belfast, Northern Ireland, the result of a union between a Catholic father and a Protestant mother. Whatever the reason, only Seamus remained privy to that which bolstered his actions.

CHAPTER

Notre Dame de Victoires Church in the Old City of Quebec was a stone structure built in the 1700s, and was a focal point on every tour. It sat on one side of a square, which served as the market place and center of activity during that era. With its cobblestone plaza and pathways that led to the church and the surrounding stone, town-house-type complexes built centuries before town houses became popular, this was the original settlement for the French immigrants to Canada who had trav-

eled up the St. Lawrence River. The town houses, all four stories high, were a reminder of similar dwellings located on Commonwealth Avenue in Boston and denoted a common wealth among its inhabitants.

The church itself was magnificent on the inside. The first thing Joseph and Renee noticed upon entry was the massive heavenly castle, which comprised the base of the altar and stretched two-thirds of the way up the wall behind it. Atop the castle peak was a

large sculpture of the Virgin Mary holding the Christ Child. The entire edifice was white and gold. Just below and to either side of the sculpture were guardian angels. Above the angels were paintings of cherubim. Written in Latin beneath the one on the left were the words DEUS PROVIDITA ("God provides"). Written beneath the one on the right were the words KEBEKA LIBERATA, ("a free Quebec"). The next thing that caught their eyes were the two large oil paintings on the wall at the right of the sanctuary. Though dark from so many years of exposure to the light in the church, it was possible to make out the holy scenes depicted in each work of art. Beneath the paintings were

six small oval oils reflecting the Stations of the Cross. Six additional oils on the opposite wall completed Christ's journey. Above the center of the sanctuary hung a wooden boat. The hand-carved vessel made some two-hundred years ago, was a replica of the boat used by Samuel de Champlain when he forged the St. Lawrence River and established the village of Quebec. As they took in the splendor, they agreed that it was the perfect location for their nuptials.

* * *

The wedding ceremony and mass was set for four o'clock in the afternoon. Beautiful music emanated from the tremendously powerful pipe organ located in a loft above the entry doors. The church was filled with Renee's family and friends and with what was left of Joseph's family. A few friends and members of the department who had not yet turned away from him due to his change in character, were also in attendance. Even Seamus, Michael, Edward and Arthur, Joseph's newly formed Irish companions, made the long drive to be present. They agreed to witness the wedding but bowed out from the festivities of the reception. A good thing, perhaps, as Joseph still had not related his connection to the police department. If confronted, however, he would not now deny anything had anyone directly asked him. He was comfortable enough with his Irish friends to afford them that honesty, but only if he were asked.

The service was in both English and French, but mostly French. When the large wooden doors opened at the completion of the ceremony, the newlyweds appeared in front of a cheering crowd. People on the street—tourists and visitors who just happened to be passing by—stopped what they were doing and began clapping their hands. Joseph and Renee happily climbed into one of the three *coleches*, horse-drawn coaches, which awaited the wedding party.

They spent most of their honeymoon in Dublin, Ireland. The airfare was a gift from Seamus.

The Limerick Inn quickly became their favorite place to vacation. The woman who owned the inn befriended the two of them and would often, after the evening meal, tell them stories about her village and its people. They vowed that some day they would return to Ireland and spend a month at the same inn.

Joseph and Renee traveled the countryside and visited a number of pubs, the most popular meeting places for men. The couple found many that allowed women to be present.

They enjoyed the Irish, finding that most all of their encounters were with people who were pleasant, friendly and outgoing. Those in the Irish Free State of Eire seemed different from those described by Seamus in his many discourses. Politics were on a local level and not much involved the "troubles to the north" as those who lived here phrased it. The country folk seemed like country folk everywhere. Perhaps the larger cities paid more attention to the greater picture for Ireland. At least that is the way Joseph balanced what Seamus had to say versus what he himself experienced.

Returning to Boston, he and Renee settled down in Joseph's parents' home. Renee began looking for work at some of the bigger city banks and managed to land herself a job at the Bank of Boston. Her position required someone with a fluency in both French and English, since the bank had significant holdings and interests in Canada.

It did not take too long before Renee realized what it was like to be married to a cop. Their hours are not their own. When serious events take place, time is not a factor. Hours, and sometimes days, go by without couples being able to see one another and the phone becomes their only means of communication.

Add to this the fact that Joseph continued to maintain his contacts with his bar buddies, as well as those who operated a variety of businesses in his district, and Renee discovered the disillusionment of what she thought would be a wonderful and exciting marriage.

After just a few months, tensions became as taut as strings on a violin. When she and Joseph saw each other all they did was argue—over everything and anything, significant or foolish. The marital tension crept into Renee's work and twice during one week, she was called in by her manager and reprimanded.

Joseph, on the other hand, began to spend more time on the streets to avoid the unpleasantness he knew there would be at home.

Even sex was not the same as it once was. When Renee tried to become romantic, she was turned off. Joseph did not take the time to give her any satisfaction through kissing, holding and loving her and arousing her with foreplay. Instead he asked no more of her than a prostitute following a time schedule. It was as if there were a number of tricks lined up for the evening and nothing more was expected than a quick shove-it-in, release, pull-it-out, time's up.

Unable to cope any longer, Renee asked for and was granted a leave of absence from work. She said that she needed to see a marriage counselor. Joseph refused to go; he would never share his inner feelings with anyone, let alone a stranger. So Renee went to stay with her mother and father for two weeks.

Joseph called her the third day she was gone. He apologized and promised that he would try and do better. He called her every day, sometimes two or three times, until he was able to convince her to return.

For the next several months everything went well. Even their sex improved, but it was still just that—sex, not love-making.

But his work habits were not to be broken. Before long, he was back into the groove of long hours and late nights. Renee tried to cope and vowed she would not break her marriage covenant; after all, divorce was absolutely taboo in the eyes of the Catholic Church, especially in her local parish church back in Quebec City.

As the pressures at home increased on Joseph, he became more and more aggressive out on the streets. He watched drug buys go down on street corners and covertly followed dealers back to their apartments, tenements, "pads" "cribs" or "squats" where he waited and watched for suppliers to come to them or for them to go to suppliers. When he thought he had enough evidence or probable cause, he would request search warrants and, with his team, usually in conjunction with the narcotics division, effect arrests.

One such bust was accomplished at a crack house in Roxbury, when no one from narcotics was available. Joseph was overwhelmed at the huge amount of cash he found in a safe. He took everything in as evidence, tagged it and insured a chain of custody so that none of it disappeared. He brought it back to the station and locked it away for the night, determined that he would count it and turn it over to the clerk the next day. Policy required that it be counted in front of another officer so that there would be no questions about what was being accounted for. Then the money would be put into an evidence bag, sealed, and the evidence tag was signed by both officers. But as team leader, he could circumvent much of what he was supposed to do.

His team members completed their reports and left the office for their respective homes. As he continued to finish off his report, the thought of so much money kept creeping into his head. Finally, the curiosity became too much for him. He took the evidence bag and opened it, hauling out the wad of cash to count it. He was amazed at the number of new-style, one-hundred dollar bills that were wrapped in elastic bands. In total he counted sixteen-thousand dollars, comprised mostly of fifties and twenties.

He started to put the money back into the bag and then hesitated. He thought to himself, *No one even knows how much there is here. And it does not matter what the perpetrators say. After all, everyone knows they lie about everything, especially if they think they can make an accusation against a cop, which they probably will anyway.*

He sat holding the money in his hands for a long time. He was alone in the office. No one would be in. It was late. *That's a lot of money to eventually go to the Feds. No one will ever know.* "Aw, what the hell, they'll never miss a few thou," he whispered to no one but himself.

He counted out three-thousand dollars, mostly in larger bills, and put the rest back into the evidence bag. "Funny," he said quietly to himself, "I never sealed the bag at the house. Maybe my subconscious knew something I didn't know." He sealed the bag now and locked it back in the drawer, stuffed the money he had held out into a paper bag and closed up the office for the night. The taste for money coursed toward greater development.

The next day he came in late. He got one of the other detectives to count the money with him, reseal the bag and sign the tag. He then had the detective take it to the clerk for safekeeping. No one ever questioned the amount of money, nor Joseph's credibility. For too long he had been known as an honest cop.

It seemed so easy, he thought to himself. *There is so much money out there and much of it is held by pukes who break the law. Who said that crime doesn't pay? They seem to be doing all right for themselves and only a few get caught. And it's always the shitbird on the street, never the big dealer. Even last night's raid was small potatoes; that amount had to have been just a piece of the pie.*

The newspapers carried the information on the raid and the arrests of the six local dealers and suppliers. They also mentioned how thirteen-thousand dollars in cash had been recovered along with an undetermined amount of crack and marijuana, the most popular junk to users. Joseph was credited with the arrests.

The more he thought, the more he became convinced that he could do better for himself and still be a hero on the streets.

C HAPTE R

It was a Tuesday evening when Joseph called his team in to set up battle plans for a drug raid to be accomplished with members from the narcotics division.

The lines between the detectives and the narcs was very thin and many times one would cross over into the other's territory without any intent to steal the other's case. And because they worked so closely, this was a normal occurrence.

There is a great deal of jealousy among divisions and among cops themselves. So often they work together in apparent harmony, yet in truth, each one is out for his or her own glory. Egos and jealousies are a nightmare in every department. It is not just in terms of promotions but also in specialized services. This can be borne out when any new program is being considered by a department, large or small. Everyone wants to get on the bandwagon.

When Boston first introduced the concept of adding a canine to its roster, a list was posted asking for those who might be interested in becoming handlers to sign up on this posted sheet.

Over the past few years, several outlying departments had made great strides in containing situations, which could have escalated into more serious events, by the use of canines. They had received good press in the media from this and it encouraged other police departments to look into this method of control and of fighting crime.

Within days, the sheet asking for officer's with an interest in the new position was filled on the front side and overran to the back side of the paper. Even when the person was chosen, changes came about as the training is rigorous and the man who had opted for the job discovered that it was not as ego-satisfying as he thought it was supposed to be, nor as easy, physically, as it appeared. He found out that the dog does not do all of the work, the handler is continually on the run and must keep the same active pace as the canine. It was not long before he decided that he no longer wanted that particular job.

The department went through several people before the right one was found to make a successful match. The greatest challenge was finding someone who now wanted to be a canine handler after everyone had heard just how demanding the job really was. The original list of sixty potential candidates dwindled to five. Add to that the fact that several personalities were injured when they were not chosen for the job in the first place and the jealousy factor resulted in the removal of many names by the same persons who at one time displayed a keen interest.

Similarly, when an additional field photographer was needed in the division, the list went on the board. It was filled within days and an officer was chosen for the job. When he discovered that his nights were not his own because of call-outs, even though he was getting paid overtime to go, he decided that he no longer wanted the job. Someone else had to be considered for the position.

Cops do not learn such lessons easily; the practice is still in effect as new positions are posted and the same people sign up, seemingly forgetting what they should have remembered from past experience.

Joseph and his team, along with members of the narcotics team, reviewed the location of a crack house that had been under surveillance for three weeks. It began as one of the detectives investigated the street sale of firearms. The lead had come from Joseph after his nightly visit to a bar on Washington Street. He had made this particular spot a hangout as he recognized several of the patrons and one in particular for whom a BOLO—be on the lookout—had been distributed to the Boston precincts. That person was Tony Marcello.

* * *

Tony "The Hammer" Marcello, had been suspected of selling guns on the street to various gang members living in the metropolitan area or frequenting Boston. Some of them included motorcycle "club" members who had come down from Manchester, New Hampshire.

Tony had spent his last four years in Walpole State Prison for the same offense. Obviously, he had every intention of going into the same venture again as it was a business he knew well and in which he made a fair amount of money. Many of the guns he acquired had been funneled through Providence, Rhode Island, where they had been stashed in an older home on Federal Hill, a location known for many years as the headquarters for Mafia don Raymond Patriarca, who spent his remaining years in the same prison as The Hammer.

Federal Hill has always been known as Rhode Island's home for Sicilian born families. It has also been one of the safest neighborhoods in all of New England. After all, who in their right mind would want to invade an area "owned" by La Cosa Nostra. The few poor souls who tried discovered that the Italian system of justice is much more swift and always more severe than anything the United States government has to offer. And there is no right of appeal nor any stay of execution.

The guns stored in that house were all stolen from homes and businesses throughout Rhode Island and the southeastern section of

Massachusetts. There was always a ready market for firearms, especially with the newer clients who were part of the growing trend toward gang participation.

The Hammer kept his ties to all of his "family" friends. It is said that even while he spent his years in prison, he was treated with the same respect accorded to Patriarca. He was allowed many gifts and favors in his private jail cell, which looked more like a motel room. And none of the inmates who were forced to live in more cramped quarters, because of the private rooms needed for the two imprisoned celebrities, complained, out of either admiration or fear.

All of the prison's residents knew the history of Raymond Patriarca as leader of the largest Mafia crime family in New England. And many had heard the story of The Hammer, who had come to the assistance of his good friend at a time when he needed help most.

Both were in prison when one of the New York crime families feared Patriarca would turn state's evidence against the Mafia—more a rumor than truth, as those who really knew Patriarca realized his deep unwavering loyalty.

A "hit" was ordered and arranged through prison guards and several inmates whose fears of retribution were greater from the larger New York-based family.

Tony Marcello had been a small-time hood. He had "graduated" from the Concord Reformatory and the Shirley Correctional Center and had furthered his education at Walpole. His years behind bars exceeded his years of freedom on the street. Most of his crimes in the early years had been misdemeanors and lower degree felonies. As an habitual offender, his crimes increased in intensity as the years passed. His last offense prior to being caught for selling illegal guns was for aggravated assault and battery with the intent to inflict permanent damage to his victim. The assault had been the result of someone making a false accusation against him for which his pride could not cope. He wanted the person, Ricci Mariani, to remember this mistake for the rest of his life.

* * *

Ricci Mariani was a weasel—a short, swarthy, grease-spot of a character who always turned up whenever there was easy money to be made, especially if it involved prostitutes. In Boston, much of the trade in women is controlled by black pimps. Seeing a pimp driving a flashy, expensive car is not confined to movie scripts. In reality, on the streets, that is a fact of life. One of the favorite pimpmobiles is the gold edition Lexus—usually white with gold trim. Often times, the pimps themselves will pull their car alongside a known hooker and wait while she passes to him a wad of cash from her latest scores. And she had better not withhold any of the money; the punishment can be deadly.

When a pimp operates an escort or massage service, he will always send one of his bodyguards with a girl to a hotel room to insure that there is no problem when the transaction is being made with the "john"—the guy who is willing to exchange money for sexual gratification. The bodyguard is an insurance policy that does not allow for any damage to the rented product. He will wait close by while the girl checks the john's driver's license and monetary resource; she does not want to get stung by the "pussy patrol"—the cops who set up prostitution stings—nor does she want to get burned by a john who does not have enough to pay for her favors. The monetary resource may include a credit card as most of these businesses now take VISA and MasterCard, usually filling in the "Description" blank with the words: "Something Special."

Ricci Mariani drove a taxicab for a living even though most of his income came from his outside dealings. His most productive commerce was as a result of standing-by at Logan Airport. Many recent arrivals, upon entering his cab and into conversation with him, would ask where the action could be found. If the fare did not ask, then Ricci might himself ask if the client was interested in any action. Usually this was an indicator of one of two amusements: gambling or ladies of the night. Ricci's business was good.

Ricci managed to keep himself unknown to those who utilized his connections. Although illegal, he would remove his identification information from the window above the back of the front seat that separates the driver from the passengers in the cab. He did not want anyone to know who he was in case something should happen, which might require him to be a part of an investigation. He knew that fares would never think to look at the number on the outside of the cab, so he only worried about what might be seen inside from the passenger compartment.

Ricci picked up a client early one evening. As they were passing through the Sumner Tunnel on the way to the Sheraton Hotel, the conversation disclosed the fact that the passenger was the CEO for Gemini Electronics, a computer manufacturing firm in Glen Rock, New Jersey. The man was coming to participate in a new products show at the Hines Auditorium next to the Sheraton. He mentioned that he needed to stock up on liquor for a hospitality suite his company was providing for prospective buyers and would the driver know where he might get his best deal on some quality spirits?

Ricci was only too pleased to help out and offered to drive to an outlet store on the way to the hotel.

Going into the package store to help carry out the alcohol, Ricci came up with an idea that he had never had the opportunity to use before. He suggested that there might be something else he could make available, which would really be pleasing to the man's most serious prospects. The man was intrigued.

Ricci explained that he knew some of the most beautiful "working girls" in the area; after all, he was a cab driver. For a certain amount of cash, an amount that would be far less than what the CEO might spend as a part of his advertising budget, he could provide private entertainment for those men who were ready to sign an order. Two additional hotel rooms, along with several magnificent hostesses at the hospitality suite willing to do whatever was required of them should they get the signal from the CEO, would round out the perfect sales promotion. The CEO told Ricci he should come to work for his company—he was a great salesman himself. The CEO was convinced to go along with the program. Perhaps, because in the back of his mind, he might be able to enjoy some of the favors of these women also. He had often dreamed of a *menage a trois*—two women in bed with him at the same time.

The CEO finally asked Ricci what his name was, after all, he did not even know with whom he was doing business. Ricci stumbled for a moment as his usual business dealings had never been so elaborate. But his usual business dealings had never involved such an important person spending such a significant amount of money, the majority of which was about to come to him. Without too much thought, he spit out the name Tony. He had no one in particular in mind when he said the name, just Tony. It could have been any Tony. It was just a name.

The CEO wanted to know Tony what? What was his last name?

Once again, mostly without thinking, Ricci remembered a guy he met in prison and he quickly added Marcello, Tony Marcello. That was a good name. And as far as he knew, Tony Marcello was still in the joint. Besides, that is a common Italian name. It could fit any of a dozen people. *Yeah*, he thought, *I am Tony Marcello.*

They stopped in front of the Sheraton and the bellmen took charge of all the luggage and the bottles of liquor. Ricci went with the CEO to the front desk while the man checked in and made arrangements for two additional rooms near the large hospitality suite his company was paying to use.

The CEO invited Ricci up to his room to finalize the arrangements for the next two evenings. Ricci went back to his cab and locked it before joining him in his room where they talked about the business at hand and where the CEO managed to elicit some other details about Ricci without being too obvious. There is no doubt that the man became a CEO by using talents not everyone else possessed. Ricci answered his questions without suspicion and managed to give answers that were more fitting to the Tony Marcello he knew from a few years ago.

As promised, Ricci supplied four very good-looking women wearing very short maids uniforms to be the hostesses at the hospitality suite. And, as though choreographed by a professional stage company, the girls knew how to act and what signal to look for from the man who was making available a very handsome sum of money for the two nights of familiar work.

The girls, by taking turns, managed to entertain eight of the men who gave on-the-spot written approval for orders from Gemini Electronics. To make sure that the girls understood exactly what was expected of them, the CEO did choose two of the girls on the first evening about two hours before dinner and the opening of the hospitality suite to share their charms with him. He was not disappointed.

Although everything appeared to go without a hitch, it didn't. Within a month after the show had closed, the CEO received calls from the attorneys of three of the new customers gained as a result of the negotiations at the hospitality suite. It seems that their clients each had suffered a venereal disease, which they had passed on to their wives. It was not a total shock to the CEO as he, too, had been plagued with a similar infection. That did not stop him from becoming intensely angry with the cab driver—Tony Marcello—for supplying whores. He paid for quality call girls, not tramps. And now, Marcello was going to pay.

The CEO hired a detective agency to track down this Marcello. The information he had learned about him from their meeting in his hotel room ought to give the agency enough to locate him.

It took about three weeks for the detectives to find the real Tony Marcello. When they found where he lived, they notified the CEO and he flew into Boston to confront the guy who had nearly destroyed his electronics business.

It was a Thursday evening. The CEO had met with a local attorney recommended by his New Jersey law firm. Both drove to the Marcello house in the lawyer's car. The CEO was quite surprised by the moderately upscale home owned, or perhaps rented, by this cab driver.

Climbing the steps to the front door, the CEO banged at it with a fervor fueled by anger. Tony came to the door and the CEO demanded to see Tony Marcello. When he said he was Tony Marcello, the CEO called him a liar, to which Tony lunged out at him and asked him who the fuck he was. The attorney tried to intervene but Tony grabbed him by the neck and asked him if he wanted to die.

Both the CEO and the attorney said there must be some mistake and could they please talk this out. Tony asked what the fuck they wanted and both began to speak at once. Tony then told them to get in the house as he was curious as to what had taken place.

Tony noticed how well dressed these men were once they came into the brightly illuminated kitchen where he had just been preparing his dinner of linguine and basil/tomato sauce.

The CEO explained what had taken place with the cab driver, the hospitality suite and the whores. It took Tony less than twenty minutes of the CEO's explanation to put a name to the person who had duped him and who had used his name. He kept this to himself as this was something he would handle. He told them that he would do some searching and perhaps with a little bit of luck he would find out who had been using his name and he would let them know when he made that discovery. They were not satisfied but there was little they could do otherwise. They left after giving Tony their business cards. The CEO wanted to go back to Logan Airport and spend time watching the cab drivers in an effort to locate the one that had damaged him, but he could not even remember the name of the cab company that owned the cab. Knowing that was fruitless, he returned to New Jersey.

Tony went looking for Ricci and within a few hours found him. At first Ricci denied everything; even remembering Tony. An hour later, Ricci wished he had never remembered the name "Tony." By the time the cops found Ricci, they figured they had another homicide on their hands.

Tony had, on numerous occasions, been guilty of assault and battery, but nothing had reached the severity of this last attack. Even when the case was heard in court after three months of continuances and delays, the victim looked as though the beating had taken place within the last few days. His face had been so brutally thrashed that his most recent photographs previous to the assault could not be compared as being the same person who now sat on the witness stand. Tony went to prison. Ricci moved to Arizona where his brother lived.

Tony had become known by the prison inmates without his having to introduce himself. The internal exchange of information by inmates is fast and accurate. In comparison, even the Presidential Hot Line has no advantage over the communications system in a prison. It was a natural that Tony should be approached by two of the other inmates who had agreed to "take out" Patriarca. Knowing how prisoners think, Tony immediately allied himself with the men, but as soon as there was an opportunity to do so, Tony alerted Patriarca of his impending doom. Tony also advised Patriarca that if the "don" could get him a few items, which would not arouse suspicion, he would be glad to show the New England *capo de tutti capi* how much respect he had for him. Patriarca agreed and within a day had supplied Tony with his request—a block of ice in a heavy plastic trash bag inside of a canvas bag. It is amazing what the right connections can do even in prison.

Where time was a significant factor, Tony had arranged with each of the two men to meet him twenty minutes apart in the shower room to finalize an idea he had for eliminating Patriarca. With the cooperation of the correctional officers who had been paid off to give these inmates a degree of free rein, the first inmate had access to the showers at a time when most of the other inmates were in the recreation yard.

Tony removed all of his clothing until he was totally naked. He set his clothes on a shelf near one of the sinks adjacent to the toilets and close to the shower area. He, then, waited in the darkened shower room. Lights would not be turned on until it was time for the inmates to take their daily wash. As the first of the two inmates entered the room at the appointed time, he was greeted with a tremendous blow to the abdomen even before he could call out to Tony that he was there. As he doubled over, this was followed by another crushing blow to the head. Losing consciousness, the inmate fell to the cement floor where his head was pulverized by no less than twenty more pounding hits by the bag of solid ice.

When Tony had completed his task, he dragged the body by its feet under one of the shower heads furthest from the entryway to the room. He then waited for the second inmate to enter.

Again, as though on schedule, the man came into the shower room whispering, "Hey! Tony!" as he entered. He, too, did not even realize what had happened when a repeat performance occurred and his head was demolished by the remainder of the block of ice Tony wielded in his hands.

Blood, chunks of skull and brain matter were everywhere in the shower room as well as on Tony's body. Tony's concentration on the task at hand was such that he did not seem to notice nor to care. In later years, Tony would recall this experience every time he saw the comedian, Gallagher, smash a watermelon on stage with a sledgehammer. Tony would smile to himself and mumble, "I can do a better job with a block of ice."

When both men were side by side under the shower head, Tony returned to the sinks and began to wash himself off. He would have used the showers if he could have had one with individual faucets. The problem is that the showers are all interconnected and under the control of the guard who holds the activation key; so he had no choice. He washed off the canvas bag and then, while he was still somewhat wet, got dressed in his prison uniform. He exited the room with the bag wrapped in some of his prison clothes, the method by which he first walked the prison's corridors without arousing anyone's curiosity, and returned to his cell.

Upon his entry to the cell, he removed the ice from the bags and dumped it in the toilet. Then he flushed the plastic and canvas bags down the toilet, even though the ice was not yet small enough to pass. Knowing that all prisons utilize a powerful suction and razor-scissors device to prevent anything from impeding the flow of waste by inmates trying to damage or clog the sewage system, Tony had no hesitation in sending these few items through the pipes.

It was two hours before discovery was made that two inmates were missing. And it was another two hours before their mutilated bodies were found. The prison went into immediate lock-down. The Massachusetts State Police were called in to investigate. A search of every cell was undertaken to locate the club or other weapon used to beat these men to death. Nothing would ever be found.

It was several days before Raymond Patriarca could summon Tony to his cell. When he did, he knew what Tony had done for him and from that point on, Tony became a member of the "family." And it was from that point on that Tony acquired a new name—The Hammer.

As for the prison guards who had arranged for the laxity in the protection of the don, both were involved in fatal traffic accidents. The first one occurred when one of the guards was on his way home from work. He was broadsided by a stolen vehicle from which the driver fled from the scene on foot. The guard died instantly. Four days later, as the second guard was leaving the funeral home where his friend's casket was open for viewing by members of the family and the correctional officers who were able to attend, a car pulled out of one of the parking spaces in the lot and hit the guard before he could reach the safety of his car. As the guard lay on the pavement, injured, people in the parking lot began to scream. The driver of the car then backed over the man and once again drove forward over the man's head, crushing it. People ran toward the car trying to stop the driver as he turned the wheel and accelerated to exit the driveway. He did not make it out before one of the people took down the registration plate number and ran into the funeral home to call 911. The car was found that night less than a mile away in a shopping center. It, too, had been stolen.

* * *

After spotting Tony in that bar, Joseph made a cellular call from the table where he was sitting in a corner with a good perspective of everyone who came in and left the establishment. He alerted headquarters as to what he was watching and requested some undercover cars "put the peek" on The Hammer when he leaves.

Once out of the bar, and using several cars to play "cat and mouse" with the suspect, it was only a matter of time before they found where he was staying.

Over the next few days, one of Boston's most notorious drug suppliers made contact with The Hammer. Surveillance was conducted with several unmarked vehicles including a van rigged to videotape and monitor activity at the house. Getting a warrant to listen in on telephone calls by tapping the lines is easier obtained through the FBI than by local departments. However, as Joseph made declarations in an affidavit for such a tap, enhancing some of the details by stretching the truth, the judge was obliged to grant the warrant.

It was determined that a transaction would take place on Tuesday. Sixteen 9 mm, semiautomatic machine-pistols were to be purchased by Juan Cardiz in exchange for $26,000 in cash. Even new in boxes, with enough ammunition for a small war, the guns would not cost this much when bought legitimately, but this was not legitimate and there could be no tracing of ownership.

The deal was to take place in the parking area behind the Mission Church on Huntington Avenue at rush hour. The guns would all be in two boxes no larger than a typewriter. The money was to be in one-hundred dollar bills and was to be banded in one-thousand dollar increments and placed in a zippered money bag. Once the money was counted inside The Hammer's car and the guns were inspected by Juan, he would unlock the back door and the boxes could be moved. The Hammer drove a dark blue Buick with deeply tinted windows. Juan drove a forest-green Jeep Wagoneer.

It would be just the two of them and with the busyness of the hour, no one would pay any attention to what they were doing. Besides it was a church, anyone passing by would think it was church business.

There was to be no action taken by the cops. They were there solely to watch the transaction, to videotape it and then to follow the suspects back to their respective locations. The van would be set up early enough so as to be out of sight yet have viewing access to what transpired.

The detectives could effect an arrest on The Hammer when he returned home. They were to be sure to follow him into the house so that anything discovered there could be seized as evidence even if it was outside of the perimeter of the crime. This was not strictly legal, but Joseph wanted everything he could find.

The narcotics team was to follow Juan and set up a stakeout on his place of business. They knew he had been operating out of a new location but they had no idea as to where until they got this break. They would take no action at this time as they wanted to see how far Juan's connections would take them.

Everything went off according to plan; not so much as one hitch. They videotaped the transaction, the narcotics people carried through on their stakeout and Joseph's crew made the arrest of The Hammer.

In The Hammer's house, they discovered a cache of handguns, all different calibers, several Colt AR-15 rifles and five crates of Chinese-made Norinco AK-47 assault rifles. Four of the assault rifles had been converted to fully automatic machine-guns.

As they began to question The Hammer, having made him aware of his constitutional rights, Joseph took over the initial interview. He made sure that The Hammer knew he was going back to prison; in fact, he pounded away at that making it as uncomfortable as possible for him. He knew that if he got The Hammer in the right frame of mind, he could get the results he wanted from him.

While Joseph questioned him, the rest of the team lightly searched the house. Joseph knew that he could stretch the law, but he wanted more. So, he advised The Hammer that he was getting a search warrant and he was going to destroy the house if necessary to make sure there was nothing hidden.

"Man, you found everything; what are you looking for?"

"Money!" stated Joseph.

"You've got all the money; you took it when we came into the house," The Hammer said.

"I've got what you consigned for," said Joseph. "Now I want whatever else you have in the house."

"I don't have nothin' else!" he shouted.

"Well, I'll have to see for myself," Joseph retorted.

"I'm tellin' ya, I got nothin' else!"

"We'll see."

While two detectives remained at the house, Joseph drove back to his office and typed up a search warrant request and affidavit. Once again, choosing his words very carefully, he added information to his affidavit that would guarantee his warrant.

Armed with this piece of paper, he made contact with an available judge and had the warrant signed. He then returned to the house and showed the signed warrant to The Hammer. Without delay, his men began to pull apart the rooms.

The house was built in the 1930s and was as solid as any with quality workmanship. It was a three-story home with a kitchen, dining room, living room and sitting room on the first floor. The second floor had three bedrooms and a bathroom off a central hall. The third floor had a bedroom, a bathroom and an attic, which also ran off a central hall.

The house was furnished with heavy furniture that matched the period of its surroundings. It was clean and well-kept by a maid who came in twice a week. What Joseph really had in mind was finding cash or a bank book, some indicator as to what The Hammer had for assets.

The minute the detectives began rummaging through the rooms, The Hammer became extremely upset.

"What the fuck is it you want, O'Fallon?" he demanded.

"I want to know what kinda money you got and where."

"What do you mean 'and where'?"

"I mean, I know you got money. I know you sell guns. I know your entire history and I know you can't live like you do without an income. I know you don't do no legitimate work. So I want to know where you got your money. And I also know that unless you tell me, you ain't ever gonna get a chance to spend it where you're going because I'm about to whack you as hard as I can. With your record, you won't be out for a long while, this time."

"Fuck you, O'Fallon—go ahead and have your fun. I ain't givin' you shit. And when my attorneys get through with you, you're gonna be lookin' for a new job. Mark my words."

Joseph turned to his men and said, "Tear the walls out if you have to. This bastard's got money hidden somewhere and I intend for us to find it."

For a while The Hammer just sat there. It was not until Detective Frank Devlin found a floor safe under a nailed-down rug in the sitting room on which an easy chair rested, that The Hammer began to wiggle in his seat.

Devlin said, "This isn't any big deal. I can get a locksmith to open this. It's not like the ones you find in convenience stores set in cement. This one's a piece a cake."

"Hey, O'Fallon," called The Hammer.

"What is it?"

"All right, you found the safe. Now what?"

"I'm gonna get it open and I'm gonna take all the cash as evidence."

"If you take that, I'll have nothin'," The Hammer said.

"Too fuckin' bad. I gave you a chance to tell me where it was, but you thought we were stupid. So, fuck you!"

"Hey, c'mon. That's everything I got!"

"Ya know something, asshole, I don't care. And I'll tell ya somethin' else. When I get through tellin' the judge and the jury how I discovered that some of the guns you sold were used by gangbangers to kill other kids who were eight and nine years old, they're gonna fuck you up the ass."

"Whattaya talkin' about? I ain't sold any guns to kids."

"Like I said, I don't care. But they're gonna think you did when I get through with them."

"Hey, O'Fallon, c'mon. You're gonna fuck me outta my money and then fuck me as well?"

"You got the picture."

The Hammer sulked down in his chair and said nothing.

Joseph went over to Detective Devlin and whispered, "You know, we don't have a chance in hell of doing anything with his money even if we do seize it. There's nothin' that gives us the right to hold it. What I think I'm gonna do is let him think we had it cleaned out and will not return it unless he turns state's evidence on some of his dealings. No sense in going to the expense of having a locksmith break in; it could be more of a problem later depending upon who he has as a lawyer."

"You're the boss," said Devlin. "What do ya want us ta do with him?"

"Take him in and 'book 'im, Dano'!" Joseph said in a voice loud enough for The Hammer to hear. "Grab all those guns and put 'em in my office."

Turning to The Hammer, Joseph said, "Tony, I'll be talkin' to you later. I'm gonna wait till the safecracker gets here and then I'm gonna take what I find as evidence. It'll be in a safe place where you can dream about it while you're back in the can," Joseph ended his conversation.

The Hammer was transported back to the precinct where he was booked and where he sat in a holding cell until Joseph returned to the station. Joseph waited for an hour and a half to pass before he went into the holding cell to retrieve The Hammer for more questioning.

"I have the power to make you a deal, Tony," Joseph said to The Hammer. "Right now, I hold all the cards. I hold an impossible 'royal flush full house' and I can make things easy on you. Your buddy, Raymond Patriarca, is dead so you have no more connections which can help you. Only I can help you. I know a way that I can get you outta this mess you're now in. It won't be easy, but I can do it. You interested?"

The Hammer looked at Joseph without saying a word. He just stared at him for several minutes. "I don't follow you," he finally said.

"If I can convince the district attorney that you're gonna turn state's evidence on the gun sale you made and are gonna tip some previous encounters into our hands, maybe the most time you'll get is two years. That'll mean early release time even with you being on probation."

"Why?" The Hammer asked.

"Why what?" Joseph responded.

"Why? Why are you willin' to do this? You figure your search warrant's bad or somethin'? You fuck up somewhere?"

"Nope. Not at all. I got you right by the short hairs if I want. All I wanna know is are you interested?"

"I don't know, man" said The Hammer, "I don't understand what you want outta this."

"I'll tell ya what I want outta this. I want to make a few good busts. And you hold the keys to the kingdom. You can make it possible for me to do a good job."

"That's it? That don't sound right to me. All you want is a coupla good busts? You been gettin' some business lately. I been readin' about ya in the papers."

"Yeah, well that's a big part a what I want."

"Oh, so there *is* more?" The Hammer said, more a statement than a question.

"Yeah, there's more. I'll discuss that with ya at a later date. There is one other thing I will mention now, though. That money you had in the safe, I haven't counted it yet. Why don't you tell me how much is there."

"You'll know soon enough, I guess. There's about a hundred fifty grand."

"Well, I hope it's all there."

"Whattaya mean by that? It better be all there!"

"Yeah, well if I count it and it's short, it's your word against mine. And you know what? My word will win."

"So that's the other part of it, is it? Your hush money. Well, how much do you think will be there?"

"Oh, I would venture to say there will be about a hundred thou, maybe a little more, maybe a little less. And you're half right. There is still something else."

"What the fuck *more* do you want?"

"Not now, later. Oh, by the way, I didn't have the locksmith come out just yet. That was going to depend upon our little talk here. But, if you tell me where to find the key, I'll make sure your money is safe."

"You know, you fuckin' suck! What's to keep me from hollerin' right now and spillin' my guts to your boss and lettin' him know that you're shakin' me down?"

"Because I could burn you right now. It'd take me thirty minutes to get that safe cracked and have my guys count out that money and make my case against you stick. If that's what you wanna do, remember the consequences."

"There's a jacket in the closet in the spare bedroom, the one with the bed with no covers. The key's in the pocket. You'll be able to find it."

Keeping to his word, Joseph worked the deal to the benefit of The Hammer. And also to his word, he kept only fifty thousand of the one-hundred and fifty-four thousand he located in the safe. The rest he left locked in the floor where he found it. His taste for money continued to increase.

CHAPTER

Joseph knew that holding as much money as he did would be a problem if he decided to bank any of it. He could put it in a safe-deposit box, which would give him access to it if he needed it. He thought about investing it, maybe with someone he trusted like Seamus O'Neill, but really, how well did he know Seamus. At least, well enough to give him ten thousand dollars several weeks ago. He would have to think on that for awhile.

One person Joseph had befriended was Terrence Maloney, a writer for the *Boston Record* and a former dockworker on Atlantic Avenue down by the wharves. As gruff and boisterous a person as he was on the docks, he was less intense outwardly as an employee of the newspaper. Joseph, at first, did not know what to make of this character. Terrence was very opinionated on every subject. Once engaged in conversation, it was only a short matter of time before one knew exactly how Terrence felt about the subject at hand. Perhaps it was their unconstrained personalities that linked together these two men. Both managed to get along with other people but neither had what might be considered true friends. In time, they became as close as any two people possibly could.

Terrence always did a great job when it came to putting into print all the criminal activities, which Joseph became involved in as he brought the perpetrators to justice. From the first time that

Terrence interviewed Joseph, the pair struck up this mutual friendship. It continued to having lunches together and to discussing some of the cases, which proved to be challenging to Joseph. It would soon grow into an association, which would last several years.

Terrence admitted one day, as they met for lunch at Legal Seafood in Brookline's Chestnut Hill Mall, that he had a craving for more independence and wished he could become a partner in some venture where he had a say in its operation. The newspaper was so weighted down with upper management and politics, he would never get such an opportunity with them.

Joseph knew that most people grumble about their job at one time or another; not everyone was always happy or satisfied with those things they do in life for work. So, out of curiosity he asked Terrence what he had in mind.

Terrence said that there was a gasoline service station up for sale in West Roxbury, not too far from his home. That is where he would like to hold an interest. It need not be some place where he had to be all the time to work, but a place where he could just have some say, knowing that he was an owner. As a youngster, he always worked with his hands and he enjoyed cars. What could be a better combination? He would have the freedom he longed for and something that would belong to him after retirement from the paper.

As they continued their discussion, Joseph made no offer nor any commitment to help, but he did keep that in the back of his mind as something to look into the next time he was in the area. He asked Terrence exactly where the business was located, making small talk as to giving his opinion once he had a chance to look it over.

Once Joseph saw the station, he asked its present owner/manager for the details of its cost and operation. The fellow had owned the filling station for fifteen years and had emphysema, which he swore was amplified by the new low-pollution gasoline being pumped into cars. It was time to retire and he was not interested in making a killing, just what would be a fair profit.

The price was definitely right. Joseph slept on this thought for a couple of days and then said to himself, what the hell, if Terrence wanted to go halves with him, why not. The income was good, besides look at all the free gasoline he could get. Also, it might be a good business in which to place some of his money.

It was on a Wednesday, some five weeks following The Hammer's incident, that Joseph again saw Terrence. They met for lunch and Joseph told Terrence that he thought the filling station was a sound idea. Terrence seemed excited to hear the positive report from his friend. He made the comment that his only hang-up was that he could not come up with all of the money required without putting himself in a precarious financial position.

"I'll tell you what," said Joseph, "if you're willing to have me as a partner, I'd be willing to go halfway and invest with you."

"You mean that, Joe?" Terrence asked.

"Of course," Joseph answered.

"Partner, you got a deal."

It was almost a month later when papers were passed giving the prior owner his retirement and making entrepreneurs out of Joseph and Terrence. The gas station was located in Joseph's area, so he could easily stop by on occasion and see how things were going. Of course, Terrence on his way home from work, would stop by and put in a few hours at the pumps and the cash register. The people who had been employed at the station remained on as they had all worked for a few years for the former owner. That in itself was unusual as most businesses of this nature have a very high turnover. At first, Terrence wanted to examine the books carefully, thinking that perhaps there had been some skimming and the employees had found this to be a lucrative money-maker. But after two months of cautious accuracy he realized what dependable and dedicated employees he really had. The reason they had stayed there was money. The old-timer had paid his help well and they appreciated it. The business did very well and Terrence continued to show good faith by increasing the hourly wages by small but significant amounts.

Things were looking up for Joseph as well. The investment that he had made with Seamus O'Neill for a piece of property to be acquired by the city finally was sold. It meant a return of twenty-five thousand dollars from his ten-thousand-dollar venture.

The day that Seamus brought the check to the Irish Pub and laid it down on the table in front of the whole crew of men who met there at their usual time, every one of them had a momentary feeling of envy and then stupidity for not taking advantage themselves of such a good, almost risk-free, deal. They ribbed Joseph about cashing the check quickly before it bounced. They questioned the validity of the check as it was drawn on an out-of-state bank, and they asked Joseph how credible a check could be in which the imprinted company name read: SOB VENTURES. Even though one might read that as son-of-a-bitch ventures, as Seamus was not an easy business man with whom to deal, the name simply stood for Seamus O'Neill Business Ventures.

As the men made small talk about their day's activities, the discussion took its usual course and the talk was again of Northern Ireland. This time Joseph had some information he wanted to share. He told them that he knew a man who had been involved in the Mafia some years ago who was supplying guns to anyone who had the money to pay for them.

Michael Meara put up his hand in a gesture as though to say "hold on a minute."

"I appreciate your input, Joseph, but where we get the weapons of war comes from a longtime underground dealer. The guns we get are designed for a heavy duty conflict, not just street shooting. I am afraid that the quantities we are talking about are far in excess of anything a former Mafia member can obtain. Perhaps years ago when there was not the sophistication, they could have done well for us. I know that they managed to locate a great deal of government equipment through unbelievable channels during the war with Vietnam, but things have changed. I hope I don't sound like I'm putting you down; it's just that I do know how to get what we need. I have been researching this for a long time. I do thank you anyway for thinking of us."

"No, I understand, Michael," Joseph said, "I just wanted to help in any way I could but, I do understand, and I do know that you are the expert."

"Oh, now *you've* been payin' a visit to the Blarney stone," Seamus said.

With that they all laughed and continued to update one another on events in Ireland.

Joseph returned home around midnight. Renee was asleep in bed and did not awaken even when he turned on the light in the bathroom adjoining their bedroom.

It was not until he crept into bed that she stirred and asked him if he was ever going to love her again.

He mumbled something followed by, "I'm tired." He then turned his back toward her and almost immediately fell asleep.

Renee began to cry. She had tried hard to make him happy but there was just something about him that had changed so much. He was not the same man he used to be. Their life together was not one of joy; in fact it was not even living—just existing while sharing a common bed. Renee made up her mind that she could no longer cope without love. Her only choices were to leave or to commit suicide because staying here was already an issue of death. She knew she could never do the latter because suicide in the Catholic Church meant only one thing, not going to heaven.

In the morning she went to work as usual. She told her newest supervisor, Joanne, that she desperately needed to talk. Joanne told her she could have as much time as she wanted; whatever was bothering Renee was important to her as well. Joanne had watched Renee for the last few months and knew two things about her: first, was her tremendous capability as management material for the bank, and second, was her intense depression, which she tried to hide from everyone as she worked hard at being an effective producer in her job. Renee asked if she could close the office door. Joanne said, "Certainly, I want you to feel comfortable."

"I am afraid that feeling comfortable is far from where I am right now," Renee said. "I have had many problems at home, as you probably already know. My husband has a very demanding job and it has made for the interference of our life together. I have tried to think of ways to make everything better, you know? But, it has not worked. I am going to go home to Quebec. I am sorry to have to leave the bank and especially to leave you. You have been very nice to me and I am thankful for that. I wish I have a different answer to my problems, but I do not. I hope that some day you may come to visit me in my home. I also hope that the Royal Bank can find for me another job. It will be an embarrassment to return and I know some will think it is my fault that my marriage did not succeed. But I must not care what others think."

"Oh, Renee, I am so sorry to hear this. You have no idea how badly I feel. You are a shining star in our department and I know that it would not be long before you would be moving into a management position here. Everyone has been watching you and commenting on what a wonderful, dedicated worker and person you are. I even know that it was a little bit of jealousy, which caused your former supervisor to be somewhat unkind to you, but she is gone, never to return."

"Thank you," said Renee. "You make me feel the best I have felt in a long time. I wish I could stay but I have not made many friends here as most of those with whom I work are married and like to do things with other couples. My husband is not like that any more. He stays alone even when he is not working. Thank you again for everything. I will always remember you."

Renee left the office and began cleaning out the few things that she had in her desk that were hers. As she looked at the picture of her husband, she hesitated for just a moment before putting it in her pocketbook, almost wondering if she should bother to keep it.

She began to weep, not enough to be noticed by the others in the office as they mostly kept to themselves. She wiped her tears with the back of her hand and quickly walked out of the office and over to the elevator. She felt that if she had said good-bye to those with whom she was friendly, she would let go with a torrent of tears, which would take more than a hand to clear away. In addition to that, she did not want to disrupt these people from the work they were getting paid to do.

Reaching the main banking floor, she went over to one of the tellers and withdrew her savings passbook and her checking account wallet from her pocketbook. She closed out both without any explanation to the teller—not that it was any of her business anyway. Then she walked toward the outside door.

As she left the building, she waved down a taxi and took that home instead of the subway, her usual mode of transportation.

Arriving home just before noon, she found herself in the house alone. Joseph had gone to work and had not even bothered to eat any breakfast at home. She went upstairs to the bedroom and packed all of her belongings into two suitcases.

Then she went downstairs to the desk, which had belonged to Joseph's father and she wrote a lengthy note to Joseph to explain her leaving. She stated that she would not be returning, that things never really worked out from before and that they, obviously, would not work again. She was sorry that she was leaving but it was not a matter of choice. She ended the letter telling him that she loved him and would always love him, but it could never be the same again. She wished him well and hoped that some day he would meet someone he felt he could share himself with—someone other than the police department.

She telephoned for a taxi and had the driver take her to Logan Airport where she was fortunate to get aboard an Air Canada plane to Montreal and a commuter plane to Quebec City.

Renee never again went to Boston. And she never again would date a policeman from any city or town or province.

For Renee, to return to Old Orchard Beach would be impossible. There were too many memories there that would never go away. Once she made her way back into the Royal Bank, she would take all her holidays in Florida where the water was warmer and where she was fifteen hundred miles from that brief part of her life that she needed to forget.

Joseph found the note and tried to call Renee—after polishing off a bottle of Irish whisky his father had kept for special occasions, which Joseph found in the liquor cabinet in the living room. No one answered her phone and there was no answering machine.

Joseph knew he had made a mistake, but like all the other ones he made in life, he put this one out of his mind and was determined to go on from there. No sense lingering or worrying over something that could not be changed. And, at this time, he had no desire for any further change.

CHAPTER 9

Roger Gallagher had been with the narcotics unit for seventeen years. His knowledge of drugs was legendary in the department and he was competent enough to become an expert witness should he ever decide to retire and make himself available to those in the private practice of law.

As Joseph became more entrenched in street activity, his leads proved out with great accuracy. He would often call Roger when he had a tip concerning a significant drug buy. On occasion there was some reciprocation as Roger's informants would let out a small bit of information relating some criminal activity more connected to Joseph's line of expertise. Both men formed an unlikely alliance where each division enjoyed a degree of autonomy. But sometimes it was necessary to join forces for the betterment of the entire department, especially in the eyes of the news media.

It was not until Joseph was invited to spend an afternoon at Roger's house, following an all night fact-finding investigation, that several events came into play.

The first was Joseph's surprise at the rather palatial home his counterpart owned in the town of Sharon. When Roger first suggested that they take a break from the office and meet at his house, he told Joseph to bring along a bathing suit so they could take advantage of the pool he had installed last summer. The pool turned out to run the full length of Roger's house. It was set in the back yard, which was enclosed by an eight-foot-high stockade fence. The pool was somewhat of a kidney shape. On one side there was a waterfall, which flowed from a cluster of huge rocks that were set about four feet above the pool itself. The remainder of the pool looked like a picture from one of those colorful tour brochures for Hawaii—with a native girl standing under a waterfall in a naturally formed lagoon in the middle of a rain forest. The sides of the pool were all large rocks accompanied by a variety of flora and fauna giving it a woodsy effect.

Roger's house was a large, two-story colonial with great pillars supporting an overhanging roof in the front. The front door was recessed back some three feet and was flanked on either side by long glass windows, which allowed a view from the outside into the entryway. The full-length windows on the front of the house went from ground level upwards to six feet. The whole layout could have come directly out of a copy of *Beautiful Homes* magazine.

After having seen this, the inside was no surprise. As Roger's wife, Anne, took Joseph on the "twenty-five-cent tour" of the house, he could not help but marvel at everything he saw. He thought to himself, one of his hosts must have come from money because Anne did not have any full-time employment.

Inside the living room was a baby grand piano with a candelabra perched on top. Liberace would have been flattered. Anne was taking piano lessons, according to Roger, and was doing very well. The remainder of the furnishings looked as though they came directly out of an Ethan Allen gallery. Each room in the twelve-room house was equally appointed.

Sitting in the shade of the lanai next to the pool, Roger and Joseph drank ice cold Coors Lights and munched on nachos with melted jalapeno cheese. They continued to discuss in depth the investigation, which was initiated the night before. As they spoke, Roger would occasionally change the subject and try to pry from Joseph information as to how Joseph managed to get such good leads into activities taking place on the streets. With each question, the answer was almost always the same, "I have some good informants." Roger kept on pressing for greater details.

Joseph, likewise, tried to extract, without being too obvious, some data from Roger as to his great wealth. Roger just claimed it was from wise investments on his part. Where he got the initial amount to invest was never revealed.

Through the course of the afternoon, Roger drank a large quantity of liquids, progressing from beer to more potent beverages. It became evident to Joseph, as Roger spoke, that something did not seem quite kosher in the way Roger had originally made his money. Just a few words dropped carelessly, or perhaps with some intent, gave Joseph the feeling that Roger's newly formed friendship with him had an ulterior motive. It was almost as if Roger wanted an alliance with him in order to have access to greater sources of money—perhaps criminal sources that could only be tapped through the threat of police intervention.

Roger made a comment stating, "Isn't it amazing in our line of work that we have authority over the lives of some people."

"Well, yeah," said Joseph, "to a degree."

"We can change people's lives almost instantaneously because we know something about them that they don't know we know. And when they are confronted by what we do know, they know that we are going to make a change in their lives one way or another."

"One way or another?" Joseph asked.

"Yeah," said Roger without elaborating.

"What do you mean by that?" Joseph asked, trying to see where this conversation would lead. Did Roger want to hint that his wealth came from scamming criminals? He could not imagine this cop, who he hardly really knew, opening a Pandora's box.

"What I mean is, and I don't want you to be offended by what I'm gonna say, I know somethin' about your business that you don't know I know. Ya see, I been workin' with this little Jew-kid who owns a computer store at Upham's Corner. His name is Nathan Berkowitz."

Suddenly, all color drained out of Joseph's face. Just the shock of those few words brought Joseph to instant sobriety. He thought that his bowels were going to let go as he felt an immediate cramping in his lower intestine. He tried to keep his hands from shaking or from dropping his can of Coors as he moved to place the beer on the tiled patio deck next to where he was seated. His thirst had gone even though the dryness forming in his mouth would have welcomed any hint of moisture. He wanted to say something but he did not know what to say. And if he had tried to speak any words, he knew they would be stuck somewhere between his diaphragm and his lips. Any words that might be expelled would be weak and tremulous. So he remained transfixed and quiet except for the loud roar produced in his head each time he swallowed and awaited the final climax.

"You see, Joe, you're good at what you do. And I'm good at what I do. You know the criminal element better than most dicks on the job. You're like a doctor who's a general practitioner. But I know drug dealers like a doctor who specializes in a particular field of medicine. I know how they think and I know how they act especially if someone is turning up the heat on them. I know them better than they know themselves."

Roger continued, "I had a reason in inviting you out here today. It was more than discussing the investigation we're working on. It's more an investigation I'm working on; one that only I am aware of. Except for you, that is. I want to hear the whole story from you, Joe. And I don't want you to bullshit me. I want to know about you and Nathan and I want to hear it from your lips."

Joseph had never been in a position such as this before. Usually he had control no matter what the situation. Even in cases of a tight pinch, he always knew how to effect the outcome he wanted; but this was different. As he sat there staring away from Roger, he knew he had no escape. Roger was in the driver's seat and had all the controls at his fingertips.

His voice somewhat hoarse, Joseph managed to say, "Why don't you tell me what you think you know and I'll tell you if you're correct."

"No," said Roger. "You tell me what you think I know and I'll tell you if I think you're full of shit."

Looking now at the ground, Joseph hesitated to say anything. His mind was enveloped with thoughts of prison—something he could never and would never tolerate. He knew how thorough a detective Roger was and he knew that Roger would not be playing this game without all the cards stacked in his favor. His options: deny everything, lie through his teeth, or tell the truth. As he considered these options he watched Roger pop the top on another can of Coors, take a shot glass of Red Roses whisky and down the latter followed by the former.

Why didn't Roger confront him with his facts at the station? That would make sense if he were going to lower the boom on him. At least there Roger would have the benefit of witnesses and a videotaping of his confession. Something was out of place; something very confusing. Finally, Joseph opted to tell how he had put the bite on Nathan Berkowitz to the tune of a thousand dollars a week.

Once he finished his story, Roger looked over at him and said, "I didn't know if I could trust you. I feel better now."

"What's that supposed to mean?" Joseph asked.

"Joe," Roger replied, "you and I hold the same rank in a job we've been at for about the same amount of time. We make the same dough. But you're not living the same as me. I told you I invested some money and the investment made good. Where do you think I got my start?"

Without waiting for an answer, he continued, "I didn't inherit any money. My wife does not come from a wealthy family. We earned it out on the streets . . . I should say I earned it out on the streets. I earned it every time I went to a call and had to put up with the shit I took from people who were less than human beings and who were stealing money in one form or another, whether it be welfare or insurance fraud or dealing drugs or armed robbery. I earned it and I figure I'm entitled to some of the money being made through drug sales. If morons want to use the stuff and are willing to pay for it and have learned nothin' from the programs against that shit, then I'm gonna get a cut of the pie and live equally as well as some of the uneducated scrotebags who pay no taxes and have the least amount to lose because they have other up-and-coming morons who are willing to do the footwork for them and take all the chances."

He went on, "I asked you not to bullshit me and you didn't. I had all the facts from Nathan and he knew enough to 'drop a dime' on you and give me the details. You see, Nathan is loyal to me but he's more loyal to himself. We had a heart-to-heart talk one night awhile back and Nathan loves Nathan and doesn't want another talk like that ever again. Besides that, Nathan can't afford to pay out bucks to too many people or he won't have any money left for himself.

"So what I'm gettin' at is this, we should work together and not independently. Between the two of us, we can make a good living without anyone being the wiser. After all, we run our own divisions reporting to lieutenants who only know what we let them know. And no one knows what we know."

Joseph finally looked up. "You don't know what I've been going through sitting here since you first brought up Berkowitz's name. I thought at first this was it, you were lowering the boom on me and I was fucked. What I couldn't understand was why you were talking to me alone. Then I figured you had the place bugged. You don't know what a relief this is. Fuck me, my stomach 's still in a turmoil." As though on cue, Joseph's stomach forced a huge burp to be projected from his throat and mouth.

"I'm sorry," said Roger. "I needed to be sure."

"How have you been able to keep all this a secret?" Joseph asked as he swept his right arm outward encompassing all of the real estate surrounding them.

"Two years ago Anne's aunt died down in Florida. I was just starting to bring in some decent money from my contacts on the street. I let everyone believe that the aunt was loaded and that Anne was the sole inheritor. Of course, there was some jealousy as I had to put up with the usual comment, 'It must be nice . . .' but what did I care. I knew I had a way to cover myself and that was all that counted. No one has ever been out here from the department; I don't have any close associates there, except now for you."

Roger had one more question: "Well, what do you think . . . can we make an alliance . . . a partnership?"

Joseph was now the one who had no choice, but that was all right. He felt better knowing that he had someone he could confide in and work with as they pursued the same goal together: satisfying their taste for money.

Chapter 10

Over the next several months, Joseph and Roger managed to score well in a number of drug raids. With the information they pooled together, most of which came from Joseph's closeness to the people on the street, they kept watch on numerous locations simultaneously in which they could determine the significance of activity and the amount of money being amassed through narcotics transactions.

Whenever their surveillance drew them to the conclusion that there was to be a large business deal, they would create an affidavit that would be plausible enough so that a judge had no qualms in signing a search warrant. Armed with that warrant, they would raid the location and skim money off the top of whatever funds were confiscated. Where two officers had to count the money and sign for it, it was a perfect match for them as they could cover for one another.

During one of the raids, they came across a large quantity of guns in a variety of calibers and makes. Many of the weapons were in crates in the cellar of the house where the arrests took place. One of the officers assisting in the search of the premises discovered the first box of guns and called out what he had found to his supervisor. Roger went down the stairs and examined the box and soon located several additional boxes also filled with guns in another part of the cellar. He sent the officer outside to his car to get a camera. While the officer was away, Roger quickly moved three of the crates away from the spot where they originally sat. When the officer returned, Roger snapped a few pictures and told the officer to get some help and move the crates out to the patrol wagon that was standing by outside. Once the boxes were removed from the cellar, except for the ones that Roger had relocated, and once the work upstairs was completed and everyone had returned to the station and the building had been secured, Roger arranged with Joseph to come back to the house and pick up the remaining crates of guns.

The guns were taken to a storage facility on Route 28 in Milton; one of those U-Stor-It buildings so popular with people on the move, with people who have no room in their homes for things they want to keep, and with people who have items to hide.

Roger had used a fictitious name to rent the unit some time back and much of what had been available space was now filled with other cartons of material. When Joseph saw the boxes he asked, out of curiosity, what was stored here.

"Well, I might as well show you rather than tell you," said Roger as he walked over to one of the nearest cartons and lifted the cover .

Looking inside, Joseph asked, "Is that what I think it is?"

"Marijuana and hashish," stated Roger matter-of-factly.

"What are you doing with it?" Joseph asked.

"Keeping it for insurance," Roger replied.

"Insurance?" Joseph questioned.

"Yeah. In case I run short of money and need to find someone to sell it for me."

"You're gonna be in the dope business?" Joseph asked.

"Why not? It's lucrative, isn't it?"

"Well, yeah. But I just thought we wanted the easy money. You're takin' an awful chance sellin' pot."

"Maybe. Everything depends on two things. One, of course, is supply and demand. I'm gettin' a supply and I know there's a demand. The other thing is findin' the right person to peddle the shit. I don't mind waitin'—the right person will come along. In the meantime, I'll just collect and store what I can. I've got about twenty-grand in weed right now."

"What about the guns?" Joseph asked. "What are we gonna do with them? Do you have an outlet?"

"Matter of fact, I do. Some a these are collectors items. I mean they have value beyond just for street sale. When I ripped open the boxes down in the cellar before we hauled them out, I checked them over. I found that quite a few of them would be good possessions for the right persons and I know the man who can handle them for us."

"Who's that?" Joseph asked.

"It's not important. Just trust me that I know what I'm doing. This is not my first dealing with guns. A guy who has some connections in Orlando owns three pawn shops down there. When he gets guns in that are of a questionable origin, he ships them out to Haiti where he has a ready market for them. He's been doing business for a dozen years and has never had any problems. Don't ask me how he manages to get the guns out of the country, all I know is that he can do it."

"So how do we get the guns down to Florida?"

"Another guy I know has an eighteen-wheeler he uses to bring huge rolls of paper from International Paper in Jay, Maine, down the east coast. He always has room for a few more boxes of stuff. Once he drops off his load, he finishes his route with my stuff and collects from my contact. Then, on his way back to Maine, usually with some other load depending upon which company has northbound material, he stops in Boston off the Southeast Expressway and meets me on Kneeland Street in Chinatown for lunch and to complete our business."

"How the fuck long have you been doing this?"

"Joseph, my boy, long enough to make a few dollars and to be livin' the good life. If I were to retire tomorrow, I would not have to worry about collectin' the little amount Social Security pays. But there's a lot more business out there so I'm gonna hold off on retiring until I am damn good and comfortable."

"I'm with you, Roger," Joseph stated before they locked the storage shed and headed out.

* * *

Stopping in at the gas station on his way home from the storage shed, Joseph was pleased to find his friend and partner, Terrence, inside the garage ringing up a sale on the cash register.

"Hey, Ter, what's up?" Joseph asked.

"They tell me it's been a busy day and it's not over yet. I was just starting to cash-up when you pulled in. We usually stay open, now, until ten o'clock. I asked the crew if they wouldn't mind putting in an extra hour at night. It seems that we are the only station in the area and the only one that keeps hours convenient to the working public. How was your day?"

"If I told ya, you wouldn't believe it. I had a good day. A lot a shit went down. We had a raid and managed to get drugs, money and guns. One a your guys was at the station so we gave him the scoop. I tried to reach you but you'd already gone for the day."

"Ain't that the way, though. Well, I can't complain. After all, I get my share of info from you and once in a while it's OK to let someone else take the story." He paused for only a quick moment and then he added, "Just don't make a habit of it."

Joseph laughed. "You don't have anything to worry about. No one writes a story like you do and no one gets me more press than you do. I know on what side my bread is buttered and I'm never going to lose sight of that."

Joseph's next stop was at the Irish Pub. His cronies had been and gone so he just took a seat at the bar and ordered a beer.

Tip, the bartender—given the nickname because he was a devoted admirer of the former speaker of the House of Representatives, Tip O'Neill—stopped to talk with him while serving up a few drinks. Things were quiet this night so he could spend some time with one of his best customers.

"Ya know, Joseph," Tip said, as he began to wipe down the water spots and rings left by condensation from the cold beer mugs and shot glasses that sat on the bar during the evening, "I think your boys are ready to do some serious deals with the IRA."

"Whattaya mean by that?" Joseph asked.

"Oh, ya don't have ta play dumb with me. I may look like I'm busy all the time and ain't payin' much attention to what goes on at the different tables, but I got ears and I got eyes that see things a lot of other folks don't see."

"Explain," said Joseph.

"Well, first of all, I got a brother who had cancer of the throat and was unable to speak. So, I had to learn how to read his lips. It became a hobby with me as I worked each day. I started to watch people when they spoke and the funny thing is, I was surprised at what a lot of them had to say when they got their fill of booze. I been watchin' you guys and I know what you been discussin'."

"Now wait a minute. You've got this all wrong; I don't care what your lipreading eyes say."

"Joseph, Joseph, Joseph . . ." Tip said with each cascading "Joseph" going down scale as if in a decrescendo. "Don't try to play games with me. I know what I saw. I don't want to argue the facts with you. What I want to tell you is that I am in agreement with you.

I've been wanting to tell Seamus but I haven't had the chance because he's usually here when things are busy. So, when you came in tonight I figured I'd tell you and you could pass it along to Seamus. I've got some money saved up and I want to support the cause for a united Ireland. Most everybody who comes here to relax agrees with what I'm tellin' you. The only thing I know that they don't know is what steps you all want to take to help the Free State gain total control of the country and independence from England."

"Look," said Joseph, "I'll pass on to Seamus what you said, but I'm not going to admit I know anything of what you're talkin'. If Seamus has something in mind, I'll let him speak to ya himself."

"Fair enough," said Tip, "fair enough."

* * *

It was a Thursday evening when Joseph was headed over to the gas station. This was the night that Terrence usually counted the week's income and prepared the night deposit along with the payroll for the employees. As Joseph drove down past the Arnold Arboretum between Roslindale and Jamaica Plain in the unmarked detective's car assigned to him, a call came over the radio advising of a holdup in progress at the gas station that he and Terrence owned.

Putting the magnetic-base blue light on the dashboard and flipping on the switch, which made his headlights flash in a wig-wag fashion, he stepped on the accelerator and began to pass what cars there were on the roadway as he made his way toward the West Roxbury location.

Within minutes he was parked alongside four marked cars that surrounded the gas station. As he got out of his car, he could make out Terrence inside the station. Standing next to him was a man wearing a Halloween mask. From what Joseph could determine, the man stood a good six and a half feet tall. He held a gun at Terrence's head and kept moving, almost jumping, back and forth as he glanced out the window and back behind Terrence. The man was extremely nervous; Joseph hoped he would not shoot Terrence because of his jumpiness and his quirky moves. He also hoped that Terrence would not take matters into his own hands and try to subdue the thief. It would not take much for Terrence to unleash his explosive temper, one that he did not often display, and to try to overpower the gunman.

It was not until the man turned his head toward the display cases, removed his mask, which had now become more of an obstruction to him, and began to move his lips, that Joseph noticed a second gunman crouched down trying not to be seen by the police who had encircled the building. This man, too, appeared to be wearing some sort of mask. It was difficult to tell how tall he might be because of his bent stature. In a way, it was to Terrence's benefit that there was more than one perpetrator; Terrence would not try anything on his own.

Joseph went up to one of the uniformed officers and inquired the status of the situation other than what was readily apparent. The officer was from a Rapid Response Unit, part of a select team of radio cars in each district designated to go immediately to the location of any significant trouble or incident in order to accomplish two consequences: first, to assess the situation and second, to provide without delay a police presence. In many instances, these officers have captured perpetrators in the act of committing a crime before the suspect has had an opportunity to escape the area.

The Rapid Response officer stated that he had been the first one on the scene and had approached the gas station with his lights off, standing by until additional units arrived and closed off the accesses to the building. The gunmen spotted the last cruiser as it pulled in and grabbed the manager and, shouting from the doorway, threatened to kill him if the cops did not leave.

"I turned on the P.A. and told him we couldn't leave the area and that their best chance was to exit the building," the officer stated.

"Have we got anyone from TPF here who could take those ass-holes down?" Joseph asked.

"I radioed for tactical assistance. No one has shown up yet."

Just as he made that statement an unmarked cruiser pulled in with the lights shut off. Hernando Vasquez got out and opened the trunk of the car and removed a high-powered rifle.

"Hey, Hernando," Joseph called out.

"Hey, Joe," Hernando called back.

"See if you can get a sight picture on the cocksucker with the gun pressed against the manager's head. If you can get one, hold it on him. If you can't, don't do anything. That manager is a friend of mine and I don't want him to get hurt."

"I'll do what I can," said Hernando as he leaned on top of the cruiser roof, strapping around his arm the unique sling designed for holding the weapon steady, and began to sight in on his prey.

Within seconds Hernando said, "I've got his head right in my crosshairs. You give the word, Sarge, and I'll do a frontal lobotomy, Mexican-style."

"Give me a minute to try and talk with the fuckers. I'll let you know when, if need be," Joseph replied.

Picking up the public address microphone in the marked cruiser, Joseph said to two gunmen, "Throw your guns out and come out with your hands high in the air!"

Once again the gunman holding Terrence shouted back, "No fuckin' way, man! You and the rest of those cops get the fuck outta here or I'm gonna ace whitey here, then do my bro' and myself."

"Don't be hasty, man. Think about this. What a waste a life that would be. We can work something out. No need of all you getting killed over money. It's just not worth it!"

"Don't fuckin' tell me what stuff's worth. Just get the fuck outta here or this guy's history. You hear me?"

Joseph ended by saying, slowly and deliberately, "If you release the hostage, we can work a deal. If you don't, you will have to take the consequences."

"What the fuck consequences you talkin', man. They ain't no consequences 'cept the ones what I jus' tol' you," the gunman responded.

Looking carefully at the position of each gunman, Joseph said to Hernando, "Do you think you have a good enough picture still to take the guy down?"

"Ready when you are, Sarge. The other dude is far enough away so that once I drop the first one, you guys can hit him."

Joseph turned to the uniformed officers closest to him and said, "When I give the word for Hernando to fire on the guy holding the hostage, you follow up with fire on the second gunman. Don't fuckin' hesitate and don't fuckin' miss! Ya got that?"

Each one nodded his head and said, "Yes, sir."

Joseph gave the word to Hernando. In less than five seconds time, Hernando's rifle emitted a loud explosion and bucked in his hand from the momentous recoil. The bullet pierced the plate glass window of the gas station. The glass hung in place momentarily before shattering and falling to the ground. As Joseph watched, he could see the top of the gunman's head lift and open up like the trunk of a car. At the same time, the uniformed officers began to fire their guns and the second gunman flew backwards from the impact of the bullets that crashed into his body along with the weight of the display cases, which fell against him as the cases were pushed by the fusillade.

Joseph ordered the men to stop firing and they rushed the building and checked out their handiwork. Both gunmen were very dead.

Terrence stood rubbing his neck where the gunman had kept the pistol pressed against it so tightly. He kicked the dead body several times as though to punish it for the discomfort that was inflicted upon himself.

"I was closing up for the night. I let everybody go home. I wanted to get the money squared away before I left and these two fucks come bursting in with guns in their hands and tell me to give them all the money I had. I started to hand over the zipper bags while I stepped on the holdup button. These shits said they wanted the rest of the money. I asked them what they were talkin' about and they said they knew I had more money because tomorrow was payday and they been watchin' me and know my routine.

"I told them this was all I had; just enough for payroll as I made nightly deposits, which they woulda known if they were payin' attention to me every night. The first fuck says I was fulla shit and he begins to go through the register, which only has a hundred bucks in it for start-up in the morning. Then he starts to paw through my desk, yankin' out the drawers and dumpin' everythin' on the floor. He musta been tossin' my stuff for ten minutes. I'm really gettin' pissed and he tells me he's gettin' pissed. He starts throwin' stuff all over the place and his partner begins goin' through the back of the garage past the display cases. It was about this time that the first guy, the one who grabbed me by the neck, spotted the cops outside. And you know what happened from there."

"You all right?" Joseph asked.

"Yeah, I'm OK," Terrence replied. He then took one more look at the gunman with no face lying there on the floor beside him. He gave the lifeless body one more swift kick. This time right in the balls. "I'd feel better if I knew he felt that."

Joseph finished up his report and reminded the uniform men to get their versions of the incident into him as soon as possible. He stayed with Terrence for a couple of hours but Terrence said for him to get some sleep, that he would be fine; in fact he wanted to start writing the story for the paper while he still had everything, especially the animosity he felt toward the scum on his floor, fresh in his mind. "Besides," Terrence said, "I don't want you giving this story to any other reporter."

It was well after midnight by the time the bodies were removed and the gas station regained some order. The emergency window repair people came immediately and put up sheets of plywood to cover the openings created from the bullets penetrating the plate glass. They would be back in the morning to replace the broken glass.

Terrence could not wait until morning to tell his employees what they had missed.

CHAPTER 11

It had been two months since the attempted holdup at the gas station. During that time Joseph had only stopped by the station sporadically as he was busy with his visits to the bars and businesses on the streets.

As Friday evening rolled around and Joseph walked into the Irish Pub, his pager vibrated on his belt. The number displayed was that of Roger's office at the station. He stopped short from continuing into the pub and made a quick about-face returning to his vehicle. He picked up the cellular phone and dialed the number shown on the pager. Roger answered.

"What's up?" Joseph asked.

"Do you know a guy named Terrence Maloney?" Roger inquired.

"Yeah, I know him pretty well. Why?"

"How well do you know him?" Roger continued.

"I met him working at the *Boston Record*. He usually does the police reports and on occasion we've been to lunch. I've helped him in a business venture, a gas station in West Roxbury. Why? What gives?" Joseph asked.

"Meet me somewhere where we can talk. I've got some information you may be interested in hearing. And don't talk to anyone until after I see you. OK?"

"You name the place, just don't make it near any of the places I frequent. I don't want anyone to know my business," Joseph stated.

"Meet me in front of the Holiday Inn in Brookline," Roger said.

"Is that the one that used to be the 1200 Beacon Street Motel?" Joseph asked.

"The same," Roger answered.

"Give me about twenty minutes and I'll be there." He then pushed the END button on the phone, placed it back in its cradle and headed out of the parking space he had occupied.

Pulling up in front of the Holiday Inn next to one of the long line of empty parking meters on Beacon Street, Joseph shut off the engine and waited for Roger to arrive. He sat there for less than two minutes when Roger's car pulled up behind him and the headlights went off. He watched Roger through the rearview mirror get out of the driver's seat.

Roger walked to Joseph's car and got in on the passenger side.

"What's goin' on?" Joseph asked.

"Look, we've been straight with each other in our business dealings, right?" Roger asked.

"Yeah, of course. Why do you ask?" Joseph queried.

"Do you know anything about this Maloney guy's background? I mean did you run a check on him or anything?" Roger asked.

"No. Why should I? I knew him from the paper and I got to know him because of all the stories he wrote about me; all the incidents I covered. We became friends. Shit, you must remember the two fucks that got blown away in the gas station in West Roxbury. That was his gas station. I guess I should say, technically, our gas station as I helped him get the financing for it." He stopped speaking for just a moment, then continued. "Just what the fuck is this all about. And don't ask me any more questions until you answer mine."

"The guy's inta dope. He's a drug peddler with a boomin' business in Charlestown. He's selling hash, Colombian gold, Maui Wowie and any other marijuana he can locate. One a my snitches fell into something last Wednesday concerning him and tipped me about him and said he ran a gas station in West Roxbury. I started an investigation as I had nothing in our files on this guy and when I checked with the city records, I found your name on the property along with his. That's why I wanted to get some input from you as to what was going on."

Joseph sat there staring at Roger with an incredulous look on his face. His mouth had dropped open and he slowly shook his head from right to left. "You gotta be shittin' me," he said. "I loaned this guy money and he's makin' enough to have done this thing on his own? I don't fuckin' believe it."

"Just a theory, Joe," said Roger, "but I figure he wanted you in the gas business with him so that if he got caught peddlin' shit you would hear about it and could protect him. If you didn't protect him, he could burn you because he could show that you were in partnership with him."

"Maybe so, but he didn't know that I had access to some money to help him out; in fact, he didn't know I would offer to help him."

"Think about this, Joe," Roger continued, "even if you only offered a small amount of money, he would have taken it just to get you onto the paperwork with him. And he baited you. He knew how to appeal to your ego with his newspaper stories. I bet he's the one who invited you to lunch first and not the other way around. He wanted you hooked."

"I can't fuckin' believe it. You make it sound like it makes sense. I got scammed. So, what's my next move?"

"I think we ought to approach him. I mean you know what I got in storage. He's evidently been in the business for a long time. I checked out his home and he's not hurtin' a bit. I don't know where he's keepin' his money, but I'm sure of two things. He's got a lot of it in cash and he's got a lot of it buried where no questions are ever asked."

"You mean like one 'a the Caribbean islands or Switzerland?" Joseph asked.

"I don't know yet, but somewhere," Roger replied.

"And how do you suggest we approach him?" Joseph asked.

"You approach him first. After all, he knows you. Lay the whole thing out for him. Tell him what you know and get his reaction. I guarantee he thinks no one knows his connection as a dealer. He operates through a dozen other peddlers who work the streets and he stays remote from all of them. He even has middle men do the negotiating so he doesn't get connected. He's so clean that he doesn't even own a gun."

"Roger, you've blown my mind. I've had people put things over on me before, but usually I'm very conscious of what goes on around me. But this one definitely got past me. OK. I'll blow *his* mind when I drop this bomb on him. No doubt whatsoever."

Roger finished up by saying, "If he needs further convincing, let me know. I've got the videos and a lot of other proof to show I know what he's doin'." He then got out of the car and walked back to his car and left.

Joseph sat for just a few minutes more, still digesting all the latest news before he started his car and headed home. He considered returning to the Irish Pub but opted to forget that this evening as he needed a clear mind to strategize how he would approach his partner, Terrence Maloney.

CHAPTER 12

With so many things going on, it would be awhile before Joseph would get back to the Irish Pub. Right now, his primary concern was focused on his most recent surprise.

He stopped by the gas station at five minutes before closing on Sunday night. He knew things would be quiet on the last day of the weekend so he purposely chose this time to speak to Terrence.

As Joseph walked into the station, Terrence said, "Just give me a minute to read the numbers off of the pumps and check the underground gas tank levels with the dipstick, then I can lock the door and we can visit. You haven't been around in a while; you must be busy."

"I've been busy. You're right. Go ahead and do your thing and I'll wait in the office."

As Joseph walked toward the office, he stopped to grab an Almond Joy from the display rack. He sat on one of the steel-backed office chairs, opened the wrapper of the candy bar and began to munch on the first of the two chocolate-coated coconut sweets.

He was still formulating in his mind how he would begin his conversation with Terrence. He wanted to gain his attention without shutting him up or turning him off.

He heard Terrence locking the door and switching off the outside lights indicating that the station was closed for the night.

Terrence walked into the office and sat down with a huff in the swivel chair behind the desk he used to do all his paperwork. "Hey! How've you been?" he asked in a fairly loud voice as he regained a second breath after having been moderately busy for the day.

"I'm great!" Joseph said. "I couldn't be any better if someone laid a hundred kilos of pot in my lap and told me I could keep the proceeds from the sale of it without any attached strings and no fear of arrest."

"What kind of an answer is that?" Terrence asked.

"The kind of an answer someone gives when he knows he's being hoodwinked by a pro," Joseph replied.

"I guess I don't follow you," said Terrence.

"I don't understand why not. After all, I'm only telling you what you already know and what I've just begun to know."

"Are we gonna talk in riddles all night or have you got something you wanna say?" Terrence asked.

"Ter, I thought I knew you pretty well. I'm finding out that there's stuff about you that I don't know. Now you don't have to deny anything because I have proof of what I'm about to say. I just want you to hear it from me and then we can discuss our options."

"What're you gettin' at?" Terrence began. "I don't. . . ."

Before Terrence could continue, Joseph said, "I know all about the business you've been doing in Charlestown. I know people who have bought and sold all flavors of marijuana purchased from you. I know how you set me up to be an insurance policy for you. And I've got video tapes of you making deals with street peddlers. Now, as I said, you can deny it if you wanta, but I can show you film of your movie star debut. Before you say anything, I want you to know that the guy who heads narcotics is also aware of everything I'm tellin' you. And we have a deal we're willin' to make with you. Now you know me well enough to know that I'm not shittin' you."

Terrence sat quietly and never said a word for a long time. When he did speak, he did so with a question. "What do you want from me? What kinda deal are you offerin'?"

"First, how long have you been in the business? And second, didn't you think I'd ever find out?"

"I been doin' this for maybe six, seven years. And, no, I thought I had myself far enough removed so that no one would know. I'd like to know how you found out, though. I'd really like to know where I screwed up."

"Enough time for that. What I want you to know now is that the deal involves unloading marijuana. There is a quantity in a storage warehouse that needs to find its way to the streets for a marketable price. And I know you can do it."

"What are you doing? Setting up some kind of a sting?" Terrence asked.

"No, not exactly. What I am doing is going into business with you. I should say, my other partner and I are going into business with you."

"I don't get it," he replied.

"Ter, you and I and another guy I know are going to work together. He and I have some quality stuff we want you to sell through your channels. There will be enough money for all of us. And you can't afford not to do this."

"You're on the level. You want me to deal for you."

"You got it, Ter."

"Man, you have just. . . ."

"Blown your mind?" Joseph asked, finishing Terrence's statement.

"Blown my mind!" Terrence continued.

CHAPTER 13

Within two months, the stash of drugs that Roger had amassed was gone. Promises of greater scores loomed ahead as he and Joseph attacked with fervor the dealers on the streets.

"Ya know, Roger," Joseph said one day when they were meeting at Roger's house, "it's hard to believe how much drug traffic we got in this city. I can't imagine what New York or Chicago must be like."

"From what I get off the teletype," Roger said, "Atlanta, Los Angeles, Dallas and all the cities in between are choking on the drug sales taking place. Even Manchester, New Hampshire, has a problem with drugs. A little city like that. So, don't be surprised. This is an epidemic which is never goin' ta get resolved. For too long it has been flourishin' and the people it buys—the lawyers, the politicians—they've kept it alive no matter what they say to the contrary. There's too much money bein' made to stop it. All it's gonna do is keep growin' so we gotta get what we can get while the gettin' is good."

"Well, I've gotta tell ya," Joseph replied, "this is the first time in my life I've been somewhat independently wealthy. My mortgage is paid off, my car loan is paid off, the stuff my folks bought when they were expectin' to live long enough to make the monthly payments out of their Social Security, even that's paid off and now

I've got a decent bank account and cash which I never thought I would ever have. I've been able to get into some small investments which have panned out and have covered my extra income. I can see how the taste for money has touched so many people. The best part is that we're only taking a share of what these scrotebags would have kept for themselves anyway."

"The best thing is," said Roger, "there's lots more to be made."

"Hey! I've had my eye on a boat for awhile now. Before long, I'm gonna buy it and head out of Portland Harbor into Casco Bay and get away from all the crap I face every day down here. I've been watchin' my pennies and I'm almost at the point where I can do this. I bet you didn't know that when you buy a boat, a cabin cruiser, which is what I want, it costs fifteen-hundred dollars a foot when you go over eighteen feet. There's this forty-four-foot Chris-Craft I been lookin' at and it's got every gadget a guy like me could ever ask for. That's gonna be my boat. And then, when I take my retirement, I'm gonna move to Maine and get away from this fuckin' city and all the animals I've had to deal with over the years.

"Did I tell ya, I'm goin' up ta Maine on vacation in August? I'm gonna visit a cousin of mine who's a lawyer in Skowhegan," Joseph continued animatedly, "and he has a summer place on a lake in Rome. They call the entire area Belgrade Lakes 'cause Rome borders on the lake that separates the towns. He says there's only a few lots left on the water and he says where I've been so lucky in my investments, I oughta think about buyin' one a them for later on. I don't have ta build right off but I can get the lot and wait until I'm ready. Maybe I'll find the right woman, get married again and settle down with an early retirement; enjoy life, ya know what I mean?"

"Jeez, slow down, will ya?" Roger responded. "Ya got me spinnin' with all your ideas. Take your time. You'll have everything you want, I guarantee it."

135

"I know, I just get excited once in awhile when I think of how well we're doin'."

"Yeah, well, it's OK to think about it, but take your time. Like they say, Rome wasn't built in a day."

"I know, Roger, I know."

"Look, I want ta get to the business at hand," Roger said. "I had word from one a my people that there's a shitload of pot comin' in by truck from Connecticut. It was picked up in Bridgeport off a fishing boat that made a connection off Long Island. I don't know where it originated or how it got past the Coast Guard, but it's supposed to be comin' in tomorrow night. It's my understandin' that it'll be unloaded in a warehouse by the Charles River somewhere close to the Mystic-Tobin Bridge. I don't have an exact location yet, but I will have before the day is out. My snitch is goin' ta page me when he gets the word on where it'll be dropped."

"I been meanin' ta ask ya, who's your C.I.?"

"Hey, give me a break. I don't ask you who your confidential informants are, so let's just keep these things to ourselves. That way, should anything unexpected ever happen, they don't get burned."

"Fair enough," Joseph replied and then changed the subject back to its original topic. "About this drop, how many people are involved?"

"Don't know," Roger replied. "If it's late in the night, which I expect it will be, prob'ly be four or five at the most. Too many more will draw attention at that hour. If it's an afternoon delivery, there'll be more so they can keep a watch on wharf activity.

"Might as well relax," Roger continued. "My beeper hasn't gone off yet."

Both men swam in Roger's pool as Anne served them snacks and drinks during the afternoon. She joined them for awhile and

Joseph thought to himself how nice it must be to have a companion like her. He had all but forgotten what a wonderful wife Renee had been, but that was a long time ago and things had changed a lot since then. He wondered what it would have been like if she had only hung in there. Then again, was she the perfect mate for him? Well, there had to be plenty of time to find out. Things were better now that money was not an issue any more.

It was almost three hours before the piercing tones of Roger's pager let them know his information was ready. As he picked up the small Motorola unit, he read the message that said, "Eleven PM. D19. B. 1000K. 4 M."

"Looks like the shipment will be at dock 19, warehouse B, at 11:00 P.M. Four men are going to off-load a thousand kilos of pot. That's about a ton. I've got to figure a way to surprise them there, take them down, hoist the stuff and transport it to our place. There's enough room now."

"Is that four men including the truck driver?" Joseph asked.

"Prob'ly in addition to him," Roger replied.

"I've got an idea," Joseph said.

"What is it?"

"There's only one way onto and off of that dock. It's the same for most of the ones down there. The people he's meetin' will be waitin' for him in the warehouse, why not stop the load before it gets to the warehouse?"

"How we gonna do that? Get a marked car to pull it over? Then we'll have to turn it in and we'll need men to impound the truck and contents and we'll miss out on the guys at the warehouse because there'll be no way to link them to the shipment."

"Ya know, Roger, for all your smarts, you're not thinkin' very well. Take a ride with me down to the docks and let's scope out the area."

"All right. I don't know what you've got in mind, but I'll listen."

Both men went inside the house and changed back into their street clothes. Joseph drove them downtown in his car. As they started out onto the wharf leading to warehouse B, Joseph reached over and tapped Roger on the arm. "Look, those eighteen-wheelers parked by the fence. That's one a the terminals for J.B. Hunt's trucks. The trucks on the outside are the independents. They lock them up and leave them there while they wait for their next shipment and waybill."

"Yeah, so?" Roger asked.

"If we block the roadway with one a those when the truck arrives, the guy will have to stop and wait for us to move so he can get by. One of us will keep his attention with the eighteen-wheeler while the other *gets* his attention and hauls him outta the truck."

Saying nothing, just listening, Roger then uttered: "Might work. How you gonna get inta the truck and start it?"

"I'll just hot-wire it. The wiring is all exposed. It's easier than tryin' ta do a car. If we get down here early enough, I'll have time to rig the rig. If there's a problem, then we go to plan B, as they say, and that will be to hit them at the warehouse. To me, this one carries a lot less risk."

"I gotta agree with ya," Roger replied.

* * *

At about nine o'clock that night, Roger drove the two of them back to the docks. They parked between two buildings. If a cruiser happened to come along, they could always say they were on a stake-out. It would put a crimp in their plans, but that was a chance they would have to take.

As luck would have it, the night turned out to be busy enough so that no patrol car had time for door checks.

Joseph eased his way out of the passenger seat of the car after pulling the bulb for the dome light from its socket so that nothing would give them away once the door was opened.

He walked over to the eighteen-wheeler that was parked nearest to the roadway leading onto the wharf. Taking from his pocket a device designed to break glass and cut seat belts in an emergency and made by Smith and Wesson, the gun manufacturers, he pulled back on the bolt of the unit and placed it against the small windbreaker window on the passenger side of the truck's cab. Releasing the bolt, it hit with enough impact to shatter the small window. This allowed Joseph to reach in and unlock the door to the truck. He then climbed inside, pocketed the glass breaking device and took from his other pocket a pair of wirecutters and three wires with alligator clips connected to each of the six ends.

Using a penlight, holding it in his mouth, he turned himself upside down on the driver's seat so that his head was underneath the dashboard. He, then, began to pull at the wires that went to the ignition switch.

The truck had a diesel engine. This meant that he would have to attach one of the wires to the primer so that the plugs could get hot enough to start the engine. Once that was done, he could jump the starter with the other wire and crank over the engine.

As a kid, he liked trucks and he knew a bit about them. One of his neighbors had a diesel engine and he was always fascinated that they could not be started like other trucks; they all needed time to be primed. He remembered thinking how crooks would not want to use one in a holdup. By the time the engine was warmed enough to turn over, the cops would have arrested them and put them in jail.

When the glow light came on, indicating that the plugs had warmed to the starting temperature, he put the second jumper wire from the battery position across to the run position and then placed the third jumper wire across the battery terminal to the starter switch and the truck came to life. He then quickly removed the jumper wire to the starter terminal. Now that the truck was running, there was no need to keep the starter motor turning; its only function was to get the main motor activated.

Knowing that the engine would start without any problem, he shut the engine down and waited until it was closer to eleven o'clock. If the truck arrived too early, they would both be out of luck as he could never get the truck energized in time.

While he sat there, he kept watch for the men, who were supposed to meet the truck, to arrive. As the only entry/exit, he knew this would be the route they would have to take.

It was nearly ten o'clock when a car pulled into the roadway from the avenue. As it came down the street, its lights were extinguished and it coasted toward the end of the wharf and turned left in the direction of warehouse B. Crouched down out of sight, Joseph raised himself only enough to peek into the windows of the black Pontiac as it eased past his vantage point. It was too dark to make out any of the figures in the car; all he could tell is that it appeared that the four men were all together.

Once it had gone by, he noticed Roger come out from where the car had been parked. He approached the passenger side of the truck and lifted himself up on the running board to the broken window.

"I'm gonna put the peek on them. I'll be back shortly," he said.

"Hey! Don't be gone too long in case the truck arrives," Joseph demanded.

"No sweat," Roger retorted.

He watched as Roger made his way down the roadway, hugging close to the buildings that lined the left-hand side. When he reached the last building, he ducked into the alleyway rather than go down to the driveway in front of the building that separated it from the wharf and the water.

Minutes seem much longer when anticipation is involved. Joseph began to get a little nervous when Roger did not return. Looking at his watch, he realized only ten minutes had passed. He tried to wait and watch without concern, but his impatience gnawed at his mind.

All of a sudden, there was a noise by the passenger side window. Joseph drew his Glock from its shoulder holster and aimed it at the window.

"Psst! It's me! Relax, will ya," Roger whispered.

"Where in the fuck did you come from? You nearly scared me outta my pants!" Joseph exclaimed in a loud return whisper.

"I found an alleyway that leads back behind all the buildings so I took that instead of making myself a target out on the street. There are four of them. They're all waiting on the loading platform of the warehouse with the overhead door open and the lights out; so they must be expectin' the truck momentarily. You better start the engine. One good thing, if this was warehouse A, the warehouse closest to us, we'd be in a pile a shit. The engine noise would alert everyone. Warehouse B is closest to the water and the noise of the river along with the traffic on the Mystic-Tobin Bridge is coverin' everything pretty well. I'll get back outta sight and wait for you to make your move."

"OK," Joseph replied.

Joseph started the engine once again. He then pushed down on the clutch and put the gearshift into first. Most of these big rigs had about a dozen forward gears, but the first gear would give him enough power to pull out and block the road fairly quickly.

He could not have had better timing. Just as he put the gearshift into first, he saw lights turn onto the roadway. Looking in the rear view mirror, he could tell that it was a truck, but much smaller than what he expected. Like the car, the truck turned out its head-lights and coasted down the street.

Joseph pulled the steering wheel hard to the left and released the clutch as he gave the accelerator a push. The big truck jumped forward and almost stalled, causing a lump to form in Joseph's throat. "Fuck me," he whispered. But the truck's engine kept on whining as it pulled ahead across the roadway. Joseph turned on the head-lights to make it look as though the truck was getting ready to leave on its late-night route.

The other truck slowed even more and finally came to a stop. The driver must have realized that the operator of the eighteen-wheeler did not know he was pulling out in front of him as he had the pickup's headlights off.

His attention being focused on the eighteen-wheeler, the driver did not see Roger approach the small truck. The window was open on the operator's side. Roger could see that the door was unlocked as the button was raised high. Keeping low and out of sight of the side mirror, he reached for the handle, pushed the button and yanked the driver out of the truck all at once.

The driver, startled, let out with an "Uhhh!" and nothing more.

The small truck lurched forward as it was still in gear. Fortu-nately, it was a standard shift truck and the engine stalled out as there was no gasoline being applied by the accelerator.

Pulling the man to the ground, Roger pounded a fist into his face before the guy knew what hit him. The man's head hit the as-phalt pavement knocking him from consciousness. Roger then turned the man over and, removing a piece of nylon rope from his pocket, tied the man's hands and feet, then took a cloth from his pocket and covered the man's eyes. He picked the man up under the armpits and half-carried, half-dragged him over to the eighteen-wheeler where Joseph was wiping down the steering wheel after having removed the jumper wires from the ignition switch. He shut off the headlights, wiped everything he had touched and exited the cab.

Roger then hoisted the bound man into the truck and shut the door.

Roger ran back to his car, got in and started the motor while Joseph ran over to the small truck, got in and restarted the motor that had stalled.

Within seconds the truck was turned around, the headlights turned on and both the truck and the car headed out to the storage locker in Milton where they would unload the pot. They had no concerns as to the truck being reported stolen, after all, who would want to be implicated in a truck filled with marijuana. Time was also on their side. It would be a while before the men waiting at the warehouse would realize that the shipment was not coming. And it would be awhile before they would be able to move the eighteen-wheeler that now blocked their path.

Arriving at the storage building, they quickly unloaded the truck and secured the facility. Joseph then drove the truck to Braintree and parked it in the lot belonging to the phone company located in the old Naval Station. The property had long ago been decommissioned and sold for commercial use. He again went through the process of wiping down the truck and then got into Roger's car and they drove back to Roger's house.

"Couldn't have been any smoother," Roger exclaimed as they pulled into Roger's driveway. "That oughta get us a healthy amount of cash once your boy has had a chance to offer it to his people. As long as he handles it wisely and doesn't dump it all at once, no one will know it was part of anyone's incoming load."

"I'll talk to him and make sure he's aware of that," Joseph answered. "Whattaya think we'll net?"

"Oh, man, that's a ton of shit. We're gonna do well here. That represents a lot a money."

* * *

The following morning Roger and Joseph had agreed to meet at the storage garage and check over their latest stash. They wanted to make sure that it was wrapped in convenient packages and not in some kind of bulk casing. And they wanted to check on the quality of the marijuana. It would be easier to determine these things with some sunlight, a better light than just that provided by the single bulb that was on the ceiling of the storeroom.

Arriving at six in the morning, a good time as no one would be likely to be at the facility at that hour, they opened the overhead door and began to move the hastily dropped-off shipment into a neater pattern on the floor in the back of the room.

Joseph took out his knife; it was a part of the same tool he had used to break the small window in the eighteen-wheeler. He cut into one of the bales that contained the valuable weed and found that the marijuana had been packaged in plastic bags, each containing about one kilo and tightly confined with duct tape. He then cut into one of the packages with a wide enough slit to expose the material inside.

Joseph let out with an "I don't fuckin' believe this! We've been screwed!"

"What're you talkin' about?" Roger called back over his shoulder as he stopped short the moving of the bales.

"This is fuckin' grass!" Joseph shouted.

"Yeah, well that's what it's supposed to be," Roger replied.

"No! I mean this is grass like what you mow on your lawn!"

"What?!"

"Take a look for yourself! They must've suspected somethin' and brought in a dummy load in case it should get hijacked and then trucked the real stuff in later."

Roger walked over to the open package, grabbed it and pulled it apart at the slit. As he stared inside at the very green grass he began to laugh. "Remember what I told you about being like a doctor—a specialist—and knowing my business better than the general practitioner?" Roger asked and then continued, "This is Micanopy Madness. This is better than Colombian Gold. It comes from a place in northern Florida called Micanopy, which looks like it should be pronounced my-canopy but properly spoken is mih-cah-no-pee with the accent on the 'no.' It's a tiny little town, which for years has been known for its antiques but most recently for two other events. Just a few years ago it had a gay bar on its outskirts, which had its doors blown off by dynamite as a protest against it. And then even more recently the movie *Doc Hollywood* with Michael J. Fox as the star, was filmed there. You may not remember it, but back in the early eighties a bunch of cops from Gainesville, which is just north of Micanopy by the way, got busted for marijuana use. The pot they were using—Micanopy Madness. It is not easy to detect because it is so green and looks just like grass from the lawn, but what it can do, that's something else. I haven't seen this stuff in a number of years. This is an excellent haul!"

"For a small town," said Joseph, "it's had its share of notoriety, hasn't it?"

"Yeah. You got that right. Now give me a hand moving the rest of this shit and let's get outta here."

"OK. You'll make me an expert in this stuff yet, Roger."

They finished their task and locked the storeroom.

"Get ahold of Terrence and let him know what we've got," Roger said. "The minute you tell him what it is, if he's as good as he's supposed to be, he'll be in a hurry to make some deals. This is worth big bucks."

"Will do," said Joseph as they each went on their way.

CR

When August arrived, Joseph headed north to Belgrade Lakes to visit with his cousin, George, the attorney. George was happy to see him and could not wait to show him the lot that was available on the lake. They caught up on each other's news since the last time they had seen one another was at Joseph's mother's funeral.

Joseph mentioned that he was also in the market to buy a boat just in case George knew anyone who sold them. He would rather buy it in Maine because he knew that it would be kept here during the winter in a dry-dock. And if there were any problems, he did not want to deal with someone down in the Boston area where he would have to wait for repairs or be recommended to someone in Maine from whom he did not make the purchase. Those things never settled well with Mainers. Of course, in the back of his mind Joseph had two reasons for wanting to do business in Maine. The first was so that no one from his department would be aware of his large expenditures. The best way to keep such things secret was to make transactions out of state. Besides that, he really liked Maine. The second reason was that he needed an outlet for some of the money he had been making. Investing in things in Maine made it easier to launder his money.

George did know someone in the boat business and the fellow had two bases of operation: one in Belgrade on Great Pond and the other in Portland close to Casco Bay. How could he be any more lucky?

On a Sunday they drove down to Portland since Charlie Ross, the owner of both marinas, happened to be working there that day. Joseph was introduced by his cousin and he told Charlie exactly what he was looking for.

"You got any idea whut a boat like whut your describin' costs?" Charlie asked in his down east accent.

"Yeah, a rough idea," Joseph replied.

"You on the take down they-ah or whut?" Charlie asked trying to be comical with his dry sense of humor.

"Yeah, I'm on the take all right. I take what I make and I invest it and it pays out pretty well. So now I'm gonna put it where I can enjoy it."

"Well, this is a pretty signif-k-nt investm-nt," Charlie said, running the consonants together as though there were no need for vowels.

"Well, the way I look at it is the same way I look at a new car. It's not an investment. It's a guaranteed loss. In an investment, ya plan to make money, not to lose it. And you know as well as I do that no vehicle ends up makin' ya money unless ya keep it as an antique."

"Ay-uh, yuh right about thayat," Charlie said. "Well, the boat you want'll run ya, with a perfessional discount 'cause a yuh cousin, leh-me see now, 'bout $60,000. Yuh'll still hafta pay tax, ya know. Six p-cent heah in Maine."

"How long will it take ya ta get it in?" Joseph asked.

The answer surprised Joseph. Being as how this old guy dealt with pencil and paper and ran two shops that looked like old garages, he never expected he would have anything more modern than a telephone.

"If'n I run it on the computah, I can see if they's any in New Englund, dontcha know?"

"OK, do that," answered Joseph.

"It'll only take me a few minutes." And with that, Charlie went into his little office and sat down at the terminal board.

George just chuckled to himself as he watched Joseph looking at the old man.

While Joseph waited, he spent his time looking over the marina and the sales office. Here was one of those prefabricated steel buildings, which can be erected on a concrete slab in a matter of a few days. It was fairly large as it needed space for one or two boats to be able to be brought into the showroom in the front of the building and space for a boat to be brought into the repair area at the rear of the building, which had an enormous overhead door opening onto a dry-dock. The dry-dock was like those garage ports used down south. It really did not do much to protect one from the elements but did provide a covering for boats, too large to be brought inside the building, to be secured while repairs were being made.

Beyond the dry-dock was the pier, which had a cradle designed to lift boats out of the water and onto the dock. When the tide was in, the water level was just six feet below the street level. When the tide was out, the drop looked like it went down some twenty feet and it was sheer. To the right of the cradle was a ramp, which led down into Casco Bay and upon which a boat on a trailer could be backed into the water. Joseph was impressed with the marina's setup.

Back inside, he noticed that the sales room was fairly compartmentalized with a large display of nautical equipment mounted on the wall to the left of the room. The shiny brass and stainless steel devices were as appealing to the eye as to the function each one performed. Just past these items was a display of electronic instruments including marine radiotelephone apparatus, cellular phones, antennas, depth-finders, fish-finders, radar, sonar, transducers and a dozen other things that would enhance the smooth operation of any water craft. Beneath the displays were racks of brochures describing the items found above. The only thing missing was the price tag; Charlie had made it a habit to always go to the book to look up pricing for people as he would try to judge those who came into his facility and then quote costs accordingly to see their reactions and what the traffic would bear.

In the center of the room, perched on two gigantic supports, was a twenty-four foot Bayliner cruiser with a sleeping compartment for four people and an inboard-outboard engine. The horsepower of the engine was not in view but, judging from its size, it appeared to be enough to make the boat fly on top of the water. The boat's blue-and-white fiberglass glistened under the fluorescent lights of the showroom. Joseph climbed on board just to get a better look at this first-class boat. As he stood behind the polished wooden wheel with its brass accouterments, he pictured himself gliding over the water between Old Orchard and Cape Elizabeth, going past Portland Head Light and Twin Lights and passing the numerous bays where bathers enjoyed the beaches.

"Got one in Pautsmuth, New Hampsheah," Charlie called out as he came back into the sales room and as Joseph awoke from his daydreaming.

"Well, tell them ta send it on up. I want it," Joseph stated as he climbed back down the steps set to the side of the Bayliner.

"I'll have 'em hold it until we get the papahwurk done and the finances approved, then I'll have 'em ship it up. Get it? Ship it up?" he asked with just the hint of a smile on his face.

"Yeah. I got it."

The men sat down at a desk cluttered with brochures on boats, marine supplies and a half-dozen other things and drew up the contract. When Joseph asked how much Charlie wanted as a down payment, Charlie said he had to get at least twenty-five percent if it was going to be financed through a bank.

"How about I give you $35,000 cash down and the rest when you have it ready for me to take out on the bay?"

"You carryin' that kinda money with you? Even bein' in Maine I wouldn't carry that kinda money," Charlie said.

"Well, Charlie, I carry somethin' else with me as well so I wasn't really worried, dontcha know?" He said, imitating Charlie.

"I'll have ya in business within the week," Charlie answered.

"Great!" said Joseph and he and George left the building.

"Don't think old Charlie has ever seen anyone come in with that much cash. Even though he's done a big business here, it's mostly been through banks," George said.

"Well, there's a first time for everything, George."

* * *

The men returned to Belgrade and went to Lake Real Estate to make arrangements for the lot of land.

When Joseph saw the lots that were available, he opted to buy three of them; the last remaining ones on this side of the lake. Joseph was going to spend out another $75,000 and the question of a mortgage never arose. George looked askance at Joseph as he made the offer, wondering just what kind of investments paid off with these kinds of rewards.

"Joe?" George queried.

"Yeah?" Joseph responded.

"Are you sure you want to spend this kind of money? I mean, you're putting out a lot in one day."

"George, I don't know what you make as an attorney, but I know you do well. I know you've got your son and a brother all milking the same firm, so there has to be money there somehow. I don't ask you who you squeeze for whatever it is you do because it's none of my business. Now, in my line of work, there are also opportunities. I'm comfortable knowing that I don't need to know how or what you do, and I expect you feel the same way about me."

"Well, uh, of course, Joe. I mean . . . I didn't mean that I, uh . . . that I . . . uh . . . ."

"No, of course you didn't, George, I understand that. Just help me with the legalities involved on these transactions and I'll be more than pleased."

"Sure, yes, of course, Joe. Whatever you need, you know that."

"Thanks, George, I knew I could count on you. By the way, for an attorney, I've never seen you stutter or hesitate the way you just did."

"Well, normally I have time to think things through. You just caught me off guard. And usually I have all the details when I'm working with a client. I just am not familiar with as much of your life as I become with a client."

"Of course, George," Joseph said smiling as he turned his head back to the business at hand.

The Realtor made out some paperwork and had Joseph sign on the dotted line making the offer "legal" as the Realtor called it. He then took a sum of money from Joseph and prepared to give him a receipt in return. The Realtor, who has been in business there for quite a number of years appeared to be in shock as he counted out the voluminous one-hundred dollar bills Joseph had just handed to him. Joseph smiled to himself as he thought this was probably the largest amount of cash the Realtor has ever received as a down payment for property.

"Well," said Joseph, "that twenty thou' just about cleans me out of what I brought here to spend. I'm glad I've kept enough to at least cover me for the remainder of my vacation. I do want to take some time down at OOB. I haven't been there since the folks passed away. And I thought I might take the place we always stayed at; it'll be empty and maybe a little lonely, but I just need to do it. I need the reminiscing because those were always good years."

"I can understand that," said George. "You know you're always welcome to stay with us; we have plenty of room especially now that all the kids are grown and out and have their own places here on the lake."

"Thanks, George. I'll stay in touch. Right now I'm hot to get onto my new toy and the next few days are going to be extra long waiting for that boat to arrive."

"At least stay for supper. Joan will be disappointed if you don't."

"You got a deal. I can do that without any hesitation. She's the best cook I know. Those Lebanese dishes she serves up are great."

"Good," said George as he and Joseph walked back toward the huge, three-story, four-thousand-square-foot, three-car garage colonial house they called "camp."

* * *

Joseph had made reservations for the cottage on Old Orchard Beach. When he pulled in to Mullen Street, he was hit with a nostalgia he did not expect. All of a sudden the years he had spent there rushed through his mind. He remembered his first trip to Maine. Meeting his friend from Montreal, John Cologgi, and his family. John was thirteen and Joseph was fifteen. At that age, even a year made a big difference, but somehow that was not important. They had become buddies and every year from that period forward, they looked to meet again during the month of August. Of course, with the passing of time and with each of them finishing school and taking full-time jobs, John's work kept him from returning to Old Orchard.

Joseph wondered as he sat there in his car, preparing to go into the cottage colony office to get the key to the house, if John has ever made a return visit to the beach. Quite a few years had passed since those early days.

He then remembered all the young girls he had met on the beach as he was growing up. When he was here during school vacations, it was inevitable that his bright red hair, enhanced by the sunlight on those hot summer days, would attract girls like bees to honey.

He remembered the first time he lost his "virginity." It was at Old Orchard. John and he had met two high school girls from New York City. They both spoke with Brooklyn accents so thick they could be cut with a knife. The boys were sitting on the wooden chairs that were placed so people could sit and look out at the ocean. It was early evening and the two girls, wearing one-piece bathing suits, were walking on the sand heading back from the amusements at the pier toward one of the motels further up the avenue.

John waved at them and without a moment's delay, they walked right up to where the boys were sitting. Joseph could not believe what he was witnessing. He was somewhat shy as they approached but the girls had no problem and did most of the talking. That made things easier. They introduced each other and told where they were from.

Diane, the brunette, took a liking to Joseph. The other girl, whose name was Selena, had dirty blond hair and was attracted to John's very blond hair that, likewise, had been bleached by the sun almost to the point of being pure white.

They sat in the chairs for about two hours when Selena said maybe they should check in at the motel so that their folks knew they were all right. Both girls promised to return, but Joseph seemed to think that this would be their first and last visit. They made the boys promise to remain there until they got back.

It was not more than twenty minutes when both girls returned, now dressed in short shorts and halter tops. Even as young as they were, both about sixteen, they were not overly well-developed but what they did have seemed to be appealing.

The girls suggested they go for a walk on the beach. They started out toward the pier, picking up flat rocks and tossing them into the ocean to see of they could make them skip on the water, and talking about the things that kids that age talk about.

Neither girl knew what she wanted out of life except that both knew they wanted to get married to successful men and have lots of children. It seems that was the case no matter what girls either boy met and talked to for as long as they could remember.

Both guys knew what they wanted. Joseph was going to become an attorney if he had the chance. And John was going to be an electrician. John's interest sparked when he and Joseph wired the entire compound where they stayed at Old Orchard with a World War II military surplus, field-phone system. Joseph's hobby had been communications and over the years he had managed to acquire a couple of sets of earphones and microphones and old telephone handsets and two Army field phones along with some old radios and a wireless microphone that allowed him to broadcast through an AM radio once it was tuned across the dial somewhere onto an empty channel.

The boys had set up wiring for the field phones underneath the cottages so that wherever they went in their imagination as they played, they could keep in constant contact with each other.

They thought they knew what direction they were going in even at that early stage of life so many years before.

As they walked along, considering each other's comments, Diane took ahold of Joseph's hand. This was a first for Joseph; he had never met anyone as forward as this girl. When Selena saw them walking hand-in-hand, she did likewise with John. They continued down the beach, past the pier and over toward one of the more remote spots, where tourists were more likely to be found during the daylight hours than the nighttime ones.

At Diane's suggestion, she and Joseph sat down to talk as John and Selena moved on down the beach. Diane began to question Joseph about girlfriends and how many he had over the years and what they used to do together. Then out of the blue, she turned her head toward Joseph and reached around his neck and gave him a kiss. He was startled but was not willing to stop the action. He was usually the one who tried to maneuver his way to this point with a girl, but that did not always work either.

Diane then moved her head down to his neck and tried to kiss him lightly under his ear. Joseph struggled to keep from wincing as this tickled him and yet he did not want it to stop. She gave him a hickey on his neck; the only thing that went through his mind was what his parents would say when they saw that big red splotch. Immediately, they would think he had a rash of some kind. He figured he would play that for all it was worth.

Diane then tried to stick her tongue in his mouth. He had never French-kissed before and he was not sure he wanted to start right now. Instead he took command and gave her a sloppy kiss on the mouth; if she wanted saliva, she was going to get it.

As they sat there, Diane refrained for a moment, just long enough to ask him, "Have you ever focked?"

It took him a minute to translate the New York accent into English.

"Have I ever fucked?" he asked back. Then without waiting for any response he said, "Oh yeah, a number of times," he lied as he did not want to appear that he was a virgin.

He then asked her the same question. She said, "Oh yeah, it's nothing special where I go to school. Everyone does it. Why? You wanna fock?"

"Uh, I hadn't thought about it. I, uh, I . . . ," he stuttered.

"Hey, if you wanna fock, we'll fock." With that she took the halter off and pulled down her short shorts. She was wearing nothing underneath either. Joseph was surprised at her breasts; all he could think about as he gawked at them were Dairy Queen ice cream cones. They stood out and came to the nipple gradually, not smoothly like a mountain on its side, but more like gradual rings. As he looked down to her pubis, a word he had never used until he became a cop, he could see in the little bit of light, which existed mostly from the nearly full moon, that she had a nice crop of dark black hair protecting the entryway to man's earthly paradise.

Because John and Selena had opted to walk further down the beach, they missed what was about to take place.

Joseph removed his pants and his jockey shorts. He was so lubricated that he began to drip all down his pants as he was taking them off. Diane giggled as she watched him and then stared as she looked at the large weapon that was about to penetrate her. For a moment she stopped short, wondering if this was such a good idea, but she had come this far and she wanted to know what it felt like to have someone inside her. Her only previous experience had been with her finger and that was not great even though she found that she could masturbate and give herself a little bit of pleasure.

Diane laid down on her shorts to keep sand from causing any discomfort and from creeping in to places where it would not be welcomed. Joseph came down on top of her but discovered that this was not as easy as everyone had said it was when discussions on the subject of "getting laid" came up at school. He began to wonder how many guys who had bragged about their conquests really had gone "all the way." As well-endowed as he was, he could not make things fit just right. It either would not go in or it would not go in far enough. Finally, facing her, he took her legs and threw them up over his shoulders and entered her with great ease. He no more than made his entry when he let out a loud moan and she did likewise. He let go with what he swore later on were two quarts of penned up semen, saved from years of desire, which could not be released even when he had jerked off in the bathroom. When they finished, she kissed him over and over again. And he felt guilty for what he had done. More guilty than when he had masturbated and tried to avoid the truth when the time came to enter the confessional on all those Sundays he went to church.

The next few weeks were agonizing. He saw her many times and even repeated the act several times; each time feeling guilty, but less so than the first time. However, his greatest concern was whether or not he had impregnated her. He would never know. This was her first and last trip to Old Orchard. He did not even keep her address in New York after she left. Nor did he give her his correct address at home in Boston. He was too afraid of finding out he had fathered a child.

* * *

Joseph reflected for another moment on the day the boys buried some old telephone wire out into the ocean. He had picked up some telephone cable that was left in the trash when the phone company was wiring a building for new equipment. The old cable was ripped out and put on a barrel relegated for the rubbish truck. It was eighty feet long and had a plastic covering and contained two-hundred wires, each one with a plastic-colored sheath. He had stripped the outer cable and made two long wires out of it by connecting them end to end. Once completed, the wires were over two-thousand feet in length.

The boys were game for an idea, which had been created in Joseph's mind over the last year as he waited for summer to arrive and the annual trip to OOB—an idea that would make use of this wire. Joseph had been thinking about this project for a long time. In his travels, he visited an Army-Navy surplus store not far from his home in Dorchester and for eighty-eight cents apiece he bought two G.I. foxhole shovels, which he kept in his room for the next trip to Maine.

The boys picked up a cloudy-white, plastic, gallon milk bottle with its top from John's mother. They found an old flashlight and removed the bulb, soldering one of the ends of each wire to the bulb's base. They then put the bulb in the milk bottle and closed it tightly, sealing the outside with water-resistant airplane glue. To the outside of the bottle they tied a fifteen-foot piece of clothesline rope and secured the other end of the rope to a cement block John had found under one of the cottages.

Early in the morning, when the sun was promising a glorious day, both boys walked out into the ocean water to the extent that they could during low tide. The timing was right and the water level was at dead low. Even though the water was freezing, they did not mind as they were on a mission and nothing was going to dissuade them. The beach was empty; even the joggers were not to be seen.

They managed to get more than two hundred feet from shore, where the water was still fairly calm as the tide had not yet turned. They dropped the cement block into the water, which was almost up to their necks, and left the bottle to float in place.

Coming back to shore, they unraveled the wire as they walked. Once on dry land, they took the shovels that Joseph had brought with him and began to bury the wire in the sand. It was easy where the sand was dry, but difficult where the sand met the water's edge. Every time they would dig, the damp sand swirled back in place. They had to work at a feverish pace in order to accomplish their task. Nature was kind to them; with every wave the motion of the deep water over the sand would bury the wire further down.

It took about three hours to secure the wire beneath the sand on the beach and have it brought up to the wooden wall, which separated the sand from the road and parking area for the cottage colony. The few people who had come out onto the beach early gave no heed to the two boys who were enjoying playing in the sand, evidently building castles with their shovels. They ran the wire up the wall in a crevice that had formed in the wood pylons from many years of pounding surf against the wall during storms.

At the top of the wall were the chairs, again, for the people to watch the ocean. Leaving the wire hidden against the wall and the fence, which separated the cottage colony from its neighboring motel, the boys waited until the tide came in and then looked through a pair of binoculars John's father had brought with him on the trip from Montreal.

With some difficulty in the blazing sun, they could just make out the bottle floating in place way off shore, narrowly being missed a couple of times by boaters who were dodging it as they raced past.

When nighttime came and the tide had again gone out and was in the process of returning to its highest point for the night, many of the tourists, also, came down to the chairs to sit in the coolness of the night where the day and where the cottages without air conditioning had been so hot.

John and Joseph brought a lantern battery down to the chairs and pulled the wire from its hiding place. They attached one of the leads to the negative post of the battery. With the second lead, they began to touch it to the positive post of the battery making the light flash out in the ocean. It was eerie seeing this clouded light, enhanced by the white, plastic, milk bottle, flashing off shore.

A few of the people noticed the light and began to ask one another what it was. One or two said it must be on a boat way out in the ocean as the light is dim and seemingly so small.

That comment was all the boys needed. They had waited for such an opportunity. Joseph began to send out three dots followed by three dashes followed by three dots as he touched the wire to the battery in that sequence.

"Oh my God," one of the men called out who had been sitting engrossed by the light off shore. "The ship's in trouble. Look it's sending Morse code. I can read it, being an old military man myself. It's an SOS."

Both boys could hardly contain themselves. They were trying not to laugh out loud and yet tears were flowing down their cheeks they were chuckling so hard. Luckily for them, no one seemed to notice them. All eyes were focused on the "sinking ship."

The old military man jumped up and ran as quickly as he could to the public pay phones that were located about halfway down Mullen Street. The boys could hear him shouting into the phone at the operator as he tried to explain in his frenzy the drama that was taking place.

Once hanging up the phone, he returned to watch the light continue to send out its signal.

Within minutes, a police car, siren screaming, turned onto Mullen Street and headed to where everyone was standing and watching. As the car came down the street, the noise of the siren and the bright flashing of the cruiser's blue lights awoke everyone vacationing there and soon the parking lot was crammed with gawkers wondering what was happening.

As people stared out at the ocean along with the policeman, Joseph and John stopped sending out the signal.

The military man pointed with authority, stating that he knows what he saw and there is a ship in danger of sinking well off shore. Some of the people who had been there when the light began to flash supported the man in his claim.

"I'm afraid we've lost her," the military man said. "The signaling has stopped. I hope you had enough sense to call out the Coast Guard," he continued as he looked directly into the face of the patrolman who had responded to the scene.

"I'm sure they've been told," said the cop.

With nothing more he could do, the cop took down the names, addresses and phone numbers of the people who said they saw the strange sight. He then left the area in his patrol car.

The military man grumbled to himself as he sat back down in his seat. His comments were not pleasant as he considered the course of action not taken by the people who should have been in charge.

When the man was back in place, Joseph again began signaling. The man almost fell over the wall and onto the sand below as he jumped up and hollered, "They're still alive! Look! And not a sign of any rescue ship in sight."

Once again, he ran to the pay phone and made a call. Once again, the same cop responded to the cottage colony but this time without any siren or lights. As the boys heard the tires turn onto Mullen Street, they again stopped sending the signal.

"I'm telling you I saw what I saw and so did these good people who are sitting here with me," the military man shouted out.

But this time, the people said they were not sure what they saw. Maybe it was just a reflection of the moon on the water.

The military man was beside himself with rage. "I cannot believe the apathy of you people. All right, then, let it be on your conscience when the remains of those poor souls float to shore." Having said his last, he removed himself from the rest of the people who were still gathered there and he returned to his motel room.

Life at the beach had been fun; it had been serious; and it had been challenging. Old Orchard was a place Joseph loved and it would always remain a part of his memory.

* * *

Joseph exited from his car and went into the cottage colony office. He obtained the key to his cottage and, at a whim, asked if the Cologgi's had ever come back to Old Orchard. It had been so many years, he was not sure if the people would even recognize the name.

Joseph could have been pushed over with a feather when he heard they had rooms at the other side of the motel. The cottage they had rented for years had been torn down in order to expand the office and put in a swimming pool. Now they were consigned to a somewhat smaller space even though there were more family members.

Joseph asked for the room numbers and after parking his car he walked over to the rooms, which were next to one another. No one answered his knock to either of the doors. He decided to take a glance down at the beach.

As he walked toward the steps, which led from the parking lot to the sand, he immediately recognized Dom Cologgi, John's father. Joseph started to wave at Dom, but Dom had a quizzical look on his face as though to say: "Are you waving at me? Do I know you?"

As Dom stared upward at Joseph, his eyes went from a pinched look on his face to an I-don't-believe-it look. Dom made the sign of the cross on his chest as he called out, "Joseph? Is that really you?"

They hugged and Dom went to get John who was down by the water with his wife and two grown kids. Dom's wife was seated up on the pavement in a metal lawn chair. She watched the commotion but did not recognize Joseph until he turned in her direction as Dom pointed her out before he went to get John.

John came running up the beach and could not believe his eyes. "How many years, Joe?" he asked. "I know you met Peggy and the kids. Of course, the kids were just infants back then. What are you doing here? Man, I have so many questions, I don't know where to begin."

He and Joseph and all of the family went to Joseph's cottage where there was much more room to sit and talk and reminisce about old times. Joseph even offered the use of the huge cottage as there were so many of them and so little space in the two motel rooms they had rented. They declined but appreciated the offer. Dom had brought his video camera with him as he wanted to record this reunion.

They each recalled old memories and good times. Dom said how much he missed Joseph's parents. He called them the nicest people he has ever known.

During the next two weeks, they spent almost all of their time together. It was like time itself had stood still and nothing but physical features had changed over the years.

On the day that Joseph picked up his boat, John and Dom went with him. Joseph had made a quick trip to Boston the day before to bring back the balance of the amount due to Charlie. John and Dom were in a slight state of shock as they watched Joseph count out the enormous sum of money and give it to the man who sold him the boat. They never said a word to Joseph, but that evening they discussed it when they were safely settled in for the night at the motel.

Every day, as long as the weather stayed sunny, they all went out on the boat. Joseph had wasted no time in getting his vessel registered and under way. He learned everything he needed to know about the boat in record time and had taken every opportunity to pass the requirements to operate such a vessel. They all agreed that there was nothing more relaxing than a boat.

Joseph was more than pleased at his newest acquisition. The boat had a semi-enclosed bridge from which he could operate all the necessary functions to maneuver over the water. Below deck was a totally enclosed operations center with all of the radio, radar and sonar equipment, which had remote controls on the upper bridge. The twin inboard engines had the latest in safety devices, which would clear out any gases produced in the engine compartment when the engines were idle and which pumped out the bilge of anything that could be hazardous to the boat or the people on board.

The cabin area, which was the foremost area of the boat, could sleep eight people comfortably and up to four additional people with some cramping of space. Walking down the four steps into the cabin, which was just forward of the enclosed control center, one would see the high sheen of the well-polished wood, which formed the base for every fixture on the boat. To the left of the stairway was the head, which had a rather large shower, toilet and sink. To the right was closet space. On the right and left side of the cabin were the beds, each one had a flexible reading light attached to the wood affixed to the wall just below the portholes, which gave natural light to these quarters. There were storage cabinets beneath the beds.

Exiting the cabin and the control center, one entered the galley. It was equipped with a refrigerator, stove, microwave oven and sink. Propane gas gave the necessary fuel for the various forms of energy on the boat and, again, every possible safety device had been thought of and included with this craft. On the opposite side of the galley was a foldaway table, seats and storage space. Above the table and the sink were two long windows that gave a great view of the outside.

Outside, the deck itself had been equipped with two captain's chairs bolted to its floor. The boat was ideal for going after sailfish or other game fish, but Joseph had them removed as fishing was not one of his favorite sports. Instead he had them replaced with seating that allowed for sunbathing and casual relaxation. Indeed, this boat was everything he could have ever wanted.

When it came time for John and his family to return to Canada, they promised to return and get together the next year. It was the closest Joseph had come to crying since his folks had passed away.

* * *

The last two weeks of his vacation, Joseph spent between boating and visiting his cousin in Rome.

George had a new secretary named Nancy, who was recently divorced, and George thought it might be good to introduce her to Joseph. He knew about Joseph's prior situation and, with all the changes that had taken place in Joseph's life, maybe it was time to meet someone new. So George took the liberty of inviting Nancy to the house for dinner on a night that Joseph planned to be there.

What began as an awkward introduction, as George did not know exactly how to play the role of Cupid, ended with the start of a great relationship.

Nancy's ethnic background was German. She was raised in a home in which her grandfather had come from the old country and had been very set in his ways. Therefore, his children were also set in their ways. However, his granddaughter was tired of the old ways and showed her independence when she broke away from the family's way of living and married the first person who paid any attention to her.

The man she married turned out to be gay. He played the part of a caring husband but could not perform the necessary function required to show the love she needed to feel. He also was a very independent person—so independent that it was only a matter of time before the two of them would be at odds with one another. When things came to a head, Nancy refused to walk out but instead threw him out with only the clothes that he owned. She held onto everything material and refused to share it with him. He fussed and complained and said he was going to get a lawyer. Resourcefully, she took a job at George's law office and made a condition of her employment that his firm would represent her.

As a result of court action, she kept everything, he got nothing.

Joseph liked her "take charge" attitude. It was not that she wanted to be boss, only that she was not ever again going to be stepped on in any manner.

After finishing their meal, another great culinary and gastronomic experience by George's wife, they retired to the den where George and Joan excused themselves feigning a need to wash the dishes as their new Maytag, supposedly and conveniently, had a problem—a suggestion at which the television commercial Maytag repairman would have shuddered.

Sitting there over the next five hours, long after George and Joan had gone to bed, they agreed to see more of one another even though that meant a long-distance relationship not too unlike the one Joseph had been involved in a long time ago.

Both did not want to rush into something that might prove fatal. They would take things slowly and if all worked out well, then they would keep things progressing.

When Joseph left the house the next day and returned to Old Orchard, he had felt more complete than he had in a long time. There was no sex; not even a thought of sex, at least on his part. And he was sure the feeling was mutual.

He did manage to see Nancy a few more times, even taking her out on his boat, before returning to Boston. He did notice, while they were on the boat, that she had an enticing figure as she wore a bathing suit well. But he was not going to let sex rule his world ever again. As the weeks passed, and as their phone calls to one another increased, he knew that something was going to evolve out of this association.

CHAPTER 15

It had been some time since Joseph had been to the Irish Pub. When he entered the bar early on the first Friday evening following his vacation, he was greeted as a long lost friend by everyone who knew him.

"I almost don't wanta ask," said Seamus with a grin on his face, "but did you find another honey while you were in Old Orchard?"

"Naw, I wasn't lookin' for anything like that," Joseph replied. "It's funny you would ask, though, 'cause my cousin introduced me to a very nice girl who, herself, has been through a bad marriage."

"Ach!" said Seamus, "Used goods, Joseph. You don't want ta get involved with used goods. I'm sorry, I know it's none of my business, but I've gone the route before and usually there's a good reason why people don't stay together. Mark my words, lad, you don't want any used goods."

"I know you aren't gonna believe this, Seamus, but this girl never had sex with her husband."

Everyone at the table just stopped and stared at Joseph. Then they all burst into laughter.

"Did she tell you that?" asked Arthur Boyle.

"Now, Joseph, we took you to be a man of the world," said Michael Meara. "You aren't really that naive, are you?"

"As a matter of fact," said Joseph, "she did tell me that. And you know what? I believed her."

To which another round of laughter ensued.

"All right," Seamus interjected, "tell us the story. You can't leave us with that little bit of information and no explanation."

"The fact of the matter is that the girl herself was somewhat naive when she met this guy. She had been brought up in a very strict German household and sex was never discussed by any of her family. You know how old-fashioned some people can be, even in this day. Anyway, the girl rebelled against her home life and took up with this guy who was very attentive to her. She was young enough never to have dated any men; of course, her family wouldn't let her go out with anyone anyway. They wanted her to wait for the proper time, as they put it.

"This guy was really good to her. So, with a romance that lasted some three weeks, he asked her to marry him and she did. She was disappointed that he wanted to have a justice of the peace perform the ceremony with only a few witnesses present. But she also knew that her family disapproved of everything she was doing with her life and they refused to support her. She knew they wouldn't even attend her wedding, in or outside of the church. She was also a little surprised at the people who attended the wedding. He told her she could have a few friends and he would do the same. So, she had her best friends from school, six of them, come to the home where the wedding was to take place.

"He, in turn, had his mother and eight of his friends at the ceremony. What bothered her was the fact that not one of his friends, who were all male, even spoke to her; in fact, they seemed to shun her. Only his mother seemed genuinely pleased. Add to that the fact that all these men huddled around her new husband and when one of them would call out congratulations to him, they all began to laugh. She sensed something was very peculiar. She shrugged it off, feeling that she could ask him about it later on.

"Now she was prepared for that part of the marriage commitment that she had heard so much about from her friends at school but the guy never touched her. She didn't know how to be aggressive, so she was in the dark about how to get his 'engine' started. That first night, they stayed up late after having dinner and going to a play. Can you picture that? Going to a play on your wedding night? They go to see a play called *Les Cages au Folles*. Some kinda French play but with English speaking actors."

"Oh my God. . . ," exclaimed Seamus. "Don't tell me. . . ."

Joseph continued, "When they got back to his house . . . get this, now, he still lives with his mother. Anyhow, when they get back to his house, she gets on some flimsy negligee and waits for him in bed. And, guess where he is? He's downstairs talking to his mother! Then he gets phone calls and by the time he goes to bed, she's asleep.

"Now she accepts this the first night. But as the next few nights start to be a near repeat of the first, she tries to get his attention, if you know what I mean. What does he do? He tells her that he has a meeting with his friends and he won't be back until late, so he goes out after one of them calls him on the phone.

"She tells her husband that they need some time together. He asks her what she wants and she tells him this living arrangement is not what she expected. She threatens to leave and he says no, whatever she wants he will do for her. Within a few days he has bought a house in Winslow, a little town outside of Waterville, Maine, and she goes hog-wild with getting furnishings for it.

"Once again, as they get settled, the phone calls start coming in and he makes excuses about having to visit with his friends. He states that he has been a bachelor for so long that it's not easy to give up one's habit of being with friends. She buys it for a while but then becomes more and more suspicious.

"One night, after a similar phone call, she decides to follow him. When he leaves the house with his friend, she gets into her car and, with the headlights out, stays far enough away from them not to be obvious. Only when she encountered traffic and someone flashed their lights at her, did she turn the headlights on. She told me she almost lost sight of them several times, but somehow managed to stay with them until they pulled into a motel on Kennedy Memorial Drive in Waterville. That's one a the main drags through the city up there. Anyhow, she waits until she sees them go into one of the rooms together and then she goes to the door and listens. She said she stood there for about twenty minutes and then began to knock. One of them came to the door and asked who it was. She put her thumb over the peek hole and in her squeakiest voice mumbled something unintelligible. When the guy asked her to repeat herself, she did the same thing again. Finally, he opened the door to better understand her and, leaning around its edge while keeping his body out of sight, she burst into the room.

"She says she almost vomited when she saw her husband in bed and this strange man, stark naked, behind the door. The guy let out with a shriek and her husband nearly fainted as he tried to hide under the bed sheets, shaking uncontrollably as he pulled the covers over himself."

"I knew the guy was a fuckin' fruit!" Seamus exclaimed.

"So," continued Joseph, "when I tell ya that she never had sex with him, she never had sex with him. Now if you want to laugh at what I started to say in the first place, go ahead."

"Well, that's too bad. I mean," said Seamus, "too bad for her having to go through that, but its gonna be real good for you in the long run."

"Let me tell ya, I ain't rushin' inta anything ever again. And she's not, either. She, at least, is mature enough emotionally, and to me, that's a plus."

"How about talkin' some business?" interjected Ed Clancy. "I got news and I think it's important we all get a chance to hear it so we can make some plans."

"Whattaya got?" asked Seamus.

"I been speakin' with Paul Finley. He's been my contact with the Sinn Fein. He says he has a port on the Atlantic Coast of Ireland in which we can unload any weapons we manage to accumulate. His instructions are specific and he won't relinquish them until he knows we're ready to transport the guns. He's lookin' to us for as much heavy equipment as we can muster. As you know, Mike and I have been out of state for the past two weeks. We've gone ahead with a commitment to pick up nearly seven tons of armament. At the moment, without going into detail, they are all stored in a warehouse in Vermont. Once we have the good faith money in hand from Ireland, we can ship the guns overseas. The good faith money will cover our cost of purchase; the balance of the money will be our profit."

At that point, Michael Meara said to Joseph, "You said some time ago that you had access to some small arms. Can you still get them?"

"Yeah, I think so. I mean I got some now but I believe I can locate more. Why the sudden change?"

"There has come a need for a few guns other than what we originally were told were needed. We have some rugged equipment, but it is my understanding that they will take anything that's offered. What have you got and what do you think you can get?"

"I've got some handguns, different calibers; and I've got some AK-47s"

"AK-47s? That would be a nice bit of frosting on the cake. See how many you can obtain, Joseph. We are definitely interested if the price is right."

"I'll get back with ya," Joseph said, finishing up the conversation.

* * *

The next night, Joseph got a call from Seamus asking him if he was able to come to the pub, he had something he wanted to discuss with him. Joseph agreed and met with Seamus at seven o'clock. None of the others had arrived yet so it was just he and Seamus sitting alone at their usual table away from the more populated section of the barroom.

"I asked ya here 'cause I got somethin' I gotta ask ya," said Seamus. "I know that Joseph O'Fallon is a common Irish name and there are prob'ly a dozen or so of them in the city. But I got to know if you're the same Joseph O'Fallon I been readin' about every once in a while in the newspapers; the one that works for the Boston Police." He stopped without saying anything further and just looked intently into Joseph's eyes.

"I told myself that I would not lie to you if you ever asked me that question, Seamus, because I respect you and I believe in what you are doing. At the first, I wasn't sure if I really did. Then, later on as I got to know you and to hear what everyone in our group had to say, I became convinced that what you were doing was right. Yes, I am the same man. I hope that doesn't change your mind about me."

"Joseph, I guess I really suspected it all along, especially as I got to know you better and as I got to read more about each news story itself. So, I had a friend of mine who is, also, on the department, but who does not know of all my interests, check you out. I am glad you told me true, lad, and I am glad you said what you just did because that makes me feel a whole lot better. I believe what you say about your feelings being in agreement with ours for *The Cause*. I won't say anything to the others if you don't want me to, not that it'll spook them, but it may be better comin' from you when you feel the time is right."

"Seamus, I have no problem letting them know right now. As I said, I would never keep this a secret from our boys. You're perfectly correct when you say I am with all of you— I am. I will let it come out in conversation as easily as I can so that it seems natural and nothing else. If you want to 'salt the mine' as it were, to make it more palatable, then please do so. I want only that all of us should continue as we have been doing."

"So be it, Joseph. The boys will be here soon and we will let things take their course. You're a good lad, Joseph O'Fallon. I'm glad you're one of us."

The conversation that night among all of the Irish cronies at that table centered on Joseph once Seamus cleverly and calculatingly weaved his news into the topics which were being discussed. It was as though they all knew that Joseph had been a cop but really had not thought to bring it up before, was Seamus so smooth in his dissertation. Joseph could not have asked for a better friend, nor a better friendship with all the men.

CHAPTER 16

It was early in the afternoon on the next day when Joseph got a tip from Rosa Hererra of something peculiar she happened to witness. Rosa was a seventy-plus-year-old woman who had been the wife of a New Bedford fisherman until his death a long time ago. She was also a cleaning woman who had worked following his death in some large and prestigious homes in Brookline. When she reached the age of sixty-five, she put in for Social Security and took her retirement from the hard labor she had done up to that period. Now she wandered the streets close to her home in Dorchester, picking up soda cans from the roadways and trash containers and turning them in for the few coins they were worth as scrap aluminum. The money she collected was not used on herself. No one knew except for Joseph, who had made her acquaintance years ago when he was a beat cop, that she then used the money she had acquired in order to help a variety of causes. After she picked up the cans, she would head home and sit in the back yard of her apartment house, and with an old hammer, flatten the cans so that they would not be as bulky to transport by bus to the scrap yard that bought them from her. It is surprising how much aluminum can be found when one dedicates oneself to recovering such seemingly useless trash.

Over the years, Rosa had given, in increments of hundred dollars, more than ten thousand dollars to people who had their tenements burned out and had lost every worldly possession, to people who had lost children to death as a result of ill health, to animal shelters, that struggled to keep enough food to feed homeless and unwanted dogs and cats, and even to the families of firefighters whose husbands were consumed by flames in multiple-alarm conflagrations. Why she picked up sticky, dirty, sometimes cigarette-butt-filled containers to accomplish her task, no one knew but Rosa herself; and she would never relinquish the answer.

If people only realized that years ago, when she was married only for a short while and living in a dilapidated house in a poor section of New Bedford, her house burned to the ground with all of their belongings in the wee hours of the morning while she waited for her husband at the docks of Narragansett Bay. Neighbors, some whom she knew but most whom she had never met, came to their assistance providing food, clothing, and even some furnishings to help fill the little apartment provided through the efforts of the Salvation Army. It was to help them get by until they again could get back on their feet. The astonishing thing was that no one ever expected anything in return. These were truly gifts from people who had never known the word apathy—people poor like her and her husband, but people whose family backgrounds originated in Portugal or the Azores and who knew the intrinsic value of helping one another when trouble arose. People, who like other Europeans at that time, felt that every neighbor was an extended part of their family. It was for this reason that Rosa felt compelled to do the things she did—what she thought of as God's work here on earth.

She had seen two men around noontime standing, talking, near a trash barrel in an alley where she was confiscating a substantial quantity of aluminum cans from a long line of similar barrels. This was a poor area and what drew her attention was the paper bag being carried by one of the men.

Paying no mind to this "street lady," this man had taken out wads of cash bound by elastic bands and had shown them to the other man before turning them over to him. She pretended not to notice what was happening. The man who had received the money crouched down in the alleyway as the other man started to walk away. Both men had been dressed like street people, were unshaven and appeared very dirty. She knew most of the people in this area and had not recognized either one of these. With her curiosity piqued, she decided to follow the man with the money when he, some ten minutes later, got up and left the alley.

Rosa would have made a great detective herself. She managed to keep the man in sight as he wandered down Dever Street and then onto Bowdoin Street where he walked for more than six blocks and eventually climbed into an older model Chevrolet Impala parked in front of a restaurant. Rosa was quick to catch up to the car before it pulled away from the curb and disappeared. She scratched down the registration plate number on the side of one of the soda cans using the key to her apartment as a stylus. She then saved the can apart from the others, hoping that she might run into her friend, Joseph O'Fallon, where she often passed him in her travels.

It was purely luck that she saw him on Columbia Road as she worked her way back to her regular "picking" ground. She walked over to him, waving the soda can in the air as she called his name.

Joseph waved back, thinking nothing of the Pepsi can she held aloft, droplets of stale soda flying about the top of her head.

"Joseph . . . Joseph!" she called out gasping in great breaths of air as she spoke. For a person well into her seventies she had amazing stamina, but this long trek had tested her ability.

"Hello, Rosa," Joseph replied. "What's up?"

"Just give me a minute to catch my breath and I'll tell you," she replied.

Taking a few moments to regain her strength, she told Joseph what she had seen. She then handed the soda can to him with the numbers and letters scratched in its side.

He took out a small wire-bound notebook and copied down the plate number.

"Was it a Massachusetts license number?" he asked.

"Yes, and it is due to be renewed next month. I noticed that, too."

"Well, thank you, Rosa. I don't know what it means, but you can bet it's not legal whatever it is. I'll see what I can find. You take care of yourself and if it turns out to be something exciting, I'll let you know." With that, he reached into his pocket and took out a twenty dollar bill and said, "Rosa, I know you won't take this for yourself, so why don't you put it toward your latest charity. OK?"

"Thank you, Joseph. That is the only way I would take it," Rosa answered as she pocketed the money and headed back to retrieve more cans.

Joseph thought to himself that chances are a car like that might be stolen, however, why go to the bother of keeping so remote from it and then going after it if it were? It would not make sense. Hopefully, the car's owner and the driver Rosa saw are one in the same.

Joseph ran the registration number through the teletype, which came back within a minute and showed the owner as a Charles Carbeau from West Roxbury. He then ran the name through the department's criminal information system and the computer came up with a long list of crimes in which he had either been involved or had been a suspect. The majority of those records were drug related.

He tried to make contact with Roger to see what dealings he may have had with Carbeau but all he got was his voice mail. He left a message just to give him a call.

Taking the latest address from the computer record, he took the printout and put it in his desk drawer. He then examined the address and tucked it in his pocket as he exited the station.

Joseph drove over to the house in West Roxbury so that he would know a little about the neighborhood. All the homes on the street were pre-World War II. Most were three-story with unattached garages at the end of fairly long driveways. Moving slowly up the street in his unmarked car, he spotted the house number that equated with the one on the printout. Carbeau's house was painted a dark brown and was trimmed in an off-white cream color. The Chevrolet Impala with the plate that matched the number given to him by Rosa was parked about halfway up the driveway. He continued past and made himself as familiar with the house as he could with only this cursory glance. He then returned to the station.

Roger had called back just minutes before Joseph entered his office and saw the MESSAGE WAITING light on his telephone. Retrieving the return call from Roger, he immediately placed another call back. Roger was there and answered the phone.

"Hey! It's me. Whattaya know about a guy named Charles Carbeau?" Joseph asked.

"Carbeau, Charles, lives in West Roxbury, about thirty-three years of age. Yeah. I know him. He's a small-time hood who deals in dope, mostly grass, once in a while he gets his hands on coke. One a my informants says he's tryin' ta get inta 'horse.' He heard that heroin is comin' back as a drug of choice because it's cheaper than coke and not so volatile as crack. I haven't had the time or the people to be watchin' him too closely. Why? Whatcha got?" Roger asked.

"A friend of mine told me she saw him doin' some kinda deal with a chunk a cash that woulda choked a horse. Says he was dressed up like a street bum and picked up a paper sack loaded with big bills wrapped in elastic bands. She followed him to his car and got his plate number and I ran it to see who he was. I got what info I could outta the computer but I never heard of the guy before this."

"I'm not surprised," Roger said. "As I tol' ya he's small time. Maybe he just hit the big time, though. I'm kinda interested in the lump a cash he got. I tell ya what I'm gonna do; I'll set a coupla guys to put the peek on him and we'll see what comes of it. I'll let them know to talk to you if I get tied up. The 'lou' has me doin' some runnin' around for him on another case right now and my time may be screwed up with him. OK?"

"Yeah, that's OK. I guess I'm lucky. My lieutenant stays the fuck away from me. He knows I do good for him so he leaves me alone."

"Fuck you," Roger said.

"Yeah, well fuck you, too. I'll catch ya later."

"OK," Roger said before hanging up his phone.

* * *

It took about a week before Joseph heard anything from the two narcs that were watching Carbeau. They said that they had put a tap on his phone line and were aware of some activity that was to take place Sunday night. The only problem was that the places he mentioned were not familiar to them; it was almost as if he were talking in code as he stated phrases such as: "next to the dump" or "at the far end of the parking lot." What dump? What parking lot? These were locations that were recognized by Carbeau's accomplices but not by anyone listening in to the conversations.

The men then stated that they had put a surveillance onto his vehicle and anyone who entered his house. But the only places he went were shopping or to the video store. They followed him into both locations each time but his activity seemed normal. They also mentioned that the guy must be a weirdo.

"Why's that?" asked Joseph as he spoke with Paul Hoffman, one of the narcotics detectives.

"He picks up porn flicks and kids cartoons," Paul responded.

"Does he have kids?" Joseph asked.

"The guy lives by himself. Once in a while over the past week a young girl by the name of Arlene Swift stops by and stays for the night. We've followed her home to Framingham to one of the dorms in the State Teachers College. She's got no record. Her folks come from Springfield. Nothing there either. My thinking is that she's a student who's linked up with Carbeau and is giving him sex in exchange for drugs. I haven't been able to get any solid evidence yet, but that's what I believe. I had a real hard time checking her health record at the college but after threatening them with a warrant, which would bring bad publicity to the school, they agreed to let me have a limited look. She has had one visit to the clinic as a result of a reaction to some kind of an overdose that proved not to be serious. And she did not give the doctor any details as to what it might have been."

"Kiddie movies, huh? When he brings the videos back, does he set them on the counter or what?" Joseph then asked.

"Now that you mention it, the last time he brought them back the girl behind the counter said just to leave them there and she would scan them as returned when she got a minute. He then said 'no'—that he would wait for Louie or Lewis to scan them because he had a bad occurrence on a previous return and the store manager claimed that he had not brought back films he had rented. He was not going through that again so he waits each time for this guy, Louie, to scan them in," Detective Hoffman stated.

"Can you guys get a background on this 'Louie' character?" Joseph asked.

"Of course. You think he's hot?" Hoffman asked.

"Could be. In the meantime, and I know it's gonna be difficult with so few people available, can you do surveillance on Louie?"

"You are askin' a lot. I'll have to check with the Sarge."

"Please, Paul, do that and let me know."

"Check," Detective Hoffman said as he left the office.

It was early Wednesday evening when the phone rang on Joseph's desk.

"Sergeant O'Fallon, can I help ya?" he answered as he picked up the receiver.

"Sarge, it's Hoffman. I think I got something for ya."

"What is it, Paul?"

"I staked out the store this afternoon. That guy, Carbeau, goes in there like clockwork every Wednesday and Saturday around four o'clock. I stayed where I could watch the clerk as Carbeau gave him his membership card and handed over the two films he was renting. He pays the guy and the guy turns to put the films on the counter on the other side of the scanner for Carbeau to pick up as he exits the store. They do that, ya know, because if he walks outta the store carrying the films past the scanner, it'll ring like it would for someone trying to take a film without payin' for it. But then I notice that the clerk takes one a the films and puts it down under the counter and picks up another one that's sittin' next to a lunch box. He does it so smoothly that I never noticed that before. Then Carbeau leaves the store with what appears to be the two videos."

"Nice work, Paul!" Joseph exclaims. "Anythin' on this guy, Louie?"

"That's the next thing. His name is Luis Alvarez. He's been working there only about a month and a half. Came in from New York. I called down there and he has a record for dope dealing. Guess what he last dealt in before he headed north?" Hoffman asked.

"Gee, I wonder if it could be heroin?"

"You got it."

"Is Sergeant Gallagher around?" Joseph asked.

"Don't know. I been out on this thing so I got no idea."

"I want to be sure he's aware of everything, that's all."

"I'll be sure to write up a report to update him," Hoffman replied. "We're gonna keep the surveillance going on Alvarez; I know he's got to be bringing in heroin from outta state."

"Hey, thanks Paul. Leave a note for your boss to give me a call, will ya?"

"Done."

* * *

In anticipation of another deal on Saturday, Joseph decided to watch Carbeau in action. Stationing himself at the video store he waited for Carbeau to arrive. Joseph walked up and down the aisles of the store reading the backs of the covers for what he thought were all twenty-thousand movies the store had to offer for rent. It was getting late, almost five-thirty. Maybe Paul had it wrong and Carbeau did not keep to a particular time. He was in the middle of the store for the second time when Carbeau came in, dropped off his latest two flicks with the fellow named Luis, and walked over to the far wall of the store where a door led to a section marked ADULTS ONLY.

It was several minutes before Carbeau came back out carrying several videos in his hand. He then went over to the young people's racks and picked up—without even looking to see the title—one of the children's films.

Joseph went to the front counter and looked at some of the previewed videos that were on sale for $9.99, while Carbeau made his way to the same counter but nearer to the cash register.

Joseph watched out of the corner of his eye as Carbeau pulled out his membership card, had the videos scanned by the magnetic reader and paid for the rentals. He then saw the clerk, Luis, walk to the opposite counter nearest to the exit of the store and put three of the videos under the counter and pull up three different ones next to a lunch box. He then placed all four on the counter and returned to the register thanking Mr. Carbeau for his business and hoping that he would enjoy his selections. With that, Carbeau walked over to the outside of the far counter, picked up the films and left the store.

While the men were exchanging their pleasantries, Joseph managed to leave the establishment and situate himself in his car where he could watch Carbeau leave.

Carbeau went to his car, got in and started it and departed from the parking lot. He drove straight home, at first not noticing the gray Ford Taurus following him from a distance.

While Joseph drove, he called on his cellular phone to Roger. Once again he got his voice mail. He left a message that he needed him to meet with him ASAP at Carbeau's location. He knew he had a big one going down. He then tried Roger's pager and left a similar message to be typed onto the pager screen; this one saying only that he had something important on his voice mail and to be sure to check it.

As Joseph parked his car toward the end of the street, he watched for Carbeau to come around to the front of the house and ascend the stairs. But no one appeared.

Joseph knew the house had a rear entrance but it was blocked from access from the driveway by a seven-foot-high fence. Carbeau had to go in by the front door. What was taking him so long?

Finally, Joseph decided to walk up the street and see what was happening. As he passed the house and crossed in front of the driveway, he quickly, but nonchalantly, glanced up at the parked car. No one was in sight.

"Now where the fuck did he go?" Joseph quietly asked himself. Looking around and seeing no one else, Joseph started up the driveway, past rose bushes and trellises laden with vines and flowers, toward the Impala. As he neared the car, a man stealthily came up behind him from the thick bushes. He had a knife in his hand. The blade had to have been a good eight inches in length. With his right hand, the man pushed the knife into the small of Joseph's back and at the same time brought his left hand around Joseph's neck.

"Who the fuck are you and what the fuck do you want?" the man asked.

"Hey man, I was just taking my nightly walk up the street and I saw you pull into the driveway and I could see that there was no place to go and when I didn't see you in your car I thought maybe you had a heart attack. I was just trying to see if I could help, that's all," Joseph lied.

"Really?" said the man, more a statement than a question. "And how do you account for the fact that I saw you following me in my rear view mirror as I drove home from town?" He pushed the knife a little harder as he said, "I want the fuckin' truth or I'm gonna leave you in the driveway with your insides on the outside. And when the cops get here I'm gonna tell them that you tried to rob me and it's gonna be my word against that of a dead man."

"Hey, c'mon, man," Joseph continued with his original lie. "I don't know anythin' about followin' you. I live just down the street in the yellow three-story. I've seen you here before. I've walked up the street here before many times. I can't help it if I happen to come home the same way you do and pull in at the same time you do. Go, look, you'll see my car is right in front of the house where I live."

"How come I never seen you before?" the man asked as he began to wonder if this guy was telling the truth and started to relax his grip and the pressure of the knife in Joseph's back.

"I don't know. I've been here for some time. Like I said, I've seen you on occasion. In fact, I've waved at your girlfriend," Joseph said as he remembered the report that Paul Hoffman gave him on the young lady he spotted at the house.

"My girlfriend? Whatt're you talkin' about?"

"Oh, I'm sorry, I thought the young lady I've seen go in and out of your house was your girlfriend. Very pretty, too."

Now Carbeau released Joseph and Joseph rubbed his back where the knife point had penetrated just below the surface of the skin and had left a small amount of blood on his shirt.

"Geez, man, I was just tryin' ta help," Joseph again said as he turned around to face the man.

"Yeah, well, you can help by mindin' your own business next time." With that the guy looked Joseph in the eye and said, "Waitaminute. I saw you in the video store. What the fuck're you tryin' ta pull?" With that, Carbeau hoisted the knife and started to grab Joseph by the back of the neck.

Before Carbeau could complete this gesture, Joseph pushed aside the knife with his left hand and thrust the forefinger and middle finger of his right hand as hard as he could into Carbeau's eyes.

Carbeau let out a bloodcurdling scream, dropped the knife, and with both of his hands covered the terrible wound, which popped his left eye out of its socket. Blood ran everywhere and Carbeau collapsed onto the driveway pavement in agony.

Joseph said, "I guess the hand is quicker than the eye. In this case, the hand is quicker than both your eyes."

At first, in shock, Carbeau lost all sense of feeling. And then as his brain realized the torment created to his face, it shut down all systems and he became unconscious.

Joseph wiped his fingers on Carbeau's shirt and then walked over and picked up the four videos as he kicked the knife out of Carbeau's reach, more a defensive reaction than anything else. After all, what could a blind man do to harm him now?

Joseph opened each of the video cases. The one with the porn flick contained just that, a movie called *Hard On*. The other three cases contained plastic baggies filled with a white substance Joseph guessed was heroine. He would wait to have Roger put it to the test to be sure.

Joseph then reached down into Carbeau's pockets and located a set of keys. He then opened the door of the Impala and unlocked the back door. He lifted Carbeau into the back seat and shut the door.

No one had responded to Carbeau's scream. Well, it was suppertime and maybe people were watching the evening news and did not hear him. Or, maybe, like Carbeau said, people thought it best to mind their own business and did not want to become involved.

Joseph walked to the front door of the house and tried the only key that resembled a house key. It worked. He opened the door and entered the living room. The house had been similar to others he had seen of this era. It was sparsely furnished but enough to be comfortable. He walked through all the rooms until he came to one that had a rolltop desk. The top was locked. Joseph looked through the keys until he found one that matched the recessed lock. He inserted the key, turned it and the desk top lifted as though on springs. It was like a miniature garage door being released. Inside the desk were books and papers. He glanced through them and decided to take them with him when he left. He then tried to open the drawers below the rolltop but they were locked and there was no apparent keyway. Once again he looked inside the area enclosed by the rolltop and he discovered a plunger on the right side of the cabinetry but toward the rear. He reached in and lifted the plunger. There was a clicking sound as it locked in place and released the latch on the drawers. Closing the rolltop, Joseph opened the first drawer. Again, there were more papers. Nothing revealing, however. The second drawer was just like the first. The third drawer seemed to be more shallow as the bottom of the drawer appeared to be at the halfway point in the drawer. He then looked at the bottom drawer that would not open. He wondered what kind of a desk he had found. As he examined it more closely, he discovered that the bottom drawer was not a drawer at all. It was made to look like one with the indentations around its perimeter as though it could be pulled open, but it was not a drawer. Joseph returned to the third drawer and this time felt around the sides and bottom of the drawer until he discovered two small pegs toward the back. He lifted the pegs and the drawer-bottom lifted out exposing the contents beneath, which went down to the base of the false fourth drawer. The desk was filled with money: hundreds, fifties, twenties and tens all bound with narrow paper wrappers. He did not know how much was there, but he knew it was a lot. The drawer was not quite full to the top so he felt pretty sure that this was all the money to be found in the house.

He went into the kitchen and looked under the sink where most people keep trash bags. Sure enough, there was a box of Glad Cinch Sacks. He took one out and went back to the desk where he unloaded the money and filled the plastic bag.

He returned to the kitchen and took some paper towels and dampened them and went back to the desk where he wiped down everything he had touched. He did this throughout the house before leaving it and walking back to his car with the money and the heroine.

He went home and again paged Roger; this time telling him to disregard his previous messages and to contact him at home ASAP.

Joseph was just starting to count the money when Roger called and apologized for not being able to get back to him sooner.

"Ya gotta come by my house," Joseph said.

"Whattaya need?" Roger inquired.

"I need you to be here as soon as you can."

"Is there a problem?" Roger asked, some anxiety in his voice.

"Naw. No problem on my part if I can keep what I found today. But it might be a problem if you decide you want some and I don't share it with you."

"I'll be right there."

It could not have taken Roger more than fifteen minutes to arrive at Joseph's front door.

"Come in!" Joseph hollered as he heard the first of Roger's knocking.

Roger walked into the kitchen and could not believe the pile of money sitting on the table. "What the fuck is that?" he asked.

"Money," Joseph said without any further explanation.

"I know it's money," Roger said exasperated. "Where did you get it?"

"From the guy I told you about—Carbeau."

"Maybe I should ask how you managed to get it."

"I just took it."

"Explain, please."

With that as an opening, Joseph gave Roger the details.

"The nice thing about it is the guy is not going to be able to finger me or anyone else; first of all because he was dealing heroin, and second of all, because he's now blind."

"What about Alvarez?" Roger asked.

"What about him? He never paid any attention to me. How's he gonna link me with anything? Besides that, we're gonna continue with our investigation on him. He's the one who's bringing in the heroin. My only concern is your guys. I mean your two detectives. They know I've been wantin' this guy. How're you gonna deal with them?"

"How am I gonna deal with them? You're out playin' cops and robbers, or maybe I should say robbers and robbers and now you wanta know how I'm gonna deal with them? Thanks a lot."

"You know what I mean. Hey, after all, half a this is yours."

His attention diverted, Roger asked, "How much is there, anyway?"

"I don't know yet. So far I'm up to eighty-six thou."

"Eighty-six thou?! You gotta be shittin' me."

"That's what I've counted up 'til you came in."

"OK. I'll find a way to deal with my guys. You convinced me."

"I kinda figured you would."

Joseph finished counting at $193,470. His next concern was what to do with the heroin. He turned it over to Roger for testing and to do with as he saw fit. Joseph did not want to deal in anything beyond the marijuana.

CHAPTER 17

Joseph awoke to the ringing of his telephone. Leaning across his pillow and lifting the receiver with one hand while rubbing his eyes with his fingers of the other hand, he managed to force the word "hello" out with a raspy, unrecognizable voice.

"Joe? That you?" came the voice from the caller.

"Who else would it be?" Joseph asked as he heard the familiar sound of his friend, Roger.

"West Roxbury Division's got a homicide," Roger stated.

"So? What's so unusual about that?" Joseph asked.

"It's your buddy, Carbeau."

"What!" Joseph shouted. "What do you mean homicide? He was hurting when I left him but no where near dying."

"No. Someone shot him. He was found in his car with three bullet holes in him; one in his chest and two in his head."

"No shit? Well, I guess I won't worry about him as a problem. Do they know who the shooter is?"

"No idea. It looks like he's been a middle man in several drug deals. That's how I happen to be aware of the shooting. I got a call at five this morning. Paperboy saw the open door of his car and blood all over the driveway. He stopped his bike to look and discovered the body. He woke a neighbor and had them call 911. Somebody must have missed getting his delivery of smack and been really pissed, I would say. Rapid Response found powder on the seat and called for our office to check it out."

"Well, now you don't have to worry about where to assign your dicks."

"For sure. I'm gonna have them spend some time on Alvarez. This couldn't've worked out better for us. It'll be interestin' to see what Alvarez does now."

"Well," said Joseph, "I guess I better get up. I won't be able to sleep any more now."

"OK. I'll speak to ya later," Roger said and hung up.

Joseph replaced the receiver, took one long stretch out on the bed, yawned and then got up. He had divided the money with Roger and had given him his share after it had been counted. Joseph had his portion piled on the floor next to his bed. He needed to get it boxed up and put safely away. He did not like to keep any large sums of money around in the off-chance that anything should happen, which would put him under scrutiny by the department. With the weekend coming up, he gave some thought to a quick trip to Maine; maybe staying up through Monday to open a safe-deposit box at one of the banks there in order to deposit this money.

He called Roger back and told him what he had in mind. Roger then asked if he wanted company on his trip.

"Sure. I'd be glad to have you ride up with me," Joseph said.

"Maybe I should give some thought to doing the same as you—as far as a safe-deposit box, I mean."

"Why not? It'd be two states away and better protected."

"Let me make some arrangements and you can pick me up at my house on Friday after work," Roger replied. "I'll just tell the wife we've got something we're investigating but I won't tell her where we're going just in case the office should call."

"Great! I'll see ya in a while."

* * *

It was ten o'clock by the time Joseph and Roger headed north on Friday evening. Joseph had called his cousin, George, to alert him that he was going to have company. George said that he already had some people staying at his house but why didn't he head over to Rome and stay at the camp. No one would be there and he could have the place to himself. The key was inside the post lamp leading up to the property. All he had to do was open the glass enclosure and feel around; he would locate it.

Joseph thanked him and said he would see him at some point in time.

Joseph and Roger drove by the storage garage and dropped off the heroin Joseph had acquired from Carbeau. Roger had done a test on it with a kit he brought from his office. The heroin had been cut several times but the street value was still significant. It would be easier selling it this way than if it had not been diluted. Shooting it up in a pure state could quickly kill the user and Joseph did not know if Terrence had contact with anyone who could thin it out.

It took them three hours to travel north, instead of the two and a quarter Joseph usually made it in, as Joseph did not want to break any speed limits or traffic laws. There was no sense having some nosy trooper looking into their car with all that money sitting in boxes in the trunk.

They slept until eight o'clock Saturday morning. After having shaved, showered, dressed and eaten breakfast, Joseph said he needed to get a post office box for any mailings that might come to him from the bank or anything else he transacted while he was there. Previously, he had used his cousin's mailing address but now he had some things he did not want his cousin to see.

They drove to the post office on Route 27 in Belgrade and Joseph filled out the application. The postmaster said that it ordinarily takes a day or so as they mail out a proof of residency to the current address, but when Joseph told him who his cousin was, the government employee said there would be no problem. He issued Joseph two keys and Joseph added Roger's name to the list of persons who would receive mail there.

As they walked out to the car, Roger said, "I appreciate your adding me to the box list."

"Well, you need a local address, too, if you're gonna have a safe-deposit box here."

"Yeah. I just hadn't given any more thought to it."

Joseph took Roger back to the lake and showed him the property he had recently purchased. He then drove over to his cousin's house and introduced Roger as a co-worker.

The three of them stood outside for a few moments and passed some small talk so that George might get to know a little something about Joseph's traveling companion. But that would be very little.

Then George asked Joseph, "When are you going to start building your little getaway?"

"I'd like to get it under way soon," Joseph replied.

"Well then, I've got someone I want you to meet."

George brought Joseph and Roger into his home and over to the living room. There were two people sitting on the couch across from George's wife, Joan.

"Joseph, Roger, I'd like you to meet Fred Nutting and his wife, Elaine," George said.

They exchanged greetings and Roger and Joseph sat down.

"Joe, Fred and his wife came in not more than ten minutes before you arrived here. Fred is the fellow who built my camp on the lake. Maybe you would like to talk to him about your plans."

As Joseph explained that he would like to have a house built, one not quite so palatial as that of his cousin, they moved into the dining room after Fred asked George if he had some paper on which he could make some notes.

Fred excused himself for a few minutes and went outside to his truck to get some sketches and photos of homes he had built. Joseph watched as Fred walked toward a new Ford pickup with an extended cab for additional passengers and a cap that covered the truck's bed. It appeared that the truck had been pampered and had never seen a day of tough work. It's bed was complete with a liner and had two Craftsman toolboxes seated on top of some wall-to-wall carpeting remnants that were as clean as the unused bedliner.

The bright, shiny, dark blue paint had been kept spotless and without any dents or nicks usually associated with the carrying of lumber. The seats and dashboard in the cab, likewise, were without any stains, mars or scratches. In fact, it looked as if polishing had been a daily ritual to both the inside and the outside of the truck. Fred, obviously, took pride in his possessions. No doubt, it was something he practiced in the building trade as well.

Fred reentered the house with a portfolio under his arm. He went into the dining room and made himself comfortable.

Seated at the dining room table, Fred began to make copious drawings of a variety of styles of homes. Joseph looked at each one and finally decided on a type he liked.

Fred gave Joseph an estimate as to the cost of such a house and Joseph said he would like to have Fred begin as soon as he could. Fred said that as soon as he had the adequate deposit, he would order the excavation, the concrete and the lumber as well as the materials for the septic system. He would, also, notify an area well-driller to set up a schedule to find water.

Joseph excused himself and went out to his car.

When he returned, Joseph plunked down twenty-thousand dollars in cash on the table and asked if that covered the "adequate deposit." Fred thought Joseph was pulling his leg, that maybe the money wasn't real. But George assured him this was the way Joseph did business. Roger just sat there, expressionless.

Fred said he estimated that the project would take about two months and that he would get started the following week. He was just finishing up on another house and did not think it would be any longer than that.

Fred then asked George if he could write up some kind of contract as he had not expected this to be a part of his visit. George went into his study and came back twenty minutes later with three printouts from his computer.

George, Joseph and Fred looked over the contract and the two involved parties signed it. George, also, kept a copy for his records. Joseph shook hands with Fred as though to solidify the agreement.

Fred still couldn't believe anyone did business like this, but he wasn't going to argue over the pile of money he had in his hand.

* * *

On Monday morning, being given some direction by George, Joseph and Roger drove into Augusta to the Gardiner Savings Institution on State Street where they each opened a safe-deposit box using their Belgrade post office box as their address.

Joseph felt a bit intimidated and hoped that it was not a bad omen that the Kennebec County Jail was diagonally across the street, and the Kennebec Court House directly across the street, from the bank.

Roger just snickered at Joseph's concern. They left the bank after making their deposits into the boxes and locking them. Now there was no need to drive slowly back to Boston; there was nothing to hide. They made the trip in two hours flat.

* * *

Joseph walked into his house as the phone was ringing. Taking long, quick strides across the entry hall, he reached for the receiver on the kitchen wall phone just as the answering machine clicked on. Picking up the receiver intercepted the outgoing message on the answering machine and Joseph spoke into the mouthpiece. "I'm here . . . hello?"

"Where you been? I've been tryin' to get you all weekend," came the voice of Terrence Maloney on the other end of the line. "I bet I've filled your answering machine with my messages."

"I had ta run an errand up north. What's up?"

"Can you stop by and see me some time real soon? I'm at the gas station today."

"Sure. I'm not workin' until later so I'll be by in a while."

"See ya when you get here," Terrence said and closed the connection.

* * *

Joseph pulled into the gas station and parked at the side of the building. Getting out of the car, he walked to the front door just as Terrence was exiting, carrying a plastic lunch box.

"Let's go over to your car so we can talk," Terrence said. "I've got employees using the office."

They got into the front seat and closed both doors.

"What's goin' on?" Joseph asked.

"I've got something for you," Terrence replied as he unlatched the cover on the lunch box and lifted it open, keeping the contents shielded from Joseph's view. "But first, I've gotta know if you can get some more of that quality Mica . . . Mica . . . Mica-stuff you had in the last batch. I never heard of it before this, but I'll tell you what, my customers like it. I mean, like it a lot!"

"I don't think so. This was just a fluke, a one of a kind deal; that's why I told ya ta try and sell it for a premium price."

"Well, I did pretty good," Terrence said as he turned the lunch box around so that Joseph could see inside.

"I like what I see," Joseph said as he stared at the money neatly stacked in the box.

"I thought you would. I've already divided the total into three equal lumps; this is yours. I've got Roger's in a cardboard box in the safe along with mine. You wanta take his or will he stop by and get it?"

"I'll tell him to see you."

"So, what didja do this weekend?"

"Went to Maine and hired a guy to get started on my house up there."

"You really like the 'sticks,' don't you?"

"Well, I've never lived in a remote place before. Used to be when I went to Maine it was at the coast and that's pretty well populated. I like being by the water. This'll be my first experience in the woods. It is by a lake, though."

"You know, my wife was born in New Hampshire near a lake. She's always talked about gettin' a place back there. I should ask her if she'd consider Maine. Maybe get a place somewhere near to you."

"If you mean it, I might be able to help you out. I know the real estate person there in Belgrade near where I'm building. I can't remember what he said about availability around the lake. I do know I got the last coupla lots near my cousin's place. It's beautiful and serene. I'm really lookin' forward to bein' up there, especially when I decide to retire. I'm sure somethin' could be worked out if you're serious about doin' somethin' up there."

"Serious as a heart attack. My wife would love to get away from the city. I tell you what . . . next time you go up, give me some notice and I'll go with you. I could use a day off anyway. Between

197

the newspaper, the gas station and our 'other' business, I haven't had a minute to myself. If I like what I see, maybe I'll just surprise her and buy a spot and do like you're doing."

"I'll let you know. Meanwhile, I wanta get this money put away and get in to work. I gotta see what I missed over the last few days."

"Don't forget me, now," Terrence said as he got out of the car.

"You don't have anything to worry about," Joseph said.

* * *

Joseph checked in at the office and made some phone calls before getting ready to go out on the street. He wanted to make the rounds, visit the places and people he had befriended as he traveled incognito, and pick up his weekly payments.

Things were fairly quiet in the department and on the streets; nothing unusual for a Monday night, though. Joseph collected his money and dropped it off at the house. He returned to his office and had the dispatcher radio Tom Dean, one of his detectives, to pick him up at the station. It had been a while since he had ridden with any of his men and he liked to keep contact with them. It was important to have some time away from the station where they felt they could talk to him alone about things that were on their minds. It also built respect for a superior officer when a subordinate was led to believe that he could have private time in which to open up to his boss and have his boss respond in a positive manner to any comments or suggestions the detective might make.

Tom had been on the job eleven years and had been promoted to detective following a lot of legwork he did in solving a gang-related shooting in Roxbury in which a woman, returning home from work as a nurse at Boston City Hospital, was randomly chosen as a victim and killed as she drove her car down Massachusetts Avenue. The gang member was completing an initiation rite that called for the killing of a person not known to him.

The woman, Jeannette Rice, had just left the parking lot at the hospital following her shift, which ended after midnight. As she drove down Massachusetts Avenue listening to some soft rock on her car radio, a shot was fired from the roof of an apartment house. The bullet smashed through the closed sunroof of her car and crashed into the top of her head. It then coursed down through her body and lodged in her spine. Death was instantaneous. She never knew what hit her. Her car, traveling at about thirty miles an hour, continued on its path for some four-hundred feet before hitting a pothole, which caused it to swerve to the left and go diagonally across an intersection before careening into a variety store on the corner. The crash set off the intrusion alarm system that quickly brought the police to the scene.

Tom had been the first car to respond to the call and to request the detectives when he discovered that it was not merely a vehicle accident but a homicide.

As a patrolman, Tom did two things that were very right in the eyes of the detective division: first, he turned over all his notes and reports to them, and second, when he had information come to him about the murder by way of the people he knew on the streets, he notified the detectives as well.

Where the murder took place in his district, he was determined to find the killer. On his time off, which was the only time he could spend as his patrol duties called for specific functions unrelated to investigations of this nature, he combed the neighborhood. After hearing that the detectives could find no motive for the murder and no suspects among the woman's family, friends or acquaintances, and that she seemingly had no enemies, he felt that the shooting had to have been a random act of violence. Such things were becoming more and more commonplace in the city as time passed and as gang wars became more prevalent.

He kept his ears open and it was only a matter of time before he heard that a teenager had fulfilled his requirement for joining a gang, known as the Intervale Street Posse, by effecting a street killing. The kid had been bragging about it to his friends. Tom pressed for the name of the new gang member as he meandered among the young people in the neighborhood. No one would say anything for fear of retribution. However, the younger brother of a girl who had been viciously raped by one of the gang members and who could not put up with her incessant nightmares as a result of the rape, and the screaming they produced while he tried to sleep, wanted revenge and was not afraid to pass what he knew on to the officer. Once having secured this information from the youngster, Tom gave it over to the detectives. With such a lead, they interrogated the teen and managed to get a confession after the discovery of the murder weapon, hidden under the floor boards in the attic, in the boy's home.

At that time, gangs in Boston were increasing in popularity among the city's youth. And they were becoming unmerciful, harsh and cruel. In one instance, the church in which a funeral was being conducted for a gang member who had been killed in a drive-by shooting was burst into by the members of a rival gang. These gangbangers began to fire guns at their opposing gang members inside the church sanctuary and one boy was stabbed nine times before they returned to the street.

There were no rules and no respect. Had it not been for innovative programs instituted by the department, gang activity would have flourished. Instead, over a few short years, this was one area that has seen a remission.

Tom was one of the few detectives who had not shown any jealousy when Joseph had been promoted to the position of detective sergeant. He had seen this detective in action and had a great admiration for him. When Joseph took the time out of his busy work schedule to speak with him, Tom was pleased. And when Joseph applied the suggestions Tom made to improve some of the facets of the detective division, his self-esteem escalated. Having Joseph ride with him this night was a plus he had not had in quite a while.

For Joseph, it was more than a character buildup for Tom; it was a way to see if anyone in the detective division was saying anything negative about him. That is not to say that Tom was a snitch or a kiss-ass; only that Tom was a person who could be trusted because he entrusted Tom to be in charge of the division when Joseph was away from the office or working the streets. And in every instance, Tom always made the correct decisions.

Joseph thought to himself that it was too bad that Tom could not be a team-player in other things. He really liked Tom, but Tom would not have gone along with Joseph's new role in life.

They rode together for three hours and they discussed a number of things, but nothing was alluded to which would indicate even a modicum of suspicion upon Joseph for any illegality. The only negative comments from his subordinates were brushed off by Joseph as mere jealousy. Tom never mentioned any names, only concerns; and because of this, Joseph had a special respect for Tom.

CHAPTER 18

It was late Friday evening when Joseph met with his friends at the Irish Pub. Seamus had asked the men to take a different table as he had something that needed to be brought up and he wanted to be sure that no one heard anything that was being said.

They moved to a cubicle at the furthermost part of the pub. At this hour, most of the men were either drinking at the bar or playing darts at the opposite end of the room.

Michael Meara was animated in a way that Joseph had never seen him act before—agitated is probably a better description. He was nervous and excited at the same time. He had passed along some information to Seamus and needed to get the opinion of everyone at the table. Seamus simply told Michael to bring it up at the meeting.

Michael began by asking the men if they had seen in the news last week that a van belonging to the FBI SWAT team had been hijacked in Memphis, Tennessee, and was later discovered in another section of the city. Most of the men had seen or heard something to that effect.

"Well, I've got to tell ya what I know," Michael said. "It was full of guns, grenade launchers, bulletproof vests, tear gas equipment, ammunition and helmets. After the people stole the van, they emptied it out of everything and then tried to set it on fire. They got away with M-16 automatic rifles and Heckler and Koch MP-5 machine guns."

"So what has that got to do with us?" Arthur Boyle asked.

"Give the lad a chance to finish explainin'," Seamus interjected.

"So," continued Michael, "I just took delivery of thirty MP-5s and M-16s along with a dozen grenade launchers, tear gas and ammunition. Do ya think there might be a connection?" he asked sarcastically.

"Ohmigod," said Joseph. "Are ya sure ya wanta take a chance on hot government weapons?"

"Joseph," Seamus said, "listen to yourself. What do you think our guns are? They may not be from the FBI but they are government issue. And they're almost all hot."

"Ya just threw me a curve, that's all," said Joseph. "I mean I never would have thought of taking FBI guns. Fuck, the Feds'll be all over the street like stink on shit. I don't think this is so good. I mean, this could really make things *hot*."

"We didn't take 'em. Somebody else did and it's possible we've just bought them—that's all," said Michael confidently. "The weapons were part of my contact's latest shipment. Not to worry, Joseph. My guy is good. Where do ya think we get our guns? They're all government issue. What about the guns you said you could get?"

"I've got a fair collection, as I said. I have them in a warehouse out by Route 128. And I know where I can get more, but my supplier is out of service for a while. As soon as he gets freed up, I can get a fairly decent number."

"We want to get these shipped out as soon as possible," Michael replied. "If the heat gets turned up, we may feel a little of it and I would rather there not be any evidence anywhere in these United States."

· "When you're ready to pick them up, I'll deliver them wherever you say," Joseph answered.

"Get them to me tomorrow. I'll store them until Arthur says to load the boats."

"That'll be shortly," said Arthur. "Ed says the money was wired to our Cayman account and can be transferred as we need it. It's in our hands now, so we can ship immediately and await the balance."

"Let's get everything outta here a week from Sunday," Seamus stated. "Arthur, take care of getting the boats ready and give us the location where to bring the guns and what time to load them on board. Michael, make the arrangements for the trucks to pick up the guns in Vermont and get them to whatever dock we are going to use. We'll meet here Thursday night and finalize everything. Is that OK with everyone?"

Each man nodded in the affirmative. As if to solidify their agreement, they called to Tip to bring drinks to the cubicle. Once they had mugs in hand, they raised them high and toasted the near completion of their long time project.

"Erin go bragh," saluted Seamus. And they all took a swig.

"Long live Ireland," toasted Ed Clancy. Again, they drew a long drink.

"To a free Irish state," pledged Arthur Boyle. A final drink before they called it a night.

* * *

All the way home, Joseph had mixed feelings. Perhaps it was the realization of the guns stolen from the FBI van; perhaps it was the close culmination of the purpose of these meetings, which he had been a part of now for so long; or perhaps it was his own emotions that had been nurtured and amplified by his association with so many pro-Irish Republic people. Whatever it was, he was an oxymoron personified.

He did not sleep well that night and wished that his old friend and mentor, Red Halloran, was still around to guide him and to tell him that this was OK because it was to the benefit of the Irish Free State.

He made a phone call to Terrence Maloney and apologized for calling so late in the night, which was in reality early morning.

"What is it?" Terrence asked.

"I need some help and I think you are the only one who can give me what I need."

"What kind of help, Joe?"

"Advice."

"Advice?"

"Yeah. Any chance you can meet with me?"

"Can it wait 'til morning?"

"I guess. I just wanta make sure I can see ya."

"Of course. Meet me at the gas station around seven-thirty. I have to be at the paper by nine. Can we get it done in a half hour?"

"I guess we'll have to."

"I'll see you there."

"Thanks, Ter," Joseph said and hung up and tried to get a few hours sleep.

* * *

"Well, I thought I had some secrets and then, all of a sudden, you knew all about them. Now," said Terrence after having been apprised by Joseph of the latest news, "you've been keeping some secrets, powerful ones, and I'm slowly finding out who the real Joseph O'Fallon truly is. I'll tell ya what I think. I think Ireland needs to be totally separate from England and I would agree with everything your friend, Seamus, and his crew are doing. In fact, if I could get to be a part of your group, I would be the first to do what I could to help. I fully believe in a free Ireland."

"Look, I don't wanta be around when they load up their ships or boats or whatever. How about making that trip with me to Maine next weekend. I guess I agree with what they're doing but I have a few reservations as far as being exposed with so much armament around."

"OK. Let's do that. We can talk more on the way up."

"Sounds good to me, Ter. Thanks for listening and for giving me your opinion."

* * *

On Thursday, as the "meeting" was called together at the Irish Pub, Joseph said that he was headed to Maine over the weekend and would not be able to meet the men at the docks on Sunday.

"There's no problem, lad," Seamus said. "You've got things to do and we have a crew to handle everything here. We're gonna be in Maine ourselves."

"What?" exclaimed Joseph. "For what?"

"Well now, lad, where do you think the best and easiest port would be to load up and ship out? There're no customs people to worry about because there are too few of them to be watchin' every activity. We're gonna head out from Kittery where the Piscataqua River meets the Atlantic by Portsmouth, New Hampshire."

"You're probably right. I defer to your expertise in these things," Joseph said.

* * *

Joseph stopped by the gas station on Friday night. He called his cousin from the office phone and asked if he could impose upon him once again and make use of the camp at the lake. There would be no problem. Terrence offered to drive his car to Maine and told Joseph to put his car into the garage bay where it would be locked up and safe for the weekend.

It was somewhat unusual to have a garage bay at a gas station/ convenience store nowadays. It seemed that most of these operations did not want the involvement of actual physical labor other than running the cash register, the credit card machine for those people who do not want to use the automatic card reader at the pump, or restocking the shelves as products are sold. But, the previous owner insisted on being able to provide some repairs to customers as his station was the only one with a mechanic in the immediate area. His one stipulation in selling the station to Terrence was that Terrence keep the repair function as a part of the business. Terrence agreed as long as he would have a mechanic available.

When Terrence took over the business, the mechanic, knowing he was good at what he did and knowing his value to the establishment, made an agreement with Terrence: he would stay as the mechanic if Terrence agreed to pay him, not a wage, but one half of the profit on all repair services. Terrence immediately went along with that idea as there was no telling how much work would actually come into the station and why pay a man by the hour to sit around if there was no repair activity.

Terrence was surprised when he saw the amount of work being done in the gas station garage. There was no doubt that the man was good at what he did and that his reputation was the reason for so many vehicles being brought in for repairs. Terrence made money and so did the mechanic.

Joseph agreed with Terrence and pulled his car into the open bay, leaving the keys with the night manager in the event that it needed to be moved so that the mechanic could have access to the garage.

The trip to Maine was uneventful. All the way north, the men spoke about their enterprises and about Joseph's isolated connection to the Irish Republican Army.

"You know, Joe, if you'd've read the articles I've written for the paper on the struggle in Northern Ireland, instead of just looking for your name in the crime section, you'd see that I've been in favor of a united Ireland, separate from British control," Terrence began as the conversation turned to the issue at hand.

"Well then, maybe you ought to come to our get-togethers at the pub. Right now, I'm just a little bit nervous with the latest purchase of firearms to be shipped overseas. I don't know if I mentioned it, but the weapons are the ones that were stolen from an FBI SWAT van in Tennessee."

"No shit!"

"Yeah, no shit. So, I know the heat's gotta be on high to locate those weapons and retrieve them. The FBI isn't gonna let go until they get their equipment back and put away the people who ripped them off."

"The arms are gettin' shipped out Sunday, right?"

"Yeah."

"So you're here, away from everything and everyone involved; so what's the problem? By Monday morning, it'll be over and done with."

"I'm just not at ease with this whole thing just the same."

"Relax. No one can connect you to the guns. Where is your link? There is none. If you're worried because of the guys you been hangin' around with, don't; there's nothing there. You meet them at a bar and get into a conversation. Who's to say that it's not an investigation you're doin'? Any correlation can be covered by the fact that you were doin' police work 'cause you overheard talk about weapons. Besides that, who's ever gonna suspect you?"

"Yeah, when you say it like that, I guess you're right. I just needed to hear it from someone else; someone I could trust in a situation like this. OK. I won't think about it again. It'll pass and that'll be it. Monday is only a coupla days away. And you're right again—by then we're in the clear."

"So relax. Tell me more about the house you're buildin'."

The next hour passed quickly as Joseph rattled off the ideas he had discussed with the builder about his new retirement home.

* * *

When Terrence walked through the front door of the camp, he could not believe his eyes. *This was a camp? This is a castle,* he thought to himself.

"My own house only has a two-car garage," Terrence said. "Why does a camp need a three-car garage? And get a load a the furnishin's. I thought I had nice things in my home, but this place looks like it was custom designed by an interior decorator for the White House. Have you been supportin' your cousin or does he just make big bucks stealin' legally from people?"

"Oh, geez, I'm glad you said that. He doesn't know anythin' about our business interests. Keep it that way, huh?"

"Naturally. I wouldn't a said anything unless it came from you, first."

"Good. No, he's a crackerjack lawyer and that's how he makes his money. He makes a lot from the looks a things. Wait'll you see his home."

They settled in for the evening and watched some TV while consuming a six-pack of Budweiser.

In the morning, they took a walk to see if any work had been done on Joseph's house. True to the builder's word, the concrete foundation had been poured. Next they went to visit George. The three of them took a ride to Lake Real Estate and spoke with the Realtor about a piece of property for Terrence. Joseph was greeted as if he were a long-lost wealthy relative. Joseph recognized that the wealthy part had a lot to do with it.

"I gotta tell ya," Joseph said to the Realtor, "my friend here does not do business in the same manner as I do. So, don't expect to be overwhelmed with a chunk of cash like before. Terry is more of a businessman than I am."

"I would not be so presumptuous," said the Realtor. "My only purpose is to find something that will fit your friend's needs."

"Good. Whattaya got left on the lake?"

"Let's take a look." With that, he pulled out a map of the lake with the existing homes and homesites. "I do have a nice piece of property four lots away from yours on a small inlet with a natural sandy beach."

"Can we take a look at it?" Terrence asked.

"Of course, we'll take my Explorer," the Realtor answered.

They drove over to the lake and got out of the car. As they approached the lot, Terrence began to smile. "You've got a deal," he said.

"I haven't even told you the price yet," the Realtor stated.

"Yeah, I know. But I don't care. I want this."

Joseph just stood and shook his head as if to say, "For a great businessman you sure don't know how to deal with Mainers."

They returned to the real estate office and, with George's assistance, they made out the paperwork. Terrence gave the Realtor a check and then asked George if they could go see the builder who was working on erecting Joseph's house.

George called Fred on his cellular phone as they drove down the driveway from the real estate office. They agreed to meet at Fred's house as he had an office attached to his garage.

The nine-mile trek to Fred's office gave Joseph ample opportunity to instruct Terrence on how to conduct business with Maine people. It took less than two hours for Terrence to strike a deal, sign a contract, and write out a deposit check. Terrence was excited at the prospect of surprising his wife with their new vacation home. It would be difficult keeping the secret until the house was completed.

"As long as we're in the area," Joseph said to Terrence after they had left Fred's office, "I might as well introduce you to Nancy, the girl I met through my cousin, George, and have been dating sporadically."

"Yeah. I remember you saying somethin' about her."

Joseph asked if he could use Terrence's cellular phone, to which Terrence replied, "You don't even have to ask. Help yourself."

Joseph punched in the numbers on the handset. Nancy picked up on the second ring.

"Hey you, it's me," Joseph said into the mouthpiece.

"Hey, where are you? You sound like you're way off in the distance."

"No. Believe it or not, I'm just about in your back yard. I'm with a friend of mine and I'm using his cell phone. We just came up to see how the building of my house was coming along."

"You gonna stop by and see me?" she said excitedly. "You better not say no!" she demanded.

"Of course. Do you think I'd come all this way and not see you?" he responded.

"Well, I should think not. I'm here. I'll be waiting. By the way, what's your friend's name?"

"Terrence Maloney."

"That's got a nice ring to it. See you when you get here."

They drove to Nancy's house after stopping to pick up a large order of Chinese food, Nancy's favorite. Even if she had already eaten lunch, Joseph knew that there is always room for Chinese food.

They spent the remainder of the afternoon visiting with Nancy. It had been a while since she and Joseph had seen one another, and something seemed to connect between them. It was kind of an electricity, a spark, an energy, which up until now had been better described as "potential" than "kinetic." Whatever it was, both Joseph and Nancy knew that this long distance relationship could not continue as each felt the need to be with the other.

As the conversation became more intimate, Terrence excused himself and took a long walk outside. Even though Joseph and Nancy had not excluded him, he felt somewhat out of place.

Although their passions were aroused, Joseph and Nancy knew that this was not the time. Joseph told her he would be up alone over the next weekend and they could make plans for their future at that time. Joseph asked Nancy if she would mind keeping an eye on his building project at the lake; after all, this, someday, could be their home. She said she would be glad to check on it for him while he was away.

On Sunday morning, Joseph and Terrence locked up the camp and headed back to Boston.

CHAPTER 19

"Smooth as silk," were Seamus's words as he described to Joseph the loading of the nearly seven tons of armament onto the fishing trawler *Sheilagh*.

Seamus was gloating with pride at the Thursday evening meeting in the Irish Pub. Joseph had not had contact with any of the men up to this point in time and he had not heard of any federal raids in which arms were seized.

The first thing Joseph did on Monday morning was to call Terrence at the newspaper to see if he was aware of anything of a similar nature. As the old saying goes, no news is good news.

Joseph had invited Terrence to join him at the meeting but Terrence thought that it would be better if Joseph went alone where the men did not know Terrence as yet. There would be plenty of time to get acquainted later.

When Joseph asked how everything went, Seamus was only too pleased to brag about the successful chain of events leading up to and including the departure of the *Sheilagh*.

"Lad, you woulda loved it!" Seamus began. "Michael drove an eighteen-wheeler truck up to Vermont last Friday evening. He and Ed loaded all of the equipment from the warehouse onto the truck. Ed operated the forklift truck over the loading dock and onto the rig, stacking the heavy boxes of weaponry toward the front.

Once everything was in place, he drove over to the Burlington Spring Water Company and had them fill the rest of the truck's space with cases of spring water. No one from the water company knew what we had on board because all of the crates were covered with canvas. Nearly a third of the truck was bottled water. We did this in case the truck should be stopped for any reason. No one would realize the true nature of the shipment.

"Michael and Ed stayed in the warehouse most all of Saturday. Late Saturday night they started out for Maine, taking back roads across New Hampshire to Kittery so as to avoid any of the weighing stations set up by the state police. We had two alternate routes we could take as we had done our homework over the past few months to determine the best passage. The boys traveled through the night and arrived in the wee hours of Sunday morning.

"Arthur and I stayed in Portsmouth Saturday night and met the truck at the docks on Sunday morning about four o'clock. The *Sheilagh* was fueled and awaiting our arrival.

"The docks were empty at that hour except for the *Sheilagh's* crew. The ship's crane and net were set up to load materials on board from the truck. With all of us workin', we had everything in place before breakfast. I settled up with the ship's captain and they set out to sea lookin' like they were goin' fishin' for the next several days. They certainly had plenty of drinking water for the next several months.

"It couldn't a gone better if I do say so myself. We all separated followin' the ship's departure and returned to the city. Michael brought the truck back to its stall, parked it and was picked up by Ed after we agreed at the docks to get together at the regular time today."

"Have ya had any word on the progress of the ship?" Joseph asked.

"We had a ship-to-shore telephone call last night and all seems to be going well. The Coast Guard showed no interest in the trawler as they look more for incoming boats than those headed out to sea."

"Well, that's a relief. I'm glad that project is finished except for the collecting of the balance due from Sinn Fein."

Once again, Tip was called over to supply drinks for the men. This night, however, the drinks kept on coming in celebration of a job well done.

Not wanting to disappoint Nancy, even though Joseph was tired more from the anxiety of the past week than anything else, he drove the long route back to Maine.

Arriving at her house around midnight, she had been waiting for him with a chilled bottle of wine. He knew this night would be a failure, more or less, as the combination of being tired along with a glass or two of wine could equal only one result: loud snoring on the couch. There was no way he would be able to stay awake, let alone perform any act of passion or sensuality the way he felt right now. He expressed to her his disappointment in not being a great date for the evening. She understood and made up the bed for him in the spare room.

The next morning he awoke late after a wonderful night's sleep. Nancy fixed what she called a hunter's breakfast of pancakes, bacon, eggs, toast, fresh fruit, orange juice and coffee. He was stuffed and thought a walk for the two of them might be in order. Nancy agreed.

They walked throughout the neighborhood. As they walked, they began to talk more about their feelings for each other. They gave some thought to their relationship and what could come of it. Returning to the house, they sat down on the couch and continued their discussion. The more they talked, the more they discovered their desire for oneness. Joseph, casually and without any thought of anything of a sexual nature, began to rub Nancy's back. She got up from where she was sitting beside him and eased herself down in his lap. He, again, began to rub her back. As she sat there, enjoying the feeling of his strong hands gently massaging her, she began to gyrate, pushing herself down further on top of him. He could feel the pressure being applied on that area between his legs. It was only spontaneous that this part of his anatomy would respond.

"Please, Joe," Nancy said softly as she turned and looked into his eyes, "I want you. I want you now."

She got up off his lap and leaned over and kissed him, first on the lips, then on his forehead, then each of his ears. It had been a long time since anyone had kissed his ears with such care. And his memory flashed back to a time so many years ago on Old Orchard Beach when a young teenager tried to put her tongue into his ear. This time was different, however. He did not squirm but instead enjoyed the pleasure this provided. In fact, the more she teased his ear, the more excited he became sexually.

He reached down, unbuttoned, and started to lower the tight jean shorts she was wearing. The problem was not with her trim tummy but getting them down over her shapely hips. He thought to himself, on a scale from one to ten, she was definitely a twelve.

Nancy had never felt so sensuous. It was as though all of her pent-up feelings were suddenly unleashed. She was more desirous of copulation than Joseph ever could have imagined. Perhaps it was animal instinct taking over, especially since she had never had the opportunity to make love with a man before. But her need was so great that she tore at her shorts and panties, her blouse and bra, not wanting to have anything between her flesh and the flesh of the man she so intensely coveted. She was now totally naked.

With hands moving ever so quickly, Joseph removed his clothes with Nancy's assistance while he was still seated on the couch.

Facing him, she climbed on top of him and let his penis slip into her saponaceous cavity. She became frenzied in her momentum as she realized for the first time in her life the pleasure of truly loving someone. It was only by sheer willpower that Joseph refused to release himself to her. His pleasure was such that he wanted it to last longer than the few moments he knew it would endure.

He knew he had lost the battle when he saw her eyes go back under her upper eyelids and she began to shout, "Fuck me! Fuck me!" And she let out a screaming moan when she had reached orgasm and he had ejaculated simultaneously.

The sweat poured off both their bodies as they relaxed from the climax. She refused to move from her position on top of him. She was expecting an immediate repeat performance, not realizing that some time is needed to regain composure and to regroup for another round.

She began to kiss him again and to attack his vulnerable ear; knowing that was a trigger for his sexual affection. Even Joseph was surprised that he was ready within minutes to return to the "battlefield of pleasures."

Their love-making continued well into the afternoon. Joseph was invited to share Nancy's bed. He relocated his overnight bag from the guest bedroom to Nancy's room.

Making their plans, the only uncertainty came about when Nancy had to decide if and when she would leave George's law firm. She enjoyed her work and felt a bonding to the people with whom she was employed.

Joseph said that he did not mind if she wanted to keep on working so long as he could plan on being with her every weekend. After all, he was busy with his own job as well and his hours were not easy on a marriage. He admitted that his first marriage fell apart solely for that reason. It really was up to her if she could cope with the separation for now. At least they would be seeing one another every weekend.

Nancy said that she had made it this far and, even though she had never felt such a satisfaction and a need for an attachment with him and him alone, she was certain that she could convince her psyche as well as her newly discovered carnal appetite that this was for the best.

When Joseph began the return trip to Boston on Sunday, he was not sure if he would be able to keep his part of the agreement as he now lusted for this woman in a way that he never would have believed previously.

CHAPTER 20

Several weeks passed with Joseph making the routine ride to Maine. The best part of his journey was that when he got there he was always in for a surprise from Nancy. She was an unusual woman with some very kinky requests. Now that she had discovered her sexuality, things became very interesting. So, although the ride was routine, the weekends never were.

* * *

Fred's prowess as a builder was reflected in the fact that he could have two crews working at the same time and be able to watch over both. The quality construction being accomplished on Joseph's house and Terrence's house was no less than superb and both men were very satisfied.

As each one neared completion, the question of furnishing each arose. Joseph asked Nancy for her help in choosing comfortable items pleasing to her as well as to him. Terrence finally had to let his wife in on the surprise as he was not an interior decorator and he knew that if *he* made the choices, they would, according to his wife, all be wrong.

Terrence was more than pleased at his wife's reaction to their vacation and retirement home. She relished the thought of being able to have some time with her husband as he worked so many hours in order to be able to pay for the many things they both enjoyed. Her first reaction was disbelief, not because he had bought the land on the lake and had the house built, but because it reminded her so much of the home of her childhood. This one was much larger but the essence was the same.

Upon completion of both projects, the men celebrated in secret. These homes away from home were, in truth, a getaway, a place out of sight, out of reach and out of knowledge of the people with whom they worked.

This celebration included only their closest confidants—business partners, family members and love partners. It was the first time Terrence would meet the Irishmen from the Irish Pub. Likewise, it was the first encounter Seamus and his crew would have with Nancy. Although Joseph had seen Terrence's wife on rare occasions, this would be the first time they would have the opportunity to speak to one another at length. And it was the first time that Roger's wife displayed any signs of jealousy. Once seeing the lakefront vacation homes Roger's friends had built, she could not understand why Roger did not build one for her.

Roger's only comment to her was, "Since when did you ever have any interest in 'doing the woods thing'? You got your castle, only twenty minutes from downtown. You'd go nuts up here. Be realistic."

To which she replied, "That's not the point. It's just that we should have one, too."

Roger refused to respond, not wanting to argue the logic, or lack thereof, with her. For the entire weekend, she did not come out of her sulking, childish mood. Fortunately, with all the activity among so many participants, her disposition did not cast a pall upon the festivities.

The 1950s Appalachian conference held in upper New York State with the heads, at that time, of the leading Mafia families would be an amplified reflection of this ceremony held at Rome, Maine; for here were a handful of gangsters passing themselves off as successful businessmen, a pretense they fully believed.

Joseph's cousin, George, was perhaps the one person most surprised by the guests. It seemed that they all talked in riddles whenever the subject of vocations emerged. He knew that two of them were cops and he knew one of them worked for a newspaper and owned a gas station and he knew that one was in real estate and that another had some connection to fishermen and still another had some affiliation with the military or appropriating military weapons and yet another had business overseas but what kind of business never came to light. And that was all he knew.

It was an odd aggregation of men with seemingly no common thread. Even their wives or girlfriends did not have similar interests. And despite their differences, here they were, all with only one thing besides Joseph that tied them together, their perpetual wealth. How could this group of people, so far beneath George's realm of educated professionals, amass such sums of money? Throughout the night, in fact, throughout the weekend, this one question haunted his every waking hour. It was a question that would remain with him for some time to come.

When the party finally ended Sunday afternoon and all the revelers had departed and all the cleaning chores had been done, Joseph returned to Boston to prepare for the next work week.

Monday promised to be busy as a number of crimes requiring detective expertise were brought to light.

CHAPTER 21

"Joe?" the voice came over the telephone handset in the detective division workroom.

"Yeah . . . Roger? That you?" Joseph responded after having picked up the receiver on the phone outside his office.

"Yuh. Got some info for you. When you get a minute, how about meeting me for a cuppa coffee?"

"Name the place."

"How about that little restaurant by Selmac's Liquors on Dudley?"

"It'll be travel time from my office," Joseph answered as he replaced the receiver in its cradle and went into his office to grab the car keys off his desk.

It took some fifteen minutes to get to the restaurant and to park his car in the only remaining vacant space on the block. It was approximately two-hundred feet beyond the restaurant.

In about a half hour, most everyone would be leaving work for the day and the traffic would be horrendous. The only good thing is that it would free up the congested parking situation, especially in front of the restaurant. Too late to do any good for Joseph who needed a space now.

Going into the restaurant, he saw Roger sipping from a coffee mug at a table near the window at a point farthest from the door.

The place was empty except for a man seated at the counter chomping on a sandwich, which oozed mayonnaise with every bite, and an older couple standing at the cash register about ready to pay their tab. He walked over to where Roger was waiting.

"Hey, whatcha got?" Joseph asked as he sat down across from Roger.

"Order your coffee now, so we won't be disturbed," Roger said in a low voice.

Looking up and over at the counter, he raised his hand to get the attention of the waitress who looked like she just stepped out of a script from a 1940s movie.

Chewing gum in an open mouth, her dyed blond-over-gray hair set in a bun on the top of her head complete with pencil stuck just above her right ear, and a nasal voice resonating at a pitch equal to a Fran Drescher with a Boston accent, the waitress came to the table with a "What can I getcha, honey?"

Joseph ordered a cup of half-and-half and a blueberry muffin.

The waitress seized the pencil from its perch in her hair and scratched down the order on a pad spotted with grease and upon which the ink from a ball-point pen would never have worked.

"Have it for ya in a sec, honey," she said as she turned and walked back toward the kitchen.

"I got word of a huge shipment coming in shortly. I mean to say *huge*," Roger said. "It's a quantity of hashish that shipped aboard a freighter from Pakistan to West Africa and is scheduled to be brought to the States. The DEA has been watching the activity but have no idea as to exactly how much to expect. It seems there's a mole in the crew giving the Drug Enforcement people some details as he can get the intelligence out. They've asked for our help."

"So what's that got to do with us?" Joseph asked. "I mean *us*, not the department."

"It means . . . ," Roger started to say when he noticed the waitress returning to the table with Joseph's order.

"Is there anything else I can get you boys?" she asked.

"No, this is fine. Thank you," Roger said.

"If ya need anything, honey," she said looking this time at Roger, "just holler. My name is Fran."

As she turned to walk away, Joseph nearly choked. "Doesn't that just figure," he said to no one, even though Roger smirked at the comment.

"Anyhow . . . where they don't have any idea as to how much is coming in, there may be an opportunity for us to score a little for ourselves. Even a few 'keys' of hash is worth a considerable amount."

"How the fuck're we gonna walk away with any of what they're bringin' in? Wherever they dock, the place'll be crawlin' with Feds."

"I haven't got it all settled in my mind yet so I don't have better details. The lou called for a task force meeting with DEA-Boston. I've got to be there. As soon as I know more, I'll let you in on what's taking place."

* * *

It was late the next afternoon when Roger called Joseph at the office.

"Get in your car and come out to the house. Have I got some news for you," Roger said.

"Let me get everyone squared away here and I'll be out," Joseph replied.

Joseph made the journey out to Sharon, pulled into the driveway and walked up to the front door. He rang the bell and Roger appeared, opening the door.

"The wife's at her aerobics class so we can talk freely. Come on in," Roger said as he stepped back to allow Joseph space enough to pass through the portal.

They went into the den. Soft music was playing on an AIWA disc system. Joseph sat down on a love seat while Roger took a seat on the recliner adjacent to it.

"This is big," Roger began. "This ship has got to be *the* major supplier of dope in the world. I mean, I've seen stuff come in from Columbia and I had always thought that was the prime growing field for not only coke but quality hash. Here I am, the expert, and I guess I was wrong. The gooks in Cambodia are a big supplier but even that doesn't amount to shit compared to what I learned today.

"As I told you yesterday," Roger continued, "the freighter went from Pakistan to West Africa to off-load a shipment that will be sent through the south of France to Germany and England. Then the ship goes to the South Atlantic and works its way north to the States.

"The next stop will be off the U.S. coast. It is supposed to rendezvous with several fishing boats, one of which is registered in Miami to a company known to be owned by a member of the Mafia. My understanding is that they make stops along the coast outside of territorial waters and link up with contacts from the coastal states. The intelligence DEA received pinpoints five locations. They know that the biggest drop-off is along the Maine coast to suppliers from New England and Canada. The Canadian connection, they feel sure, comes up the St. Lawrence River. The problem with Maine is that there are so many coves along its rocky coast. They're not sure of an exact spot on land. They believe that a secondary drop site will be in Boston and will serve as a distribution center for southern New England. As yet, their details are very sketchy. It seems their mole has not been able to verify anything more. He's on board the ship now and his covert satellite transmissions must be done only as he has the opportunity. Can you imagine what they would do to him if they caught him? Torture is a mild word compared to what he would have to suffer."

"I can't think of anyone wanting to chance working under-cover like that—I don't care how much money I was being paid," Joseph said.

"There's no fuckin' way I would do that either," Roger re-plied. "Anyway, he's got communications with the DEA. I ques-tioned how he managed to get radio equipment on board, but all they would tell me is that it's tiny and was secreted on his person and disguised in his seabag; and because of its size, it's very low power and needs direct aim at the satellite to work. So there is no problem of detection as far as an outgoing signal by anyone on the ship.

"According to what the Agency knows, as soon as the New England drop is to take place, they'll set a confirmation of latitude and longitude and a stealth-type submarine will track them as quickly as it can get to the given coordinates.

"The New England drop is supposed to be the last on their schedule, so I assume the sub will be following the boats heading inland. Canadian officials have been given the same information as we have and are in concert with the DEA efforts.

"DEA is to let us know what to expect, and where, in the city. They're gonna keep us apprised of every move. They don't wanta raid the fishing boat when it hits shore; they want to wait until the stuff has been picked up by the locals. This way, they don't jeopar-dize finding out who the New England dealers are; they wanta put as many of them outta business as they can. The raids will all be done locally. They need the help of the cops because there aren't enough agents to do the whole job themselves. That's where we come in." Roger paused to let everything sink in.

"Go ahead," Joseph said. "I'm followin' ya. What's the plan?"

"We wait at the drop-off location as backups to DEA. When they give the word, we help make the arrests and confiscate the contraband. I don't know, because DEA doesn't know, how they're gonna transport the dope into the city. If it's by truck, we'll have to look for an opportune time to take a share. We'll have to play that by ear. I guess we'll have to play the whole thing by ear no matter how they bring it in."

"Are you sure you wanta take a chance with this? I mean, we've done some risky shit, but this is right in front of the Feds," Joseph asked.

"Hey, we'll see how it looks and decide from there. We don't have anything else goin' for us right now, so let's do some shoppin' around. OK?"

"You're the boss," Joseph said. "I just hope you know what you're doing. Geez, now I'm gettin' ta sound like one a those actors in a 'B' movie. I'll wait for your call. In the meantime, I better get back to work. I've gotta catch up on some cases."

Joseph returned to the office and went over the specifics on cases his people were investigating. He called Jan Ridlon into his office. She had been working on a prostitution ring operating out of one of the city's better class hotels. Through an arrangement with the night clerk, a room was being set aside for use by the ladies of the night. Jan was at the stage to effect seven arrests including that of the night clerk for pandering and being an accessory to prostitution. Joseph wanted to be sure his newest detective had all her facts in place on the affidavit so that there would be no problem in obtaining the arrest warrants. Jan had done a superb job.

Joseph was fortunate. His detectives were good at what they did and in almost all instances never needed any interference on his part. He trusted them and they responded in kind by doing quality work, which generally, resulted in lengthy jail time for the perpetrators.

* * *

Roger's call came in at two o'clock Wednesday morning.

"The ship is just north of Bermuda," Roger said. "The Miami drop has been made and there are three vessels heading in its direction from the peninsula off Annapolis, Maryland. DEA thinks that they're the contacts for the central states. At the rate they're going, it looks like Friday morning will be the target date for Maine. The freighter will be making its rendezvous north of Bangor, but that's all we have so far for a location."

"Any more word on how the stuff'll come into the city?" Joseph asked.

"Nope. Nothin'," Roger answered. "We prob'ly won't know 'til the last minute."

"OK. Well, I'm sittin' tight," Joseph replied as he closed out the conversation.

* * *

On Thursday night, Joseph invited Terrence to the weekly meeting at the Irish Pub. After introducing everyone to Terrence, Seamus gave a soliloquy on his beloved Ireland. He made Terrence feel right at home and, after hearing Terrence's innermost thoughts concerning the Irish Free State and being familiar with some of his newspaper editorials, everyone at the table felt very comfortable with him.

Seamus had no problem bragging about how he had participated in a delivery of arms to the IRA.

Joseph was mildly surprised. After all, *he* knew Terrence, whereas these men had just met him. Then he guessed that it must have been felt that where he had brought Terrence in, he must be an all-right guy.

The table was beginning to get small now that so many people were sharing that space. They decided to move another one of these heavy pieces of furniture and try to couple them together to make one big table. The only quandary was that the tables were round and there would be no way to make them fit. It did not matter. As long as they could reach their drinks, that was all that counted.

Ed Clancy said that the *Sheilagh* had reached Ireland. The call had come in that morning and the weapons had been taken by lorries to a barn where they could be issued to the IRA mercenaries. Everything was better than expected, according to the telephone message. This would now put the IRA on a more equal footing with the British soldiers. This was good news not only for the IRA but for the Irish Pub clan as well. All they waited for now was the final payment to the Cayman bank. They could then split the proceeds according to how each one participated.

Joseph got home about one-thirty in the morning. At three-ten, with less than two hours of sleep, his phone rang. It took him several minutes to awaken enough to clear his mind and to respond more lucidly to the business at hand.

Roger's voice was calling to him from the receiving end of the telephone handset. "Joe? You awake?"

"Yeah, yeah, I hear ya," he said. "What's up?"

"They're here," Roger said.

"Who's here?"

"The ship."

"Will you quit speaking in riddles?! What're ya . . . the ship! The ship's in Maine?" Joseph suddenly shouted.

"Well, not exactly in Maine. It just transferred its load over to two trawlers. One, as expected, has a Canadian registration. The other one's from Maine. The sub has locked onto the Maine boat and is tracking northwest toward Calais. As quickly as I hear anything more, I'll call ya."

"Oh, man," Joseph said. "I was sleeping so soundly and now I've gotta headache. This better be worth it. I'll talk to ya later."

* * *

When Joseph finally decided to get up, his alarm clock showed that it was nine-thirty. The first thing that hit him was his own breath. It smelled of stale booze. At least his headache had disappeared.

He went into the bathroom and brushed his teeth and gargled with a mouthful of Listerine. He hated the taste of that stuff, but it worked.

He took care of his bodily functions, shaved, showered and started to get dressed. As he pulled on his pants, he heard a buzzing sound and realized that his vibrating pager was dancing across the top of his bureau. He picked it up and saw Roger's office number displayed. The pager had gone off while he had been in the shower. Cinching his belt, he crossed the bedroom and noticed the red light flickering on the telephone answering machine. He pushed the message recall button.

"Now, where the fuck are you?" came Roger's voice on the tape. "Call me ASAP." Then there was a click indicating his disconnection.

Joseph picked up the phone and dialed the direct line number to Roger's office at the station. He answered.

"Nice message," Joseph said.

"So, where were you?"

"In the shower. Unlike you, I do take them," Joseph retorted sarcastically.

"We got to get down to the docks in Charlestown," Roger stated. "The shipment is coming in by boat, not by truck. It left Maine about seven-thirty. The DEA will meet us to set up the sting."

"I'll be right in," Joseph said as he hung up the receiver and quickly finished dressing.

Roger was waiting in his car as Joseph pulled into his parking space. He jumped out of his Taurus and into the passenger seat of Roger's car.

"What didja hear?" Joseph asked as Roger tore out of the lot and headed toward Charlestown.

"The boat dropped anchor in a narrow inlet just south of Calais. The water was too shallow for the sub to get in close so they sent two scuba divers in. From their vantage point, it appeared that the boat just sat there for about an hour. With the darkness before dawn, they could not see a hell of a lot.

"They could hear men talking loudly but that was about all. Then at first light, they hoisted anchor and headed north.

"The scuba divers were about to return to the sub and follow the boat until they spotted another boat in a natural cave in the rocks in the inlet behind where the first boat had dropped anchor."

"Why would they bother to do that? Why a second *boat*?"

"Pretty cozy—they must have been watching for the Coast Guard while they transferred the hash from their boat onto the one hidden in the cave. If they got stopped, they could show that their trawler was empty. And if the Coast Guard was watching them, they would follow the trawler north and if the Coast Guard inter- cepted the trawler, it would be found to be empty.

"The divers returned to the sub and reported their findings. The sub stayed underwater until about an hour later when it ob- served the second boat leave from the supposedly empty cave. The boat headed out on a southerly course followed by the submarine. As they approached Boston, it was evident that this would be the drop-off point. What confirmed Charlestown was a short, coded message from the mole on the mother ship. Now you know what I know except that, according to the sub commander, the boat is named *Priscilla's Folly*."

"Well, it ought to be easy enough to spot," said Joseph. "All we have to look for are the dealer's cars as they line up to pick up their portion of the goods."

"DEA will be crawlin' all over the place with the guys I've assigned to be backup. Remember, there are more of us than them."

Roger drove onto the docks and met with the agent-in-charge. Handing Roger a Motorola portable with an earphone attached, the agent said, "Just so we're all on the same wavelength."

"Very clever remark," Joseph mumbled to Roger who gave back a look that implied, "behave yourself."

"This way we won't have any communications problem," the agent continued. "Also, all of my people are wearing dark blue windbreakers with DEA emblazoned in white on the back. Once they get into position to effect an arrest, they will put them on. So, keep an eye out for them."

More than an hour passed before there was a noticeable change on the docks. The first alert came when one of the agents called over the radio that he had made an identification on a male subject driving a late model sports car. The car pulled onto the dock and parked near a loading platform. Within minutes, more men appeared from various places. Men dressed as laborers and dock workers stood by as a fishing trawler, black and white in color, made its way up the channel and over to the dock area where these men had gathered. The name on the back of the boat, *Priscilla's Folly*, could easily be seen as it backed into the slip for docking. A pickup truck and a Chevrolet Blazer soon made their way to the same spot.

As though orchestrated by a well-known, experienced conductor, the men from the ship began to off-load plastic crates, sorting them by number and allocating them to one or another of the vehicles, loading them according to their agreement.

A command was given over the portable radios by the agent-in-charge to close in and take down the suspects. As the order was being radioed, the Boston Police harbor boat made its way up the channel in an effort to block the trawler from making any escape.

Seeing the patrol boat, the captain of *Priscilla's Folly* shouted something and everyone started to scatter.

As quickly as these men moved, they were not fast enough to avoid being surrounded by the agents in their blue windbreakers covering bulletproof vests and accompanied by the Boston Police narcotics team.

Several of the suspects were subdued as they tried to run from the area. Closing in on the men remaining near the trawler, a short burst of machine-gun fire erupted from behind the pickup truck, which was parked nearest to the loading platform. Everyone took cover wherever they could find a barrier as bullets crashed into buildings, barrels, pallets and vehicles.

From on board the trawler, the captain grabbed a MAC-11 machine-gun and began to fire at the men on shore. While he kept the police and the DEA agents pinned down, one of his crew hacked away with one of the boat's fire-axes at the mooring lines on the boat.

Once the lines were cut, the captain turned on the boat's ignition, threw the gear into forward, and gunned the engine, narrowly missing the police patrol boat's bow.

The patrol boat began to chase the trawler even as crew members fired upon it. It was too dangerous for the patrol boat's crew to return fire as it was in line with some of the law enforcement personnel on the docks. On shore, bullets were flying everywhere. The DEA agents had managed to take four into custody and had determined that they were up against five other armed aggressors.

Three of the agents had donned full protective gear and were taking positions, which gave them clear views of the suspects. The man behind the pickup was their primary target. They wanted to get that automatic weapon contained. Every few seconds, the machine-gunner would raise up, fire off a short volley and then duck back down. Watching his cadence, one of the agents raised up just seconds before the machine-gunner. When the suspect lifted himself up to fire, he was greeted with three rapidly-fired shots from the agent's M-16 automatic rifle. Each bullet, as it struck, tore out chunks of skull as it exited from the back of the perpetrator's head. Having nearly removed his head completely from his neck, the only piece of his body remaining above his shoulders was that part of his skeletal backbone, which had supported his cranium.

A suspect who had dropped below the loading dock and was at the edge of the channel water, had been firing a semiautomatic, machine-pistol in the direction of Roger and Joseph who had only their Glock handguns for protection. They, wisely, opted to remain in place rather than try anything heroic . . . or stupid.

With the machine-gunner out of the way, the agents could concentrate on the other shooters.

Speaking to one another on their portable radios, they agreed to focus on this one subject beneath the docks while the Boston narcotics officers fired at the other three men. Like the first casualty, the suspect would pop up, fire a few rounds, and then duck down. All three agents set their sights on the spot where the man would appear. The next time he lifted his head, shots rang out and the man flew backwards as though he had been hit in the chest with a sledge hammer. The impact knocked him back nearly seven feet. There was a splash as his body hit the water in a reverse belly flop.

One shooter, his attention being drawn to this last casualty, turned away from the drug agents just long enough for the narcotics team to hit him with so much lead that his dead body would register an increase in weight of some two pounds. The two last suspects, upon seeing their comrades killed, and themselves being in the most vulnerable of positions, decided that they did not want to play this game any longer. They threw out their weapons, cast their hands in the air and shouted for the agents to stop shooting. They stood up and were also taken into custody.

The *Priscilla's Folly* could not outrun the patrol boat and it was only a matter of time before the captain and crew ran out of time and ammunition. When it was in the clear, the patrol boat fired at the trawler's hull and the trawler began to take on massive amounts of water. One lucky shot, because it was difficult to aim while riding the waves created by the trawler, hit the boat's engine compartment causing the engine to all but stop.

As the patrol boat approached, the captain and crew put their hands in the air in a gesture of surrender. They were, likewise, taken into custody and their trawler was towed back to the dock. Above the loading platform, while the DEA crew brought in transportation for the prisoners, Roger offered to make arrangements to convey the hashish. It was agreed to bring it to the police station for inventory.

As the men started to off-load the last of the hash on the *Priscilla's Folly*, Roger directed Joseph to drive the pickup truck to the station and two other men to bring the Chevrolet and the sports car. Roger radioed for a wagon to come and pick up what was left of the bricks of hashish that were being removed from the trawler. With all of the activity, Roger told Joseph to bring the truck to the opposite end of the docks to where he would meet him with his car. Joseph took off and waited as instructed. When Roger arrived, he opened the trunk and put four of the large plastic containers inside. He then closed the trunk and followed the pickup to the station.

As the clean-up took place on the docks with additional help from the police department and the office of the medical examiner, and as the prisoners were being booked at the station, an inventory was taken and signed for by the DEA chief. The only exceptions, of course, were the four plastic containers in the trunk of Roger's car.

Everyone congratulated one another on a job well done recalling, as cops are prone to do, each and every minuscule aspect—some real, some invented—and then repeating their own individual participation over and over several times. The station was inundated by television, radio and newspaper media wanting details of the raid and shootings.

When Terrence got the word, he could not wait to piece together the actual happenings, which he knew would be accurate coming from his friend and most valuable player, Joseph O'Fallon.

Terrence arrived at the station to gain, firsthand, all the factors leading up to the event. He, along with the rest of the news media, had to wait nearly two hours as Joseph and all of the other officers involved in the raid were being debriefed. This session could have been completed within an hour's time, however no one was allowed to give a press release other than the police commissioner who had to be located and called in to headquarters. Rank has its privileges and being the media star-performer was accorded only to the man in that position.

Once the commissioner finished his spiel, Joseph would leak some of the "left-out" facts to his friend, Terrence, who would not name the source of these significant bits of information. When Terrence wrote his news stories, it always seemed as though he was right on the scene as the action was taking place.

Roger took Terrence aside at one point during the press conference and told him it would be in his best interest to call him back at the station once he finished writing his story.

"What's up?" Terrence asked.

"I have a little something for you but I can't discuss it here. It would prob'ly be better if we could meet at the gas station later tonight."

"I can do that," Terrence replied.

The Westminster Chimes at St. Joseph's Church had just struck the eleventh hour as Roger pulled into the gas station following his receiving Terrence's phone call not twenty minutes earlier. Terrence was inside the station and, on seeing Roger's car pull in, he raised the overhead garage door giving Roger access to an empty bay. Going into the open stall, Roger waited while Terrence shut the open door. The bay was dark to maintain the effect that the station was closed.

"So, whattaya got?" Terrence asked.

"You think you had some good shit outta that cargo we got from down South?" was Roger's question as a reply. "Wait'll ya see what I brought you."

With that, Roger opened the trunk and lifted out the first of the four plastic boxes. "Where can I open this?" Terrence asked.

"Here. Come inta my office. No one can see in."

Roger followed Terrence into the small enclosure and set the box on top of the paper-littered desk. He snapped the seal on the box and opened the cover.

Terrence gave a low whistle as he immediately recognized the quality of the hashish displayed before him.

"Well," Terrence began, "I assume that this is part of the haul taken in the raid. I was too late to catch a glimpse when the drug agents brought it into the police department."

"You got it," Roger replied. "You're gonna hafta destroy these boxes because there's nothin' like them around here. They came in from Pakistan and ya don't need anyone linking you to this haul."

"No sweat! I'll take care of all the details."

Roger helped Terrence unload the remaining three plastic boxes, and move his car out of the bay, while Terrence brought his tow truck in and then hoisted the boxes onto the back of the truck under the canvas that covered the towing rig.

Roger then left to go home.

CHAPTER 22

One Saturday morning, as Joseph stopped by the gas station to fill the tank in his own personal vehicle, he noticed a young girl sitting behind Terrence's desk in the office.

Calling Terrence's attention, he asked, "Who's the babe?"

"Huh? Oh, her?" Terrence replied. "She's a local kid, needed a job. So, I'm having her straighten out my desk."

Looking at the pert, five foot seven inch brunette with soft green eyes, and from what he could see, a very shapely figure, Joseph asked, "Is that all she's straightening out?"

"Hey! What the fuck do you care? I don't tell you how to run your life."

"Hey, Ter, no offense. I'm just givin' ya a little jab. How old is she anyway?"

"She's nineteen. Why?"

"No reason. Just curious. You're not lettin' her see anything she shouldn't see, are ya? And I don't mean your willy-wong."

"What do you take me for? Stupid?"

"No. Just makin' sure. We don't need to let our peckers confuse our thinkin'."

"Man, you let the oddest things bother you."

"Maybe, but I get nervous when someone I need to have ultimate trust in decides he needs a little action on the side."

"Hey! You don't need ta worry about me. I can take care of myself. I've done pretty well without your help over the last few years."

"I guess I can't argue with that. I'll mind my own business . . . at least, until I think it interferes with our business."

"Look. You find any problem like that and you let me know. I've got too much going for me as well to lose it on some chick. OK?"

Joseph just nodded his head and waved good-bye as he turned and left the gas station.

* * *

Not two weeks passed when Joseph again stopped by the gas station. This time it was well after closing. He saw that the office light was still on and illuminated part of the repair bay area. Joseph parked in front of the convenience section of the gas station, went to the front door and knocked. At first, no one seemed to respond. He hammered on the door loudly and within a minute Terrence appeared and unlocked the door but hesitated to let Joseph in.

With a questioning look on his face, Joseph asked, "What gives?"

"Uh . . . I've got some personal business I'm workin' on."

"So, you're tellin' me I can't come in?" queried Joseph.

"Not right now, Joe," Terrence countered.

"Well, when do ya want me ta come back?"

"Just give me about uuuuh . . . a half hour."

"You sure you'll be *done* in a half hour?" Joseph asked.

"Fuck off, Joe, will ya!"

Joseph gave a nasty laugh as he walked back to his car, got in and drove away.

Joseph circled the block and, shutting off his lights, parked where he could get a good view of the front of the gas station.

Within about ten minutes, the office light went off and Joseph could make out the newly hired female employee running from the front door to a car parked at the side of the building. Joseph waited for another ten minutes before approaching the gas station. During that time, he noticed the office light come back on.

This time when he knocked at the door, Terrence greeted him holding a can of Miller Lite in his right hand.

"Come on in, Joe," Terrence called out. "Can I get ya a beer?"

Still smiling, Joseph said, "Naw. Not thirsty. Thanks." And he walked inside the station.

"What are ya grinnin' for?" Terrence asked.

"Oh, nothing," Joseph replied.

"Well," Terrence said. "What's up?"

"Maybe I should have asked you that about twenty minutes ago."

"Are we gonna start that again?"

"Nope. I'm just here checkin' ta see how you're doin' dumpin' the hash."

"I've had ta go easy because that was a hot item in the news," Terrence stated.

"Good thinkin', Ter. You're prob'ly smart in holdin' off for a bit."

"Anything else?" Terrence asked.

"Nope. That was it. I've gotta get going so I can get some sleep. You comin' to Thursday night's meeting at the pub?"

"Yeah," Terrence replied with an animated lilt in his voice, relieved that the subject concerning his newest employee was no longer being pursued.

"Well, I'll see ya then if not beforehand."

With that, Joseph left the station and went home.

* * *

Joseph had tried to keep his promise to Nancy by driving to Maine on the weekends. However, a few managed to slip by with nothing more than a telephone call. He was very apologetic and Nancy seemed to be forgiving. He vowed, not only to Nancy but also to himself, that he would get back on track.

When Friday rolled around, he told his lieutenant that he would not be in to work that evening but would return for his shift on Monday night. Joseph made the all-too-familiar drive to Rome having called Nancy on his cellular phone as he was passing north through Topsfield. She was thrilled to hear that he was actually on his way and she promised him a special treat. Joseph did not dare ask what that might be as he did not want her to think of something so kinky as to be more torture than pleasure.

Since the completion of his camp, they made it a standard practice to stay there rather than at her house.

* * *

On Saturday morning, he and Nancy took a walk around the lake. He had made it a habit to check out Terrence's property for any problems where it was unoccupied most of the time. He knew that with winter coming, Terrence would not be as likely to head north.

Nancy and Joseph drove to Portland where they had lunch at F. Parker Reidy's Restaurant. This had become one of their favorite eateries; they liked the old bank atmosphere it projected with a huge steel safe with an open door on what had been the upper floor just above the table where they were seated; they also loved the teriyaki steak the chef prepared. After lunch they went out for the afternoon on Casco Bay on Joseph's boat. They stayed in town for supper, returning late to the house in Rome.

Climbing into bed, they watched the beginning of a new moon over the lake. The second floor picture window gave a magnificent panoramic view of this section of Belgrade Lakes.

Suddenly, Joseph sat bolt upright in the bed and looked across the lake in the direction of Terrence's house. Seeing a light flicker in an upstairs bedroom, Joseph jumped out of bed, pulled on his clothes, grabbed his gun, and told Nancy he would be right back.

"What's the matter?" Nancy asked, some fear in her voice.

"I think Terrence has company but just doesn't know it yet."

"What do you mean?"

"I just saw some lights moving around in his place."

"Do you want me to call the sheriff's office?"

"Let me check it out, first."

"Be careful!" Nancy commanded.

Before leaving the house, Joseph grabbed a military-style flashlight, which he had owned since his Old Orchard days. It was one of those lights that is angled at ninety degrees just above the battery compartment, has a belt hook on the back, and has interchangeable lenses, one of which is red in color. The red lens allowed for not being easily seen in the dark. Affixing the red lens as he went out of the front door, he turned the light on only as necessary to find his way around the lake through the woods.

The back of Terrence's house had a staircase leading from a second floor deck down to the water. The deck was accessible from both of the upstairs bedrooms. Joseph felt that he could get his best surveillance from the top of the steps.

Gingerly climbing the stairs, he crawled across the deck to a position where he could look into the bedroom in which he had seen the light flicker. As he gazed into the room, the door to the attached bathroom opened spilling light out into the bedroom. He crouched there transfixed as he waited to see who would pass through the open door. He nearly choked as he watched the young girl from Terrence's gas station walk out and cross the room toward the bed stark-naked. She really was beautiful. She had what Roger would have called a nice set of headlights—breasts that were firm and upright and not much more than a mouthful—and a perfectly rounded butt, also firm. As she approached the bed, the covers suddenly lifted and Joseph nearly burst out laughing when he saw Terrence flat on his back. What was comical was that he could not tell which was bigger, Terrence's tummy or his penis.

The girl did not bother to lie down on the mattress but immediately climbed on top of Terrence. Either she was really enjoying herself or she was an exceptional actress who should have been nominated for an Academy Award. Her gestures, gyrations, facial features, and loud moans almost made Joseph want to stop watching this live action performance and race back to bed with Nancy.

Joseph eased himself back across the deck keeping close to its wooden surface so as to prevent his being seen although there was no way Terrence would have noticed him where his concentration was focused entirely on his current pleasure. In fact, Joseph thought, he could have stood up, danced the Irish jig in front of the glass door and neither one of the lovers would have been distracted.

Making his way down the steps, he took the red lens off the flashlight, illuminated his pathway with the clear, bright light and strolled back to his house without any anxiety over being caught.

Nancy greeted him at the door, knowing that he was returning based upon the fact that she could see his flashlight well in advance as he crossed the adjacent properties.

"What was it?" Nancy asked as he came through the door.

"Well, it seems that Terrence is *up*." Joseph's double entendre was not picked up by Nancy as she had not been privy to the clandestine entertainment across the lake.

"Did you speak to him?" she asked.

"No, he was uhhhh . . . deep into some new project and when I saw that it was him, I decided not to disturb his concentration."

CHAPTER 23

Joseph awoke to loud banging on the front door of his house. He had worked the last few nights and had been in a sound sleep after keeping some very late hours. He took a quick look at the clock before getting out of bed. It was just after two a.m.

He mumbled to himself, "Who the fuck can that be at this hour?"

He took his Glock from its holster where it always hung on a hook on the back of his bedside table. It was out of sight in case anyone should ever surprise him—he would have a return surprise for any uninvited guest.

Going down the stairs to the first floor, Joseph crossed to the front door and looked through the security lens in its center only to discover Roger standing outside.

"What're you doin' here at this hour?" Joseph asked after opening the door.

"Just let me in and close the door," Roger answered. "It's cold out here this hour of the morning."

"What's the problem?" Joseph then asked as he opened the door for Roger to come inside.

"That raid with the DEA. Do you recall anyone watchin' us make the transfer to my car?"

"No. Why?" Joseph asked as they stood there in the entryway in the dark.

"'Cause a friend of mine in DEA called me tonight and asked if I knew anything about an investigation being done in our department. I told him no and asked him what he had heard. He said that investigators from the Boston Police anticorruption unit had been in to see the local director and the only thing he was aware of was it's supposed to concern a recent supply of hashish. Now it may not be our division, but unless I miss my guess, ours is the only one that participated in a raid with hash."

"I told ya this one could be dangerous and maybe we shudda stayed out of it."

"Yeah, well, it's done now so what we gotta do is make sure we covered our tracks."

Joseph thought for a minute and then said, "Well, first off, there was no one saw us do the deed. Think about it. They were all busy at the dock. Everyone can be accounted for. On top a that, just remember where we did the transfer—it was at the far end a the dock. There's water on two sides a the pier and there's a twelve-foot wall on the warehouse, next to the driveway going in, that covers two sides of the pier as well. You couldn't even do a surveillance there unless you were across the channel with a high-power set a binoculars. And nothing like that was set up. Also, nothing revealing took place back at the station, so it can't have anything to do with our end. Maybe, just maybe, it's claims being made by the perps themselves. We can counter anything they say as a lie—just tryin' ta burn cops. So, what's your worry?"

"I wasn't worried," Roger said. "I just wanta make sure we're on top a things. If I was worried, it'd show. It'll take a lot more'n rumors, no matter where they originate, to bother me. I've been through so much shit in this department over the years I worked here; and, I learned a long time ago that, if you let them get to you, rumors can kill ya."

"Well, I'm not worried either. I just don't like being caught with my pants down. I'll do some nosin' around as well and see what I can come up with."

"OK," said Roger. "I'll catch ya later. I just didn't know if you'd heard anything and I like to be sure we both know what's goin' on around us."

"So," said Joseph not willing to let go of the original conversation, "what was your reason for comin' here in the middle of the night if you weren't worried?"

"Like I said, I just wanted to be sure you knew what I knew. I didn't want someone from Internal Affairs hittin' you up for answers on somethin' you might not've been aware of. I didn't want them to get to you before I did. That's all."

Joseph thought about Roger's response for a minute before making his final comment for the night.

"OK. Makes sense to me. Go get some rest and I'll see ya later."

Roger let himself out of the house and went home.

* * *

It was a dreary, rainy night in the city when Joseph headed to the Irish Pub. As he pulled up near the front of the building he could see Terrence's truck parked toward the end of the block. The rain was heavy enough to cause a flow of water to rush along the street gutters, carrying with it the accumulation of litter—mostly candy wrappers and small potato chip bags—which seems to gather in between the semi-weekly rounds made by the street cleaners during the early morning hours.

Joseph sat for a moment watching—almost staring—daydreaming as this colorful armada of pilotless, miniature ships aimlessly floated by. Even in the fast-moving, brackish water, there was something here almost tranquil and serene.

When the rain let up a bit, he got out of his car and ran to the pub's front door.

The rainy weather seemed to bring more people in for drinks. Quite a few businessmen who worked downtown would often stop for a brew before returning home for the evening. This night, the pub was packed and the noise level reminded Joseph of the days when he used to hit a place called The Lounge next to Fenway Park following a Red Sox game. It did not matter if they won or lost, the bar would always be full and boisterous as there was either jubilation over a victory or loud bemoaning over a defeat.

The men were in their usual spot with two tables pulled together in anticipation of everyone's arrival. They were all laughing tumultuously although it could not be heard over the din of the other patrons.

As Joseph walked to the tables, Seamus called out to him.

"You're missing some very funny stories, Joseph. Terrence has a great sense of humor. He's had us in stitches here for the last twenty minutes,"

"I'm sure he has. How is everyone tonight?"

Almost in unison, each one answered in a positive mode. Why would everyone not be in a good frame of mind, the long-awaited money from the Cayman Bank had arrived and had been shared among the men who had taken part in the gunrunning to Ireland.

Joseph was the last to arrive. Seamus had waited for everyone to be present before he read a letter given to him by Ed Clancy. It had been sent by Michael O'Rourke, a member of Sinn Fein, and was carried by a courier aboard an Aer Lingus flight that landed in Boston on Wednesday.

"This morning, when I opened my office for the day, I was handed the letter that Seamus is holding," Ed said. "The man who brought it to me is a friend of mine who lives in Larne in the North.

I'm glad you're all here as I wanted Seamus to read it so that all of you would know the status of things on the other side."

With that, Seamus opened the envelope and began to speak. "The letter is coded and somewhat brief. You should all get its meaning as I read it without any explanation. If you have any problem understanding any part, stop me and I will tell you exactly what it implies. The reason for the coding, of course, is only to protect us and the courier.

> To My Family in Boston,
>
> I write to you to let you know that all is well here now. Your gifts to us, including the special heavy clothing, have been very well received as they were needed desperately. All of your cousins here are indebted to all of you for your generosity. They have posted to you a small gift in return and which you should have, by this time, received.
>
> As you know, the fighting in Belfast has taken its toll. For a while it was hard on us as we learned of the deaths of some whom we knew. Over the past weeks we have seen the opposite forces suffer many more casualties and we can relate to their losses.
>
> For now, we send to you our love. Keep us in your hearts and pray the Rosary for us.
>
> Timothy Hennessey

"Timothy was born in Ireland but came to the United States as a young man. He joined the Marines while he was here and learned battle plans and tactics from our military. He is simply letting us know in his letter that he received the arms, ammunition and bullet-proof vests and that they have sent payment in return. He also tells us that even though our side has taken some hits, the Brits have received worse because of what we shipped across. The only part you might not have figured out is 'pray the Rosary.' What he's sayin' is if we get more equipment, they can always use it."

Seamus ordered another round for everyone at the tables and told the waitress to bring three to Joseph so that he could get caught up. Joseph declined as he was still, technically, on duty.

Some of the pub's patrons were obviously feeling no pain and no anxiety over the foul weather as they tried to sing their own version of "When Irish Eyes Are Smiling." It probably would not have been too bad if only one of them would sing at a time, however, when one would begin, they would all join in and the notes were more sour than the lemons used to garnish some of the drinks being served.

Finally, Terrence could stand no more of what he called caterwauling. He stood up and when the next break came between stanzas, he began to sing. At first, when he announced to the men at his table what he was about to do, the men at his tables were ready to burst into laughter as they anticipated some drunken rendition of this age old favorite.

Terrence opened his mouth and out poured the most beautiful and powerful tenor voice the men had ever heard. Luciano Pavarotti had nothing on Terrence Maloney. Within seconds, the entire pub silenced to allow Terrence's musical talent to fill the room. If not for his booming voice, one could have heard a pin drop on the hardwood floor.

When he finished, there was dead silence, then a tumultuous clapping of hands and whistles and shouts of "Encore!"

Terrence raised his hands and silenced the crowd. He then started to sing, again *a cappella*, the words to "Danny Boy."

His singing was so magnificent and so moving that, as he reached the end of the first verse, people had closed in around him and many had tears in their eyes—men and women alike.

Never had the Irish Pub been treated to such an overwhelming experience. Many people asked who this Irish singer was. They wanted to know his name. Several people asked if this was part of the pub's entertainment and when could they expect to hear him again.

Tip, the bartender, came over, stopping in the middle of taking orders and pouring drinks, and asked Terrence if he would consider doing some singing on an on-going basis, to which Terrence declined but did promise to give a "concert" on occasion.

He did sing another song, "My Rose of Tralee," in response to pressure from all the people in the pub, but wanted them to understand that this would be the last one for the evening.

Undaunted and unabashed, no one wanted him to quit after completing the song, so he agreed to end where he began with "Irish Eyes." Only, this time, he invited everyone to join in with him. The biggest difference was that the larger chorus of better voices drowned out those that gave an attempt earlier. All around, it was no longer a problem of cacophony but a rather mellow and pleasingly harmonious blend of utterances.

People in the pub began to buy Terrence drinks by the pitcherful. A few wanted to pull up chairs and join him but he very nicely and firmly negated their overt request.

* * *

It was nearly midnight when Joseph's pager began to vibrate on his belt indicating a phone message was summoning his attention. He glanced at the face of the unit and read the office number for the detective division in his precinct. The number was followed by 911, which meant that it was an emergency.

Walking swiftly out to where he was parked, Joseph called the station on his car cellular phone and spoke with Jan Ridlon. She said his crew was off at a hostage situation on Alexander Street near

Upham's Corner. The details were very limited and his presence was required as soon as he could get there.

He closed the connection and reached down and picked up his revolving blue light. He set it on the dashboard of the car and plugged it into the cigarette lighter. He pulled away from the curb letting the blue flash pierce deep into the darkness of the night. The rain had stopped quite some time earlier as evidenced by the drying of the water on the streets.

Joseph only tapped the electronic siren switch twice at intersections, which showed a bit of activity as he sped to the location given by dispatch. It took less than ten minutes to cross this section of the city. He drove down Alexander Street, picked up the microphone and signed *adam robert*, meaning he had arrived at the scene.

The street was blocked with police cars, marked and unmarked. Neighbors were watching and wondering what was happening.

As he got out of his car, he saw Paul Hoffman crouched with two uniform officers behind an unmarked car. He approached them quickly and knelt down beside them.

"I didn't think it'd take you long to get here," Paul said. "I'll tell ya what we got. The guy inside the brown house over there," Paul pointed to a house on the even-numbered side of the street, "is holding his 'ex' at gunpoint. She lives there and took out a restraining order against him because, according to the copy we got at the station, he threatened to kill her if she divorced him. They been separated for two months. He came over today after being served the order. She heard someone forcing the rear kitchen door and called the cops. It turned out to be him. He got in before the Rapid Response car got here. When they knocked at the door, he fired a shot through the center panel just missing the uniform cop. The guy shouted through the door that he had explosives and if he set them off it would level the neighborhood."

"Do we have any confirmation of that?" Joseph asked.

"No. Not yet. We been tryin' ta get the phone number for the broad but she had it changed to an unlisted one after receiving the threats. We're waitin' for NYNEX to get us that number so we can call inta the house."

"What's the guy's name?"

"Arthur Godbout," Paul replied.

"Has he got a history?"

"Yeah. He's a winner. He beat his first wife until she left him. We have a long record of abuse calls to this house over the last few years. He married this one last year and since then the uniforms've been here at least a dozen times. Same complaint."

"What about with explosives?"

"Naw. This one's a first in that category."

As they crouched, talking, one of the uniform officers ran up with a slip of paper in his hand. There was a phone number written in pencil on its surface.

"This the number for the house?" Joseph asked.

"Yes, sir," replied the young cop.

"Good enough. Thanks." Joseph went back to his car and reached in and took out his portable cell phone. He dialed the number and it rang without being answered. He went back to the other car and asked Paul to turn on the public address mode, which was a part of the electronic siren in the car.

Paul switched the unit to P.A. and handed Joseph the microphone.

"You, in the house, Arthur Godbout," Joseph called through the PA, which caused a reverberation of his voice to echo up and down Alexander Street. "I'm tryin' ta reach you on the phone in the house. Answer it, will ya? I want ta talk with you."

There was some kind of response but it was unintelligible.

Joseph dialed the number once again. Still no one answered. He let it ring without stopping until, finally, Arthur picked up the receiver.

"What the fuck do you want?" Godbout shouted into the mouthpiece. "I got nothin' to say to you cops. Why don't you just get the fuck outta here. 'Cause if you don't, I'm gonna blow the head offa this fuckin' cunt bitch."

"Arthur," Joseph began, "you got nothing to gain and everything to lose if you do something you're gonna regret by lettin' your anger control you. It won't be like last time if you hurt your wife. You stand to be sent away forever if you harm her."

"Harm her?" he responded with an incredulous question. "I'm gonna fuckin' kill her."

"Look, Arthur, is it worth goin' ta jail over some woman? I mean, you can back outta this right now and we can get you some help and you won't hafta spend any time in jail. But you gotta back out now."

"Oh no. I'm not gonna spend any time in some mental institution. I know what you mean when you say you're gonna get me some help. Forget it. I'm not talkin' any more."

"Wait a minute, Arthur. Let me talk to your wife for a second."

"She ain't my wife. She dumped me. So, she ain't my wife. She's nothin' but a fuckin' slut now."

"Well, let me speak to her for a second anyway."

"What for?"

"I just want ta be sure she's OK."

"She's OK right now, but that's not gonna be for long."

Joseph could hear a woman crying in the background.

Turning to Paul and covering the mouthpiece of the phone, Joseph said, "You better get a hostage negotiator down here pronto. I'm no good at this shit. With my luck, if the guy does have explosives, he'll set 'em off and the whole lot of us will go up in a puff a smoke. Oh, and just so we don't get yanked up by the short hairs, ya better get the uniform guys to evacuate these buildings."

"OK, chief," Paul said, somewhat relieved to get out of his crouched position.

Joseph put the phone back to his ear and said, "You gonna let me talk to her or what?"

"You don't need ta talk to her. I told ya, she's OK."

"You know, if I don't talk to her, I'm gonna assume she's dead. And, if that's the case, we're gonna come in and get you."

"I wouldn't do that, if I were you," Arthur replied.

"Why not?"

"'Cause you and all your fuckin' buddies and every fuckin' asshole on this block will be blown to little pieces. I told *you*, or whoever came to the door, that I got explosives. I ain't shittin' ya, and if you want a sample, I'll be glad ta toss some out to ya."

"No. I believe ya," Joseph said. "Ya don't have ta prove anything to me."

Joseph was trying to buy time as he thought to himself, *Now what the fuck do I do?* He wished the negotiator was here now so he could turn the stress of this case over to him letting the negotiator do what he does best.

"Well I'm tired of talking," Arthur said, "I . . ."

"No! Wait a minute!" Joseph interjected. "There's gotta be some way we can resolve whatever it is that's ignited your fuse." *Not such a good choice of words*, Joseph thought. "You don't really want ta kill her. Why throw away your life because a her. Think about it, Art. Don't make the biggest mistake of your life. You kill her, she wins and you lose because she's dead, but you're gonna be in the slammer the rest of your life. She'll be free and you'll be locked away."

"Hey," said Arthur, "What're you? Some kinda shrink? And don't call me Art. You don't know me and I hate that nickname. I don't give a fuck about her, about you or about me. Just like I don't give a fuck about anybody in this neighborhood. Fuck 'em all!" With that he hung up the phone.

Joseph hollered at Paul, "Where's that friggin' negotiator? This cock-sucker's ready to pop his 'ex' and I'm outta stuff ta say."

"They got a hold a one from state police. She should be here shortly."

"She? She? This guy's on a rampage over a woman and they're gonna send a 'she' to try and calm him down? Are they nuts?" Joseph's questions came rapidly as he asked them with a look of incredulity on his face.

"Don't ask me," Paul replied. "I told 'em what we had and they said she was the only one available at this hour."

"I think having *no one* woulda been better than a female at this juncture." Joseph paused and then said, "I've got to think this out." He made his way back to his car, got in and sat there for about ten minutes before returning to where Paul had again crouched next to his car.

"He broke in through the rear door, right?" Joseph asked.

"Yeah. It goes inta the kitchen," Paul answered.

"And she made the call presumably from her bedroom as the hour was late and that would be the furthest point away from the kitchen."

"That'd be my guess."

"Look, somehow you gotta get him back on the phone. I'm gonna try and get inta the house. Maybe I can get the drop on him before he whacks her and sets off his fireworks," Joseph said.

"Are you crazy? Why not wait 'til the negotiator gets here and let's see what she can do?"

"I don't want ta take that chance. My gut feeling is he'll do her in if he talks to a female."

"You're the boss. You do what ya want. I'd just rather have it on someone else's neck than yours."

"I appreciate that Paul. How many uniform guys we got out back?"

"Three."

"Good. I'll have them stand by in case I need them. No sense having too many people in the house at once; any noise could give away that we're in there. Give me your backup gun. I want to tuck it in my shoe." Joseph knew that Paul always carried a very small .380 automatic pistol with him in addition to his assigned, regulation firearm.

Paul gave it to him without question.

Joseph went around to the back of the house and met with the officers who were stationed there. He explained to them what he had in mind and opted to have one of them come in as far as the kitchen in case he needed a quick backup. Freddie Tavares followed Joseph up the steps and through the open door into the kitchen. When Arthur had first burst into the house, he did not want to give his ex-wife the opportunity to escape. He never returned to close or secure the broken door.

The kitchen was in darkness. It took a few minutes for both Joseph and Freddie to adjust to the complete lack of light, unlike the outdoors, which had a partial moon shining.

As they oriented themselves, they could make out the hallway entry directly in front of them between the refrigerator on the left and a counter on the right. They crossed the kitchen floor gingerly as there was vinyl tile there, which could make a crackling sound if caution were not exercised. Beyond that was carpeting, which would conceal any footsteps.

Joseph had Freddie wait inside the hallway about three feet past the kitchen door and about seven feet from the base of the stairs leading to the second floor. The stairs were to the right.

To the left side of the hallway was an entry into the dining room. A dim sheen reflected from the floor suggested that the floor was a polished wood. Just past that, also on the left, was a similar entry to the living room. Both rooms were in darkness except for the streetlights, which filtered in through the unshaded windows.

As Joseph slowly walked down the hallway and looked up the stairs, he could see a night light illuminating the second floor access to the bedrooms. The stairs were unusual in that they curved to form almost a perfect spiral in which the top stair was directly above the bottom stair and ended toward the front of the house. *This must have been built by someone with bucks when this neighborhood had class*, Joseph thought to himself. *Lotta changes over the years.*

Fortunately, the stairs leading up were carpeted with the same wall-to-wall as in the downstairs hall and living room. This would reduce any sound going up the steps. Still, Joseph walked as though they might creak.

He was on the fourth step when he heard the phone ring.

Excellent, he thought to himself as he worked his way to the top of the stairs.

He could see a faint light coming from underneath the closed bedroom door immediately to his left and at the front of the house. It was one of three bedrooms on this floor. Just past that bedroom, again at the front of the house was the second bedroom. The door to this one was open. Down the hallway leading to the back of the house was a bathroom with an open door and the third bedroom. It, also, was in darkness with the door open.

Listening intently, he heard a man's voice coming from behind the closed bedroom door. Unable to make out exactly what he was saying, it was obvious that he was on the phone as there were lengthy pauses in between his speaking.

At one point, the man's voice elevated and Joseph could make out several popular expletives.

Joseph got down into a prone position on the floor and pulled himself along the top of the stairs to where he was next to the closed door. Putting the right side of his face on the carpet, he tried to peek into the room via the gap between the bottom of the door and the threshold, which was not carpeted.

He could see a pair of man's shoes and ankles about ten feet from the door. They were stationary as the man stood near a wide bureau. To the right, he could see a woman's bare feet next to the bed. They were spread apart and tied to each of the two end legs of the bed. She had to be either sitting or lying on its edge judging from the position of her feet.

He could also see a small suitcase between the bureau and the bed. It appeared to be open. He could not tell its contents but guessed it might have to do with the explosives Arthur had threatened to use.

Suddenly, he became aware of something breathing close to his ear. He jerked his head around and discovered a cat sniffing at him. His sudden movement caused the cat to be frightened, jump and run in fear. It clambered across the upstairs hallway and bounced up on top of a table between the bathroom and the front bedrooms knocking a framed picture off the table and onto the floor.

To Joseph, the sound was deafening. He lifted himself up quickly and hugged the wall along the staircase to the left of the bedroom door.

The noise was enough to get Arthur's attention as he yanked the door from the bedroom open and thrust the gun in his hand toward the sound of the disturbance.

He saw the cat and realized the animal had caused the picture to fall from the table resulting in the muffled noise on the carpeted floor. He moved back into the room leaving the door open.

This would probably have been an ideal time for Joseph to make his move. The only problem was, not knowing what Arthur had to trigger the explosives he touted, Joseph did not want to try anything that might make him let go of an activation switch and set off the charge. He had seen in training films that not all explosive devices required timers or push-buttons; some had release mechanisms, which meant that letting the pressure off of a previously pushed button can activate an explosion.

Joseph remained where he was, breathing a quiet sigh of relief. It was short-lived. From his left side came a harsh jab from the muzzle of a handgun being held by Arthur. The gun was pressed up against Joseph's left temple.

"Didn't think I saw you, didja?" the voice of Arthur asked as he now leaned around the corner of the doorway from the bedroom. "Real easy, now. Take your left hand and give me your gun. I see the bulge in your waistband."

Joseph used his thumb and forefinger to take the weapon from its concealed holster and hand it to Arthur.

"Now get up and come inside. You know, you're a fuckin' moron. There was no need a ya comin' in here. Now I'm gonna have ta kill ya. And you thinking my life is a waste? What about yours? You shudda stayed outside." He paused for a moment and then asked, "Anybody else with ya?"

As Joseph started to get up he answered, "Look for yourself. I'm it. They told me I was outta my mind ta come in."

"Well ya shudda listened to 'em. Now it's too late. Didja think you were gonna be a hero or something?"

"No. I just wanted both of you to come out alive. That's all."

"Well, wasn't that thoughtful of ya," Arthur said sarcastically. "Get inside and sit down on the bed next to the bitch. See, I told ya she was fine."

Joseph was taken back as he entered the room and saw Arthur's ex-wife lying naked on the bed, her wrists tied to the two bedposts at the head of the bed. She had a facecloth stuffed in her mouth, secured by a kerchief knotted at the back of her neck. Between her legs was the broken handle of a broom, the splintered end pointing toward her vagina. It was evident that Arthur had not yet plunged the device into her crotch even though he had taken care to separate the fleshy walls of the entryway so that access and torture could be made easier. Beneath the dark patch of hair was a pool of urine. In fear, she must have lost control of her bladder.

"Nice pussy, huh?" Arthur asked. "She decided it was nice enough to share with another guy and give me my walkin' papers. I gave this cunt everything she wanted and this is how she treats me."

The girl started shaking her head and making unintelligible sounds through the gag in her mouth, obviously objecting to what her ex-husband was saying.

Joseph's eyes shifted from Mrs. Godbout back toward Arthur. As Joseph turned in his direction, he glanced into the open suitcase and saw several sticks of dynamite wrapped tightly together with friction tape. A blasting cap was inserted into the center of the sticks with two wires protruding from the top of it. The wires went to a clear plastic box through which Joseph could see a number of dry-cell batteries, a circuit board with a variety of electronic components connected to it, and a wire-type antenna. The sticks of dynamite were leaking nitroglycerin, which was not uncommon; it is the reason most were packed in sawdust when being stored.

Hanging on Arthur's belt was a hand-held transmitter, which looked like a garage door opener, the only difference being a metal guard over the activation button to prevent an accidental pushing of the button.

Had Joseph only known this was what Arthur was intending to use, he could have taken him down and secured the device.

Department policy has always been not to give up one's weapon under any circumstance. Joseph's concern was for the people in the neighborhood and this would have to be seen as an exceptional case. After all, it is not a usual occurrence to have someone threaten to blow up an entire block. It was with that in mind, plus the fact that he knew he had a second weapon, that he allowed Arthur to take his gun.

Downstairs, Freddie listened to the exchange that had taken place over the last few minutes. Not wanting to go against specific orders, he hesitated to leave his position. Finally, he decided to take the chance. He took everything off his gun belt that he thought might make noise. Taking his Glock from its holster, he worked his way quietly up the stairs, stopping at the last few in order not to be seen.

Mimicking Joseph, although he did not realize it, he listened to determine what the perpetrator might be doing. He heard him speaking to Joseph and could tell by the increase or decrease in volume whether or not the guy was facing toward the doorway or away from it.

When it seemed that he was not facing in his direction, Freddie took a careful look into the room, then ducked back behind the wall.

Seeing some motion, Joseph realized that Freddie was in the hall. He now felt better about taking action.

In an effort to distract Arthur, Joseph leaned toward the suitcase full of dynamite and asked somewhat loudly, "Hey, what've you got here, anyway?"

Arthur told him to sit back on the bed, that he would find out soon enough. For just a moment his attention was turned away from the door. It was long enough for Freddie to get up and stand in the opening. As Freddie made his move, the phone again began to ring. Arthur quickly turned and started to swear at the interruption. As he did, he saw Freddie in the open doorway and tried to take aim with his gun. This was a first for Freddie, he had never fired his gun before in the line of duty. His instinct to protect himself took over. Without any more thought than that, he fired his gun before Arthur could line up his weapon on Freddie. The bullet caught him in the lower abdomen. All it did was throw him off balance and cause him to drop his gun as he grabbed for the entrance to the wound. With great determination, he reached for the transmitter on his belt, but not before Joseph leapt from the bed with both arms extended. He slammed into Arthur's midsection where Freddie's bullet had pierced his body, bringing him down onto the floor and forcing blood to spurt out of the open laceration.

Joseph grabbed ahold of the transmitter and ripped it from Arthur's belt as blood squirted into his face and left eye from the impact to Arthur's open wound. He tossed it across the room and told Freddie to take it, but to be careful not to let anything touch the button under the metal guard.

Arthur had a reserve of strength; he pushed up against Joseph nearly throwing him in the air as he cast him aside. He reached around behind himself and tried to grab ahold of Joseph's Glock, which he had slipped into his belt after taking it from him out in the hallway.

Joseph could not believe the power within this man. He knew that some people who are mentally challenged can have superhuman strength but he never would have categorized anger as giving the same results.

As Freddie retrieved the transmitter and carefully protected it, Joseph struggled to regain control while Arthur stood up once again.

Arthur managed to get the gun out of his belt and was bringing it into a firing position when Joseph realized what was happening. Arthur was unaware of the small gun belonging to Paul Hoffman tucked in Joseph's shoe.

Joseph, while still halfway between sitting and standing, reached under his pant leg and gripped the .380. As Arthur started to lower the gun on Joseph, Joseph raised and fired his weapon all in one action. The bullet went straight up through Arthur's jaw and brain and opened a large cavity in the top of his skull spewing red and gray matter all over the ceiling.

Arthur's ex-wife, who had been in a near state of shock over all that *had* and *was* taking place, lapsed into unconsciousness.

"Nice shot," was the only comment from Freddie.

Joseph stood up, took the transmitter from Freddie, and sent him down to get the bomb squad to respond to the scene. He also had him request Health and Hospitals to send an ambulance for Mrs. Godbout and the medical examiner for the deceased.

Joseph remained in the room to protect the scene. While he waited, he untied Mrs. Godbout, removed the gag from her mouth, pulled her up toward the head of the bed to get her legs on top of the mattress itself and her buttocks out of the cold, wet urine she had released, and covered her over with the blanket from the bed. He then retrieved his gun, sat down on the bed next to the still unconscious woman and took out his notebook and scribbled down some of the information regarding this latest incident.

The only person not satisfied with the outcome of this event was the hostage negotiator from state police. She wanted to speak to Joseph's superiors in the worst way. All during his stay in the room, she complained about being prevented from utilizing her expertise in this field and how she could have talked this man out of his killing mission.

It was odd that she never mentioned the fact that on the two occasions she did place telephone calls to Arthur Godbout that in the first call he blew up at her and hung up the phone and in the second he said that he would like to have her join him in the room so he could kill her, too.

When Joseph left the house after all the officials arrived, she accosted him on the street asking him who the hell he thought he was taking everything into his own hands.

Joseph stopped in his tracks, turned and looked at her and simply said, "You know what? You need a man. You can never be one yourself, so why not quit trying." Then he walked away.

It was five o'clock in the morning when he finally got home and retired for the night.

CHAPTER 24

During Joseph's next tour of duty at the station, he pulled aside Tom Dean and asked him for a favor. Where Tom was well-connected with two of the investigators working in Internal Affairs, would he find out if anything was being stirred up involving their division.

"What's goin' on?" Tom asked.

"I really don't know but word has it that one of our divisions is being looked into for a possible violation of departmental policy concerning seized or confiscated drugs."

"What's that got to do with us? We don't have any responsibility in that area."

"Only remotely. Don't lose sight of the fact that some of our business has to do with drug dealers and informants."

"Yeah. OK. I'll see what I can find."

With that, Tom got up from his desk and exited from the office.

* * *

"Boy, they're being cagey with this one," Tom said as he walked through the door into Joseph's private office.

"What's that?" Joseph asked.

"That thing you asked me to do about an internal investigation. I couldn't get them to open up, so my guess is it might have something to do with our district."

"Our district, or our division?" Joseph asked.

"Shit, Joe, it couldn't be our division. We'd know if it had something to do with us and that's ridiculous."

"Yeah. You're right," Joseph said not sounding very convincing to himself let alone to Tom.

Tom said, "I'll keep working on it and if I hear anything more, I'll let you know. He then walked out of the office and sat down at his desk.

Meanwhile, Joseph began to sweat a little bit, wondering to himself where he might have screwed up. He began to recount all of the people and incidents with whom and in which he had participated as far as his money-making interests were concerned.

Two things happened that evening that got his attention. First, Tom had dispatch call him on the radio in order to have Joseph meet him back at the station. When Joseph arrived, he could see that Tom was visibly upset.

"What's the problem, Tom?"

"It's you, Joe!" Tom whispered emphatically.

"Whattaya mean?" Joseph asked.

Again Tom said, "It's you! Your name is the one being bandied about relative to this investigation. Do you have any idea what's goin' on?"

"You know as much as I do," Joseph replied. "I got no idea what's happening. You don't know why they'd be asking about me, do ya?"

"Naw, Joe. Shit, if I'd have heard anything, I'd a told ya. Don't ya have any idea what's goin' on?"

"No, I don't, and that's what's worryin' me."

* * *

The second thing that happened was when Joseph headed home for the evening.

As Joseph drove up the street toward his house, he spotted a familiar looking car in the driveway to the apartment complex, which was some five-hundred feet down the street and on the opposite side from where he lived. What drew his attention to the car was the fact that it was backed into the driveway. As he passed the car, he recognized the registration plate as belonging to the department. He observed two men sitting in the darkened vehicle. The only reason he saw them was because their outline had been highlighted by the streetlight, which illuminated the driveway and which shone through the rear window of the car.

Joseph continued up the street and pulled into his driveway. He shut off his engine, got out of his car, and locked it as he always did upon his return home from work.

He then went into his house and, closing the curtains, he turned on a light in the living room and switched on the television to channel four. Again, following his usual habits.

He quickly walked through the rooms to the back of the house and exited from the rear door onto the back porch and down the five steps that led to the back yard. Jumping the fence, which separated his house from that of his next door neighbor to the right, he swiftly ran across that back yard and continued on the same bearing for three more yards and then walked out to the street. He was well out of sight of the unmarked car, which was now more than eight hundred feet in the other direction.

Joseph crossed the street so that he would be on the same side as the apartment complex. He then walked down the street toward the parked surveillance car and when he was within a distance just out of sight of the car, he ducked down a pathway leading to the rear of the house adjacent to the apartment complex. Once at the back of the house, he went across the back yard and jumped the four foot chain-link fence, which assured privacy by the homeowner from the tenants living in the apartment building. He was fortunate that the few dogs, which lived in the neighborhood, were not aroused by the trespassing through their yards. With the current leash and noise laws, dogs were to be kept inside during the nighttime hours.

The parking lot for the apartment house was full. Joseph worked his way between the cars to the driveway, which led from the parking lot, past the unmarked car to the street. Alongside the building, about three feet away from the brickwork foundation, were a row of shrubs about three feet in height and going the length of the building. Joseph bent down and moving like a man with a serious hunchedback made his way over to where the unmarked car sat with its engine idling. The noise of the engine's exhaust covered any sounds he might make even though he could see that the passenger side window was open to allow the smoke of a cigarette to escape.

As he neared the window, he could hear the men inside the car talking.

". . . but I know he's a cautious guy. If he's making contact with anyone, it'd have to be some place other than at his house," the first voice said.

"They all make mistakes sooner or later. Believe me, I've been doing this work for the past six years and I can tell when someone's dirty. He'll make the same errors the others have done in the past. It's too bad, in one way, because he had a good, clean record. But he must have fucked up somewhere for the administration to have ordered us to watch him. Ever since I've been on this case, I've smelled something rotten. He covers himself pretty well, but still, there's something just not right," the second voice said.

"Have you been able to track anything money-wise?"

"Like I said, he covers himself pretty well. He has an account at Fleet Bank but that hasn't turned up anything unusual. He's got about sixty thousand in savings, which isn't much considering he's been on the job for so many years. He's got a checking account with about twenty-eight hundred in it. He's got no mortgage, as far as I can see, on his house and he doesn't owe anything on his car. There really isn't anything to go on there. Nothing that appears out of the ordinary. Maybe that's why I'm more suspicious of him; he seems too clean. I even checked with his former wife. She lives up in Canada in Quebec City. When I called her, she said she doesn't want anything more to do with him. I figured that would be a good opening so I asked her point blank if he had ever been involved in anything to do with drugs. She said that he may be a bastard in a lot of ways, but he was never dishonest. She was cute the way she called him a bastard. It really wasn't her word; it was more mine. She called him a *bête*, that's the French word for beast. When I asked her what she meant, she said she didn't know what to call him in English. I suggested bastard and she thought that sounded correct. I guess he was hard to live with because she said he was always working. That was my next clue to why I suspect something's not right."

"What's our next step if no one shows up?"

"Well, I really don't expect anyone to show up. We'll just wait until he shuts off the lights and then we'll cancel out for the night."

Joseph thought to himself as he backed away from his hiding place, *Well, I hope you gentlemen have a good long night.*

He returned to his house the same way he came. Once inside, he got ready for bed in the darkness of his bedroom and never shut the downstairs lights off.

Joseph awoke at ten o'clock the next morning following a sound night's sleep. Most people, finding themselves in any position of being spied upon or questioned over even a hint of illegal activity, would probably have spent a sleepless night of anxiety, worry or concern. Joseph's unnatural ability to cope with such things was just a reflection of his capability to deal with stress on the job.

He called Nancy on the phone and said he would be up on Thursday. He needed a break and a long weekend with her was exactly the thing to relax him. She was overjoyed. In the back of her mind was a desire to discuss the possibility of marriage. She knew he was about ready to make a commitment based upon some of his comments over the last several weeks especially. The way he sounded on the phone this morning, she felt his vulnerability was at its most advantageous level.

Shortly after hanging up, Joseph's pager began to vibrate. The phone number on its display window was not one which he recognized. However, as it ended with 911, he knew it had to be someone with whom he worked.

He dialed the number and Roger answered on the first ring.

"Your line was busy so I paged you," Roger said.

"Yeah. I was talking to Nancy. Where are you? I don't recognize the number."

"I'm in a phone booth not too far from my house. I've got some info for you and I didn't want it coming over the station's recorded lines."

"Whattaya got?" Joseph asked.

"First of all, be careful where you go and who you see. You've got company following you night and day. I don't know yet who or what's behind this but I do know I.A. is keeping an eye on you. Even my L.T. got an inquiry to check on anything our division has worked with you. Good thing I'm on top a things or it could've gone beyond me. So you don't have a worry as far as I'm concerned 'cause I'll take care of anything on this end.

"Now, second of all," Roger continued, "in order for me to do this, we're gonna have ta stay sterile. In other words, we contact each other by pager and pay phone. We don't need I.A. linking us together."

"OK. That's a good idea. And thanks for tellin' me, Roger, but I was already aware that I'm being watched. Two guys were on my street last night. I caught a glimpse of them when I went home. So, I put the peek on them and listened in on part of their conversation. They never even saw me sneak up on 'em. So, I've got a heads-up on some a what's going on."

"Good enough. I'll talk to ya later and I'll let ya know what I dig up."

"Thanks, Roger," Joseph said and hung up the phone.

* * *

Joseph called his cousin, George, and told him he was coming up for the weekend. He asked George if he had some time available as he had a legal problem and needed to get some advice.

"How early can you get here on Thursday?" George asked.

"You name the time, I'll be there."

"How about ten o'clock?"

"See ya then," Joseph said and completed the conversation with George by asking to speak with Nancy.

Joseph explained to Nancy that he would see her at George's office on Thursday as he had some business to discuss with him first. So, rather than her taking off both days from work, he suggested that she only take a half-day on Thursday and all of Friday. She agreed.

* * *

When Joseph arrived in Skowhegan at George's office, he began explaining to his cousin how he was under some kind of internal investigation.

"Look," said George, "let me explain something to you before you say too much. I'm in a kind of quandary here—a catch 22—I need you to tell me the problem and if the investigation has to do with some illegal activity for which you are suspected of committing. If there is an actual base for the allegations, then I don't want to know that. If this case goes to court, I want to defend you on my belief in your innocence. OK?"

Without giving Joseph time to respond, George continued, "But if there is no foundation for the accusations being made against you, then I want all the details. Understood?"

"Yeah. OK, George. Give me a minute to think about where to begin," Joseph said.

"Take your time. Do you need some note paper or a pen to help you get your thoughts together?" George asked.

"No, I'll be fine."

"OK. I'm going to step out of the office for a moment. I want to make sure we won't be disturbed and at the same time check on any messages."

"Sure. Go ahead," Joseph said as George got up from behind his desk and went out to his secretary, closing the office door as he passed through.

When George returned some ten minutes later, Joseph had chronicled his story in his mind and was prepared to present it from the beginning to the latest event.

He spoke for nearly two hours with only minor interruptions by George who asked rather broad questions on certain of the details Joseph revealed. They were phrased in such a manner so as not to delve into those specifics which might be incriminating to his client.

Joseph, likewise, was careful in imparting his information in order that he would keep to those instructions given to him by his attorney at the onset of their meeting.

From everything George had to say, Joseph had no problem as there was no *prima facie* evidence on anything which might be construed as factual. There were, as yet, no witness accounts of any wrongdoing. These would be needed to corroborate any of the circumstantial hearsay presently being taken as gospel truth.

George made copious notes and began a file for Joseph, different from the one that recorded his real estate transactions.

Whether George believed all that he heard from his cousin is questionable; after all, he was an observer when Joseph made some very large cash dealings. But, those could be explained or rationalized. For sure, he did not know all of Joseph's business—legitimate or otherwise.

George advised Joseph to keep in touch and to let him know of any new revelations.

Joseph said he would, thanked his cousin, then left for the day with Nancy, who had been patiently waiting at her desk for him to complete his business. Knowing how much time was allotted for Joseph's appointment, she did not want to tackle anything new during the last twenty minutes but opted to relax and concentrate on what tactics she might take for the weekend to accomplish her ultimate desire.

Looking for the right opportunity, Nancy hinted at her underlying hope all during the beginning of the weekend.

She and Joseph went into Portland on Saturday to take the boat out for one last time while the weather was still conducive to being on the bay. They arrived at ten o'clock that morning and, setting out on the water, headed for one of the small, uninhabited islands. Although the air temperature was cool, the water temperature at this time of the year was at its warmest, the underlying sand having absorbed the intense sunlight of the summer.

They dropped anchor just off shore. With no one around, they swam naked for about a half-hour, then scrambled back aboard the boat and the warmth it provided.

Once below deck, Nancy turned on her charm. They made love once again before returning to port.

After eating a very late lunch at their usual spot, they drove to the Maine Mall where Joseph said he needed to look at some computer accessories at Lechmere Sales, but steered Nancy into J.M. Pollack Jewelers where, to her surprise, he asked her to make a choice in engagement rings.

Joseph paid for the ring with cash. The ring was a bit large but with the use of a ring-guard, adjustment-insert, it was made to fit perfectly. Joseph put the box into his pocket and carried it there until they got back to the house.

Once there, Joseph took out the ring and formally asked Nancy for her hand in marriage.

"Oh, Joe," she said playing cute, "I really don't know."

"Fine," he said smugly, "I'll just take it back to the store."

"The hell you will!" she said with a mock anger. "Put that on my finger, now."

She paused as he slipped the ring in place and gave her a peck on the cheek.

"Oh, Joe, it is beautiful. I love you so much. Thank you. Thank you."

"Thank you, Nancy, for being who you are and for being the girl for me. I love you; I really love you."

They set a date just before Christmas. They decided to get married by a priest who was a friend of George and to invite only those closest to them as guests.

A friend of Nancy's would do the catering and help with the decorating. Even though it was months away, the excitement was building within her.

Joseph drove back to Boston Sunday evening. As he crossed the Mystic-Tobin Bridge, his pager began to play its familiar vibration. He saw another unfamiliar number in the display and knew it had to be Roger. He took the second exit leading to downtown and stopped by the parking garage where there was an outside phone. He dialed the number and Roger answered.

"Have I got something interestin' ta tell you," Roger began.

"Yeah? What's that?"

"I told ya I'd do some diggin' and I did. I know who did what and why."

"OK. Tell me what ya got."

"You know Tom Martin?"

"The detective?" Joseph asked.

"The same," Roger replied.

"What about him?"

"He's your problem."

"Whattaya mean by that?"

"He's the one who's been feedin' I.A. with questions about you. He initiated the investigation."

"Any idea why?" Joseph asked.

"You're gonna love this . . . he's jealous."

"What? Jealous of what?"

"All the publicity you get in the *Record* by Terrence."

"And that's it? You gotta be shittin' me!"

"No shit. I spoke with one a his guys; a guy I know real good. He told me how Martin's been bitchin' and moanin' about you. He thinks he got somethin' on you outta that raid at Nathan's Computer Store. You remember, you called him in on those Egyptians, or whatever they were, shop-liftin' those computers. And then you took over the drug find that the uniform officers discovered. He says no one seems to know what happened to that case."

"Fucker should mind his own business. I'm glad you located the source, now I know what I'm up against. What about Nathan?"

"Like I told ya before, he won't say nothin'. He and I got a special relationship. In fact, it was through him I got the lead on who was spookin' ya. Because a Martin's information, I.A. paid him a visit. He almost shit himself he was so scared a burnin' me. So, he kept his mouth shut. By the way, he cleaned out his back room, he now does his business only by orders and he delivers out of his truck. He said that when they started to nose around his storage room, the place was so antiseptic that a drug dog wouldn't a been able to pick up a scent. The kid did good for us. He even claimed the cops were mistaken with their stories. To top that off, he moved all his stuff outta his house. He's growin' it in an underground cellar way at the back of his property. I don't know if I told ya, but he owns several acres and he and a friend built the greenhouse together. He was so paranoid after your visit, he made all the changes and put in video equipment to watch his place. Like I said to ya when we first discussed our business concerning him, he can't afford to pay off anyone else."

"Well," said Joseph, "all I want ta do is get Martin. I'll have ta think a how I'm gonna do it, but mark my words, he'll get a little taste a what he's put me through."

"Well, at least he doesn't know that you're aware a him being the snitch."

"Yeah," said Joseph. "I'm countin' on that. I need him ta think I'm still out there calling him in on anything that involves his sector.

"Hey, Roger," Joseph continued, "thanks for everything. I owe ya big for this one."

"No problem, Joe," Roger responded. "I'll stay in touch."

* * *

During the next several weeks, Joseph intensified his investigative work looking for just the right opportunity to burn Tom Martin.

He did get involved in two major incidents; one had to do with car thefts in which stolen autos were being dumped in Joseph's district after having been stripped clean of all usable parts. Every one of the cars was stolen out of Martin's area.

The cars were all late model, high-price vehicles; the most popular being Hondas, Ford Explorers, and the Lexus. The cars were taken to an unknown location, stripped, and the remaining skeletal frame was somehow being left in rundown sections of Roxbury and Dorchester or in abandoned lots, which once housed commercial businesses or tenements.

The only tip came from a patrol unit in which the driver turned his cruiser to chase a car speeding down Blue Hill Avenue. Calling in the registration plate on the car as he made his U-turn in the middle of the road, the radio response came back indicating that the car was stolen. It took the officer a moment to maneuver his car around so that he could begin the chase. When the stolen vehicle, which was now about a quarter of a mile ahead of the marked patrol car, turned down Glenway Street, the cruiser, with its lights and siren going, narrowed the gap.

As the cruiser turned onto Glenway, the stolen car was nowhere in sight. The patrol officer drove the length of the rather short street to the end and looked up and down the main, connecting street in both directions but the stolen car had disappeared. He retraced his route on Glenway and began to check all the side streets. He searched every driveway but to no avail. He could locate nothing. It was as though the car he was chasing had completely vanished.

There were no people he could ask as the streets were empty except for several parked cars and an eighteen-wheeler truck. The truck was the only vehicle that seemed out of place as there was no one keeping watch over it while it was parked in this neighborhood, which has been an area of a number of thefts. And it was peculiar to have such a truck trying to make a pickup or delivery where this was zoned residential with no commercial buildings.

Being suspicious and alert, the officer took down the truck's plate number. He then discovered that the cab was unlocked. He checked inside and found the truck's registration and ownership papers. He copied down all the information in his notebook.

Checking the rig itself, he found that the overhead door did not have a locking device, yet the door would not open. He made a note of that as well.

The truck was registered to Alliance Auto Services in Dorchester at an address about three miles away. Although the officer knew nothing about the business, he was determined to give them a call and ask why their truck was left open and unattended in this section of the city.

When the officer radioed in that the car had disappeared, two other radio units responded to assist. Before too long, an unmarked detective car also showed up on the scene. The first officer relayed to Detective Jan Ridlon all the details of the chase. Lastly, he told her about the truck parked on the street.

The detective also examined the truck, made some notes and told the officer she would take over questioning the truck's owner.

Looking up and down Glenway Street, Jan could only figure that the truck's operator was either in one of the houses on the street or that he had a problem with the truck and had left to get help.

Once satisfied that the stolen car was, indeed, gone, the responding officers along with the detective went to Dunkin' Donuts for coffee. They were there not more than twenty minutes. Upon leaving, Jan took one more drive down Glenway Street. She was surprised to see that the eighteen-wheeler truck was no longer there. She notified Boston Control by radio to have area cars see if they spot the truck and, if so, to call her.

No luck. The truck had gotten enough of a head-start to be long gone.

Jan now had a strange feeling about the truck and she wanted to pass her concern on to her sergeant when he arrived for duty. Within an hour of Joseph's signing-in for work, Jan stopped at the station. She advised him of the stolen car chase and of the car's disappearance. She then told him about the eighteen-wheeler and its quick exit from the area. He agreed with her gut instinct and asked her what she suspected.

"It wouldn't surprise me to find that stolen car inside that truck, especially where the overhead door would not open and there was no external lock," she said.

"Let's take a look at the garage that owns the truck. Maybe we'll get a clue from that," Joseph said.

They took Jan's unmarked car and drove to a spot near the garage; parking far enough away so as not to be seen, yet close enough so that they could keep an eye on it and have access to it if necessary.

Walking by the garage, acting as though they were talking to one another, Jan looked past Joseph and into the open bay door. The eighteen-wheeler was backed inside. The garage was divided by Sheetrocked walls so that it was impossible to see what else might be inside. It was big enough, judging from the outside of the building, to have held six eighteen-wheelers parked three in the front and three in the back.

They had hoped to get a better view. With no one around, Jan said she wanted to go in and see if she could get some idea of what was stored there. At first, Joseph objected, but then thought she would have a better chance as a female than he would if he was to nose around.

She left Joseph standing outside as she entered the building.

Jan noticed that the truck was backed up to a loading dock, but that the dock was enclosed so as not to allow anyone to be able to see beyond the back of the rig.

Facing into the bay, there was little more than six feet of open space on the left of the truck. This meant that there had to be at least twenty feet of enclosed space on the other side of the left hand wall. To the right of the truck was an open space of about ten feet and two solid doors on the right hand wall. On the other side of that wall there was, perhaps, another ten feet of enclosed space based upon what could be determined by the outside wall of the building.

As Jan walked over to the first door nearest to the rear of the truck as well as the rear wall of the exposed part of the garage, she was about to put her hand on the door knob when it suddenly opened. The startled face of a big, black man greeted her with, "Who da fuck are you? And, what da fuck do ya want here?"

"I'm sorry," Jan began. "I was just walking with my husband and I needed to go to the bathroom. I was hoping there was one in this garage. I know I should have gone before we left the apartment. I thought this door might be a bathroom. Do you have one? I really have to pee." She spoke so rapidly and was so convincing by her flighty-ness, the man believed her.

"Yeah. Dat's da secon' do', da one what's closes' to da street. Where's yo' husban'?"

"He's standing just outside the garage," she said as she quickly trotted to the bathroom, went inside and closed the door.

Taking one look at the filthy toilet, she was glad she really did not have to go. There was no way she would even squat above the seat, let alone sit down on it. She flushed the toilet and ran the water in an equally dirty sink. Taking a paper towel and scrunching it up, she opened the door and gave a big sigh of relief. The man was still standing in the garage.

She thanked him for letting her use the facilities as she walked toward the open bay door and the street beyond it.

Seeing Joseph still standing at the corner of the building, she said rather loudly, "Thank goodness this place had a bathroom. The man inside was kind enough to let me use it just in the nick of time."

Catching the hint, Joseph said, "Well, I hate to say I told you so, but you really shudda gone before we left."

"I know. You're right. You always are," Jan said as they continued to walk down the street.

Once out of hearing distance, Joseph asked, "What did you find out? Anything?"

She told him the layout of the garage from what she could see. "I did manage to get a peek inside that farthest door when the guy came out. There's a shitload of car parts back there and a couple of guys in coveralls, from the reflection I could see off of some chrome on the floor."

"Looks like your gut feeling might be right."

"Where do we go from here?"

"I've gotta get Tom Martin's group involved. I mean the car was stolen out of his district and it's a good possibility it'll be found, at least in part, in this garage. So, it's a joint case with us if we can come up with it."

"I just hate to give it all away," Jan said.

"No. We'll work a deal. After all, it was your idea to check this out and to go inside. Don't worry, even if he doesn't want to share it, he won't have a choice."

After calling in on her cell phone to have a surveillance team watch the garage, they met with the undercover officers and gave them the rundown. Then Joseph and Jan returned to the station.

Joseph dialed Tom Martin's number and he answered on the second ring. "Detective Division, Martin."

"Tom?" Joseph asked.

"Yeah, who's this?"

"Joe O'Fallon."

There was a long silence.

"What can I do for ya, Joe?" Tom asked.

"I got a lead on your stolen cars. One a my detectives found a chop shop in our district and I have a surveillance team watchin' the place. Thought you might like to know and get down here where this is your case."

"Who do ya want me ta work with?" Tom asked.

"Jan Ridlon's the detective. She'll give ya the heads-up on everything."

"Is she there now?"

"Yup."

"Tell her I'm on my way."

"You got it."

"Oh, and thanks."

"Hey Tom, no problem. I mean, you'd do the same for me, right?" Joseph asked.

"Of course," said Tom as he hung up.

Of course, thought Joseph.

* * *

The second incident that Joseph turned over to Tom Martin involved the theft of jewelry from a private home. Again, the theft had taken place in Tom's territory but the items had been fenced in Joseph's area.

Joseph got the lead on this one from one of the people who frequented the bar on Norfolk Street. It was not so much that he got a tip but more that he was approached by a man who offered to sell him a watch. The man said he had seen him in the bar on occasion and thought he might like a deal on a quality watch.

Joseph said he was interested and asked how much. The guy said he could have it for three-hundred dollars cash. Joseph said he didn't have that kind of money to spend on a watch and turned away. The guy quickly ran around to the other side of Joseph, again getting into his face.

"C'mon, man. Make me an offer. I can work with ya, man," the guy said.

"Well, let me take another look at it," Joseph replied.

"Sure, man, sure. Here, help yourself." And he handed the watch over to Joseph. The watch was a Movado. The value, Joseph knew, was somewhere around a thousand dollars.

"It is a nice watch," Joseph said, "but I don't know if it's worth any more than a hundred fifty dollars."

"A hundred-fifty dollars! Man, that's a five-hundred dollar watch. If I didn't need the money, man, I wouldn't be sellin' it. I paid top dollar for that watch, man. I'm willin' ta deal, but I can't give it away, man."

"OK. I tell ya what; I'll go two-hundred dollars but no more. I wasn't really lookin' ta buy a watch. I'm more inclined to try and find a necklace for my wife."

"You lookin' for a necklace? I got a couple since I broke up with my woman. I'll tell ya what I can do. You buy my watch and I'll give ya a great deal on one a these." With that, he took two gold necklaces out of his pocket and showed them to Joseph.

"How much for the long one?" Joseph asked.

"A 'C' note."

"Tell ya what I'll do. I'll give ya three hundred for the watch and necklace. That's it. If ya can do it, we got a deal; if not, you can forget about it." Joseph again turned away and waved for the bartender to bring him another drink.

"OK, man. You drive a tough deal, but OK. You got the dough?"

"Yeah. Right here in my pocket. And I might be interested in that other necklace, but I'll have ta hold off for about a week 'til I get my next paycheck."

"Hey, man, I'm here every week, same day, same time. I'll have it and if ya know of anyone else needs some jewelry, I got just a few pieces left. Ya know, man, like bracelets and earrings. OK, let me see your money."

Joseph pulled three one-hundred dollar bills out of his pocket and exchanged them for the two items. The guy pocketed the money and said, "See ya next week, man." Then the guy left the barroom.

Joseph walked over to the window and watched the guy walk down Norfolk Street. He put down his drink and went out to follow him at a distance. The guy walked as far as the bus stop and waited for the next bus to come along. Joseph went back and got his car and drove to within a hundred feet of the bus stop. The bus was just pulling up as he stopped.

He watched the guy climb on board and he followed the bus for eight stops when the guy finally got off and walked down a side street.

Joseph parked the car, got out, and ran to the side street. Looking down the street, he was in time to see the guy climbing the stairs to an apartment house. Joseph walked down the street and made a mental note of the number to the building.

When he returned to the station, he checked the hot list for stolen jewelry and came up with the two items he had in his pocket. The watch was easy—it had serial numbers to match the missing item. The necklace had no such identification. With this information, he put in a call for Tom Martin, but he had gone home for the night. *Typical eight-hour wooss*, Joseph thought to himself as he considered Tom Martin. He left a message on Martin's voice mail to call him as he had another hot lead for him.

When Tom Martin finally returned the call to him, Joseph turned the information he had over to Tom in total, taking no part in the action himself.

Joseph knew that he would have no trouble convincing Tom Martin to take a third case in Tom's district. Once he set him up, he would burn him bad.

The opportunity came a week later. Joseph had word through Roger, from a reliable informant, that a drug-buy was going to go down in Tom's area. It involved a sizable quantity of marijuana.

Joseph stopped by Nathan's Computer Store and told Nathan he needed a couple of large Baggies of his stash. Nathan, of course, complied. Joseph then went home with his contraband and pulled a thousand dollars out of his closet. In the morning, he would go to the bank and get the money changed to all twenty-dollar bills. He would have the teller put them in an envelope so that his fingerprints would not be on any of them. He would then, using rubber gloves, transfer the money into another envelope and wrap it in cloth so he could carry out his plan without his fingerprints on anything.

The drug-buy was scheduled for the next night at eleven o'clock. It was to take place in an abandoned house on Seaver Street. Joseph took a ride over to the location to scout it out. Once satisfied that he knew how to effect his idea, he went home.

Calling Tom Martin in the morning, after running his errands, Joseph advised him that one of his snitches had given him a lead on a drug-and-gun buy that would take place that night. Joseph said he did not have all the details yet, but was supposed to have exact information later in the day.

Tom appreciated the lead and said he would have his team ready to go.

Using rubber gloves, Joseph took the marijuana he got from Nathan and wrapped it in cloth after he replaced the Baggies with new ones, untouched by his hands. He wanted to take no chances so everything needed to be clean. He then put the wrapped money and pot in a plastic shopping bag he saved from his last grocery purchase at Star Market and placed it in his car.

Joseph arranged to borrow Terrence's tow truck and after picking it up at the garage, he transferred the plastic bag from his car into the truck's cab. Terrence was only too happy to cooperate after hearing about Tom Martin's ploy. Joseph did not want anything to appear suspicious to Tom Martin and, had Martin seen his car in the location of the drug-buy, he might have wondered why it was there as Joseph said he was not participating in this drug/gun deal as it was not in his area.

At nine o'clock that evening, Joseph called Tom back and filled him in on the remaining details saying that his snitch just called and gave the information to him.

"Doesn't leave us much time ta get set up," Tom said.

"No. I know. But sometimes we can't have what we want, can we?" Joseph said more as a statement than a question.

"Yeah. Well, we'll let ya know how we make out."

"Good luck," said Joseph as he ended the call.

Joseph drove the truck over near the location on Seaver Street, managing to arrive prior to Tom and his crew. He parked at the curb in the darkest section of the street, on the opposite side from where the house was located. He had pulled in front of two older model cars, one of which appeared to be abandoned as it had no registration plates, and waited.

Within minutes, two cars drove down the street stopping to let off three men from each car. The cars then drove the length of the street and stopped, pulling into a driveway by an unoccupied house with NO TRESPASSING signs and PROPERTY CONDEMNED signs affixed to the building.

Joseph watched as the two drivers came up the street in his direction. He recognized Tom from a distance and ducked down in the truck's cab so as not to be seen as the men passed by on the other side of the street.

He sat up and looked through the rear window of the truck as Tom and the other driver moved quickly to get into position to watch the location where the buy was to take place. Joseph could see most of the men go inside the building. Two others were outside, making themselves inconspicuous in the driveway by the abandoned house.

About a quarter to eleven, a car drove slowly down the street past the tow truck and turned into a driveway about two hundred feet from where Joseph was parked. It backed out and drove up the street and took a left onto the main drag. A few minutes later, the car again came down Seaver Street, this time it pulled into a driveway across from the abandoned house. Once again it backed out of the driveway and drove up the street to the main road. It came down a third time with its lights off and stopped just past the abandoned house, parking on the street. Whoever was in the car was smoking something as there was a reddish glow, which could be seen through the front windshield. The suspect sat there without making any attempt to exit the car.

Shortly thereafter, an old man could be seen walking down the street carrying a large bag over his shoulder. As he slowly approached the abandoned building, he stopped, picked up something on the sidewalk, and then continued to the driveway of the building where he turned in. He could not have been more than a few feet from the undercover detectives.

The car door opened and a man got out holding an envelope. He walked over to the front steps of the house, stopped, looked around for a moment, tossed his cigarette to the ground and ascended the steps.

The door on the passenger side of the car then opened and a second man got out. He stood by the car for a minute, scratched his head as he looked up and down the street almost as if he was not sure he was in the right place, and then followed the first man up the stairs.

With all eyes being on these three characters, Joseph felt this was the time to make his move. Not knowing if Tom's car was locked or unlocked, he took Terrence's "Slim Jim" from the truck along with the plastic grocery bag. He opened the truck door, which he had heavily oiled that afternoon to avoid any squeaks. He had, also, removed the bulb from the inside dome light so that it would not illuminate when the door was opened. He then closed the door easily and made his way down the street to Tom's car.

He tried all the doors on the unmarked police car but they were locked. Taking the Slim Jim, he slipped it down between the operator's side window and the frame and worked it up and down in several places until it hit the right spot. Lifting gingerly, the door's lock unlatched.

Joseph opened the door and sat inside. He knew the interior light would not go on as all department cars have that disabled as part of the "police package" from the factory. He took the money and marijuana out of the grocery bag and out of the cloth. Still wearing rubber gloves, he placed both under the passenger side seat of the car, wedging them snugly enough so as not to slide out when the car was moving or stopping.

He got out of the car and locked the door before closing it.

Crossing the street, he found a place to hide and waited for Tom and his team to return.

It was a solid twenty minutes before he saw movement coming from up the street. It was not much longer before he could make out the detectives carrying several items and escorting three handcuffed subjects toward the parked cars. As they closed the distance between themselves and the cars, Joseph saw another vehicle coming down the street; he recognized the familiar light bar on the roof of a patrol wagon. Tom must have radioed for a wagon to pick up the prisoners and to meet them at the location of the parked cars. Two of the detectives remained with the car that was parked in front of the abandoned house awaiting a tow to the impound yard.

Joseph watched as the items being carried by the officers were put into the back seat of Tom's car. The prisoners were put inside the wagon, which left, once all were on board, for processing at the station. The old man turned out not to be old at all, but a young man who had tried to disguise himself.

Joseph heard Tom say that he would wait up the street with the other detectives until the flatbed vehicle arrived to take away the impounded car.

Everyone else cleared the scene.

It was nearly a half hour before Tom, the two detectives, and the car were gone from the street. Joseph walked back to the truck and headed over to Terrence's garage.

In the morning, Joseph went to a pay phone and paged Roger. His response was immediate.

"What's up," Roger said without even questioning who had paged him.

"Knew it was me, huh?" Joseph asked.

"Yup," was his response.

"I need a favor."

"Name it."

"I've planted stuff in Tom Martin's car. I did it at that location you gave me for that drug-buy. Somehow, word has got to get to I.A. that he's skimmin' off the top of confiscated evidence. Can you get someone to drop a dime on him?"

"Let me handle it. By this afternoon, he'll be squirmin'. By the way, how did you convince him to go on a drug bust without involving narcotics?"

"I told him it was drugs and guns. I knew he'd bite if it involved guns."

"Nice work."

"Thanks for everything, Roger. I knew I could depend on you."

"Catch ya later."

They hung up the phones.

True to his word, Roger managed to have a reliable informant, known to most of the people in Roger's division, lay out a scenario concerning Tom Martin to one of the detectives assigned to Internal Affairs and who, previously, worked narcotics. The informant's name would not be revealed to Tom; only that it was from a very reliable source.

All of a sudden, there was a shift of heat from Joseph to Tom. Questions were now raised as to why Tom Martin had tried to point a finger at Joseph O'Fallon. Had he been trying to create a smoke screen to cover his own activities?

Hard as he might try later on, Tom could not make a link to Joseph on this, but it did not mean that he did not believe Joseph's hand was involved somewhere.

* * *

Joseph got back to his normal routine now that his concerns were alleviated. As he made his trips to Maine, he enjoyed watching the change of scenery as the seasons brought a variety of colors to the trees and, before long, fine snowflakes began to fall, creating an entirely new landscape.

Joseph's visits with Nancy followed a steady course. Every weekend, without fail, he managed to work his schedule so that they could be together.

The weekend before Thanksgiving, he and Nancy drove to a farm out in the country where they bought an eighteen-pound turkey and a variety of freshly picked apples. He had taken the week off from work. He would do the same in December for his wedding. The fireplace he had built in the camp was finally put to use and was very cozy as he and Nancy often curled up together in front of it while soft music played over the speakers installed all around the living room.

There were only the two of them for Thanksgiving but that was all right. Some day they planned on having a family and then the table would be full. As they spoke about this, following a gourmet's delight of a dinner, Nancy said she had something to tell Joseph; something that she had wanted to tell him since last week. They were again in front of the fireplace, lying on the carpet.

"Is it something good?" he asked.

"You be the judge of that," she answered and went quiet for a few minutes.

"Well are you gonna tell me or make me guess?"

"Hmmm. . . ." she said. "How would you feel about becoming a father?"

"You already know how I feel. What've we been discussing here for the past hour?" Joseph said with a mocking smile on his face.

"I mean now?"

Joseph's face lost its smile and he just looked at her in silence for a moment. "Whattaya mean now?"

"I'm pregnant," she said matter-of-factly.

Almost as though Nancy were speaking in some unknown foreign language, Joseph had the most peculiar look come over him. His eyebrows wrinkled and then relaxed two or three times and he had a stupefied smile begin to form and then stop a few times.

"You're pregnant?" He said it almost in a whisper.

"That's what the doctor tells me."

Then with a shout, "You're *pregnant*! Wow! That's great! I can't believe it. You mean, I'm gonna be a father?"

"For a detective, I'd of thought you'd have figured that part out. After all, one does go with the other," she said sarcastically. "I wasn't sure how you'd react. I hoped I knew you well enough to expect something positive."

"Positive? I couldn't be any more positive. This is wonderful. In a month we'll be married and no one will know anything later on except a slightly premature baby. By the way, did I tell you how much I love you?"

Before Nancy could answer, he said, "I just love you so much there is no way to measure it."

She beamed at his words and reached over across him and kissed him with a heart full of passion.

* * *

Over the weekend following Thanksgiving, Joseph, while walking around the lake, noticed Terrence's girlfriend's car parked in the driveway of Terrence's camp.

Joseph knocked at the door and Terrence looked out of the upstairs window, pulling aside the curtain carefully to see who was at the door. Seeing Joseph, he tapped on the window to get his attention. He then waved at Joseph holding up a hand to tell him he would be right down.

"Hey, Joe, I kinda figured you'd be up this weekend," Terrence said as he opened the door.

"I see you have company, again."

"Again? Whattaya mean, 'again'?"

"Oh, a while back when I was checkin' your place, I saw her up here with you."

"No fuckin' way."

"Yeah, fuckin' way. You don't really want me ta tell ya what I saw, do ya?"

"You didn't see shit!"

"How about your little nymph running across your bedroom from the bathroom wearin' just her birthday suit and then jumpin' on top a your 'leaning tower a Pisa'?"

"What are ya, a friggin' voyeur pervert?"

"No. Like I said, I was checkin' your house and didn't see any car in the driveway but I did see lights going on so I tried to do the neighborly thing and protect your property. I didn't realize what a *huge weapon* was guarding your house."

"Ya know, you're a fuckin' wise ass. I don't know why I like you so much."

"Prob'ly 'cause I can keep my mouth shut and I feed you good stories for your paper."

"Yeah. Prob'ly."

"So, now that I'm here, you gonna invite me in?"

"Sure," said Terrence. "Come on in. Ya might as well meet her."

Terrence introduced his honey to Joseph. She was wearing a very short, sheer negligee top over bright red, brief panties. *She does have a great body*, Joseph thought.

"How the hell did you manage to latch onta that," Joseph finally asked, his curiosity eating at him for months and not caring that she heard what he had to say.

"I think it's my . . ."

Before he could finish, Joseph interjected as the girl, Gloria, smiled, "Don't say your weapon, 'cause I've seen it."

". . .personality." Terrence completed his sentence.

"Right," said Joseph. "That's what I thought."

Terrence told Gloria to get Joseph a cold beer. When she was gone, Joseph said, "C'mon, Terr, what gives? How'd ya land that babe?"

"I told ya, she came inta the gas station lookin' for work."

"Yeah . . . and. . . ."

"I guess we just hit it off. At first I thought it might be money, but she drops her wages on me like I'm workin' for her. I asked her one day what she sees in me and she told me it's my personality. I think she's some kinda groupie. Instead a hangin' around cops, she finds something in my editorials that agree with her. I tell ya what. I don't care what it is, I'm just glad I got it."

"Got what?" Gloria asked, entering the room with two cold Miller Lites and a tray filled with crackers, cheese and chips.

"Got a great doll like you," Terrence replied.

She just smiled as she handed both men their drinks and set the tray down on the coffee table next to where they were standing.

"Why don't you boys sit down?" Gloria asked. "I'll go up and get changed. If you need anything, just holler and I'll get it for you."

With that Gloria left the room and went up the stairs.

"I've gotta tell ya, Terr, she seems like a nice girl. You sure she's only nineteen?"

"Yeah. Hard to believe 'cause she acts older."

"Oh geez," said Joseph. "Let me use your phone and get Nancy over here. I don't want her to think I've forgotten about her and left her out a things."

Terrence handed Joseph a portable cordless phone and Joseph placed the call to Nancy, telling her to come by.

They spent the afternoon together and got to know Gloria.

Joseph and Nancy thought the best thing was just to mind their own business and not comment or draw any conclusions as far as how Terrence lives his life.

* * *

The week before Christmas was rushed as Nancy and her best friend, Anna, worked feverishly to prepare for the wedding. They had set the date for Christmas Eve at seven o'clock. Joseph had thought they would have a problem getting the priest for that time as he had an evening mass. However, the mass was set for eleven that night so that it would end exactly on the stroke of midnight, Christmas. The only promise that Joseph and Nancy had to make to the priest in return for his agreeing to officiate at the wedding was that they would come to that midnight service. It was arranged that the wedding would take place in the church and that the reception would be afterwards at Joseph's house. Joseph's first marriage had ended with an annulment so Joseph was free, technically, to marry again without breaking any church rules. Joseph and Nancy attended several weeks of marriage classes with the priest as that was a requirement of the church.

The time between Thanksgiving and Christmas was the most exciting either Joseph or Nancy had ever enjoyed together. Going out two weeks before Christmas, on a chilly Saturday morning with just a hint of snow in the air, they went looking for a Christmas tree that would fit nicely in Joseph's living room.

Driving into the village of Belgrade Lakes, they found a tree that was just right at the general store next to the little bridge famous for its large population of ducks and that leads from Belgrade to Rome. Purchasing the tree and tying it securely to the roof of

Joseph's car, they could not wait to get it home and set up in place. They stopped at Nancy's house and picked up her tree stand and a variety of lights, which she had bought in anticipation of their Christmas together. Returning to Joseph's house, they spent the whole afternoon trimming the tree.

Responding to a call from Nancy, her best friend, Anna, stopped by to lend a hand and to go over the finishing touches Nancy would want for the wedding reception now less than two weeks away.

CHAPTER 25

Christmas Eve, the wedding, Midnight Mass, Christmas Day . . . all just a memory now. Everything went so well, so opposite the many times when life or fate keeps special events or occasions from going the way they were perfectly planned.

It seemed so recent that all of this took place, yet here it was almost spring. It was difficult keeping the same schedule as before, especially with Nancy in her condition, carrying such a large package in front of her. Even though she needed to have Joseph around on a more constant basis, she tried to keep that feeling to herself.

Meanwhile, Joseph's mode of operation had suffered an interruption when he received a form letter, with his name imprinted at the top, from the Internal Revenue Service. It was an audit to be held in their Boston office in twenty days.

Joseph knew whose handiwork was involved here. No doubt, Tom Martin was trying to destroy him again. Tom was still under a watch by the Internal Affairs Division following a paid suspension from duty while its investigation of him continued.

Joseph could not let go. He needed one more jab at Tom Martin and decided to call Roger for some help after having thought up one final retribution against Tom. He paged Roger from a pay phone and awaited his return call. He had to wait nearly a half hour.

"Shit, I thought you'd never get back to me," Joseph said.

"Well your paging is not always at the most convenient times. It is late and I do have some husbandly obligations to take care of here at home," Roger replied.

"Oops . . . sorry about that. I hope I didn't cause you any *coitus interruptus* or *penis deflatus*."

"Almost. Good thing I have a determined power of concentration. What is it you want, anyway."

"You know the problem that seems to be continuing because of Tom Martin? I have an idea to get him out of my hair for good."

"You're not goin' ta get him whacked, are ya?"

"Shit, no. I'll go just so far with someone and that's all."

"So, whattaya got in mind this time?" Roger asked.

"I need some heroin. Just a small quantity. Just enough to get it into his bloodstream so that if he's tested, it shows positive. Then I'll puncture his arms with needle tracks and make him look like a pin cushion. He'll look like he's been usin' a long time."

"You're shittin' me, right? You're not really plannin' ta do this, are ya?"

"You're fuckin'-A-right I am. Can you get me the stuff or not?"

"I can get you the horse and I can get you a needle. But how do you plan to get it into him?"

"I honestly don't know," said Joseph. "All I do know is that this would be the last straw for him."

"You're right. Joseph, Are you sure you want ta go that far."

"Look at what the fucker's done ta me. Yah, I want ta go that far. This'll end it for sure. If you got any ideas on how ta do it, let me know."

"I'll tell ya," said Roger, "the only thing I can think of is slippin' him a Mickey."

"Well, the guy is a drinker. I know that for sure. When I was watchin' him I discovered that he likes to hit a bar in Dedham 'cause that's far enough away from the station. No one from work goes there. Instead he meets Jim Beam for a little solace. Lately, he's been there an awful lot; I'd say from the pressure he's been under which he caused for himself."

Joseph was well aware of Tom's routine. He established a regular pattern during the week. To be sure of it, Joseph would follow Tom to the bar, wait outside for about an hour, and then go in himself. There was Tom, always alone and always at the same table. Keeping out of sight, he would watch Tom sit and order drinks and, often, talk to himself. Tom never left the bar without being totally inebriated. And, on more than one occasion, Tom, incapable of driving himself home, would sleep in his car through the night.

"I do have something that would prob'ly work," said Roger. "There's a new drug being peddled on the streets. I came across it when I did a raid on a place a while back. It's called Rohypnol. It's primary use is as a sedative prior to surgery. European countries are using it exclusively as it has not yet been approved as an anesthetic in the States."

Little did Roger know that it was destined to become a powerful illegal device, very popular among young men as a means to take advantage of unsuspecting young women. If a guy dropped a tablet into a woman's alcoholic beverage, within a short span of minutes the drug would cause her to become helpless. Her muscles relaxed, rendering her unconscious, and she would have no memory of what was happening. In time, the drug would come to be known as "Roofies" or the date-rape drug.

"If you were to drop one of these tabs into Tom's drink," Roger continued, "he'd go unconscious in minutes and you could follow through with your plan. I've got a few if you want to try them."

"Perfect. That's just what I need. Meet me tomorrow and I'll get them from you. OK?"

"Where do ya want ta meet? At Terrence's garage?"

"Yeah. Good idea. It'll give me a chance to ask him if he's familiar with this drug."

"See ya tomorrow," Roger said and hung up.

* * *

They met at the garage around noontime. Terrence was fascinated with the story on Rohypnol and wondered where it could be bought. He knew a lot of guys who would give anything for something like that. He decided to inquire from some of the people he worked with on the wire services if they had any knowledge of it. It would make a great story if it really worked.

Joseph picked up the three items from Roger: the Rohypnol, the heroin and two brand-new B-D syringes still in their plastic packages.

Joseph waited until Friday when the bar would be full of people. He saw Tom Martin pull up and park in the lot next to the place and then go inside. As before, Joseph waited about an hour and then went into the bar. He took a table in the back, not too far from where Tom Martin was sitting. There were four empty glasses on Tom's table and a fifth one half full. He was not drinking from shot glasses, but from water glasses. What the bartender was doing was not legal. He was allowing Tom to drink beyond the state of drunkenness. The bartender could be found liable should Tom take his car and cause an accident or kill somebody in his condition.

Joseph watched as Tom would, on occasion, put his head down on the table almost as though he were sobbing. For a moment he felt sorry for the detective, but not long enough to make any difference. As the night wore on, the amount of time Tom spent mumbling to himself and lolling on the table top increased.

At one point in time, the waitress did come over and ask Tom if he did not think that he had enough for the night. Tom responded in a growling, slobbering voice that he did not need some young cunt telling him when he had enough. Handing her a twenty-dollar bill, he told her he was sorry for what he said and would she accept that money as an apology. Of course, she would. In fact, if she thought he would keep tipping her in a similar way, she would keep his drinks coming until dawn and he could call her anything he liked.

Joseph ordered the same drink as Tom, requesting a tall glass rather than a shot glass. When it arrived at his table, he took the little foil package of Rohypnol from his pocket and tore it open. He plunked one of the tablets into the glass and stirred it until it dissolved. When he saw Tom again put his head down on the table top, he got up and began to walk over in Tom's direction. No one noticed him as there were other people standing or walking or just too busy with their own conversations.

Brushing by the table, he put down his drink near Tom's right arm and picked up one of the empty glasses that was still sitting there. He kept moving until he was a few feet from the table and then pretended to drink from the empty glass he had picked up. He wandered over to the bar and asked the bartender for a refill. The bartender took the glass, put it into the dirty glass rack, and took a fresh glass and filled it with another drink. Joseph pointed to his table and asked the bartender to have the waitress bring the bill when she had a minute. This would be his last drink for the night. The bartender told him he would make sure she saw him before long.

Joseph returned to his table and sat down. He watched Tom as Tom finally, after a very long time, again sat erect. Taking the glass, which he thought was left there by the waitress, Tom downed his drink in one quick swallow.

Not more than twenty minutes passed and Joseph could see a very profound change come over Tom, even as drunk as he was.

When his head hit the table this time, it was with a loud thump. Joseph got up and made his way over to Tom's table and sat down in front of him.

"Tom?" Joseph asked. "You OK?"

Tom could not even respond. He tried to lift his head but it was no use. He was in another world. Joseph waved for the waitress. When she came over, he asked her how much he had to drink. She became immediately fearful as she did not know who this person was. If he was a Dedham cop, she knew she and the bartender would be in a world of shit.

"Uhhh . . . I don't know. I didn't . . . I haven't been uhhh . . . giving him his drinks. Only just the last couple. I think he must have had some at the bar. I can look when I get his check. Is he ready to leave?" she asked.

"Just get me the check and I'll give him a hand to get him outta here. You know, Dedham's been sendin' in undercover cops watchin' this place. You could be in a lotta trouble if there's one in here to-night. I've seen this guy in here before. I just felt sorry for him and I don't want him ta get rolled if he leaves here like this. I tell ya what. You get the bill and look in his pockets. I'll be a witness that you didn't take any more than whatcha supposed ta. You can hold his wallet here until he wakes up. I'll leave him a note that you got it. OK?"

"Uh. . . .Yeah . . . OK . . . I guess I can do that." She then went away for a few minutes and returned with a tab. "He owes twenty-eight dollars; I guess he had more than I realized."

Sure, Joe thought.

"Well, take a look in his pockets and see what he has," Joseph instructed.

"Aw gee, I don't think I outta be the one puttin' my hands in a guy's pants."

"He ain't gonna know," Joseph said. "Besides, it'll prob'ly be the biggest thrill he's had in a long time."

She giggled. "You're prob'ly right. OK, but you're my witness." She then reached into his front right pocket. He had two twenties there. She also checked his left pocket but that only had a quarter and a set of keys. He had a wallet in his left hip pocket but that was empty, not even a credit card. His right hip pocket had a crumpled up handkerchief.

"Look," Joseph said. "Why dontcha take the two twenties. That'll cover the tab and also your tip. OK?"

"Hey. OK. Thanks," she said as she took and put the money in her pocket.

"Do ya need any help with him?" she then asked.

"No. I seen his car out there. I can get him into it and he can sleep it off."

"Gee, that's really nice of ya."

"Well, like I said, I feel sorry for the guy."

"Hey, you take care. I'll see ya again sometime maybe."

"Yeah, take care," said Joseph as he half-walked, half-carried Tom out of the bar.

Getting Tom's keys out of his pocket, Joseph found the car key and unlocked the door. He sat Tom in the driver's seat and closed the door. Taking the key, he went to the passenger side and unlocked that door and got in. Rolling up Tom's right-hand sleeve, he then took the package with the heroin and the needles out of his pocket. He had brought rubber gloves, a spoon, a small bottle of water and a cigarette lighter with him and poured the powder with a few drops of water into the spoon. He put on the gloves. Heating the base of the spoon with the lighter, he watched as the powder liquefied. He took the syringe and putting the needle into the liquid, he began to draw it up inside the glass tube. Once in place, he found by the light of the flame of the cigarette lighter, a fat vein on Tom's arm into which he jabbed the needle. There was not so much as a twitch from Tom. He squeezed the plunger on the syringe and watched as the liquid emptied out of the tube and into Tom's arm. He then withdrew the needle. Next, he used the same needle and jabbed a line of marks down Tom's arm. Each time he inserted the needle, he did so somewhat roughly so as to leave significant tracks. He had not expected the amount of bleeding that resulted. He reached into Tom's hip pocket, took out a handkerchief and wiped the blood from his arm. Then he took Tom's left arm and made the same inoculations. For some reason the bleeding was not as prolific.

Completing his task, Joseph rolled Tom's sleeves back down and took the syringe and placed it into Tom's left hand, insuring that Tom's fingerprints would cover the surface. He also put Tom's thumb on the top of the plunger. He then put the syringe and the foil, which had carried the heroin, inside Tom's glove compartment and locked it. He put Tom's handkerchief back in his pocket, put his key in the ignition, got out of the car and pushed the button to activate the electric locks. He shut the door. Tom never stirred.

In the morning, Joseph paged Roger and upon his return call, explained to Roger all that he had done. "Let him try and get out a this one," Joseph said. "That stuff'll be in his bloodstream long enough so that when another test is taken, such as the ones he's had to take since that marijuana was discovered in his car, he'll be found to be a user."

Tom never figured out what happened to him. He had no way of explaining anything and so decided to remain hidden away until his suspension was over. He also went to see a doctor about the odd feelings he had been having; his mind was not his own. And he wanted to know what might have caused the odd sores he discovered on his arms.

It could have been like a cat and mouse game, had Joseph decided to keep on playing. However, he thought it might be better just to let things stand the way they were; after all, it would probably become very obvious that Tom Martin was being framed if other irregularities surfaced following Tom's knowledge that he was under surveillance.

Coupled with a newly restored emphasis by the department's Internal Affairs unit to examine more of Joseph's life and activities based upon an indication that he was now being subjected to an IRS audit, as evidenced by an inquiry into his wages by that authority, Joseph actually considered the possibility of an early retirement.

If Joseph put in for his retirement, any Internal Affairs action would cease. Therefore, no criminal prosecution would likely ensue. He knew that the IRS would find nothing. He was too careful in the way he conducted his finances. So, that, for him, was not a worry.

Maybe, just maybe, this idea of leaving the department was not such a bad thought, though. Also, he could see Nancy's need to have him around, especially now. He would wait to see if the heat on him intensified. If it did, the decision would be made for him.

He considered his current assets: the fact that he had two pieces of real estate paid for without any obligation; a tremendous amount of cash from the weekly collections from Nathan Berkowitz and Francesco Gianni; his share of money from the guns sent to Ireland; the money he split with Terrence and Roger in the drugs they managed to unload; and, of course, the value of his boat. He also thought about the income he could expect to receive from early retirement, and what income would not continue from his private dealings.

He knew he could live fairly well with what he had amassed. He also knew that his parents' house, the one in which he had spent most of his life, could be a source of income should he either rent it or sell it.

CHAPTER 26

On August 31st, Joseph took his early retirement. That night, a huge party was held at the Pier Four Restaurant down by Boston Wharf. Several of Joseph's co-workers who had known him most of his career arranged to "roast" him following the dinner.

Some time after the roast, the police superintendent, the commissioner, the chief of the department, the captain of his district and his division lieutenant came forward and presented him with an award: a plaque for his many years of dedication to the Boston Police Department. The plaque had a gold detective's badge in its center and was mounted on a large, highly polished piece of wood with computerized engraving that looked like cursive handwriting. It showed his years of service and a flowery sentence thanking him for his devotion to the department. It was signed by the administration. They also conferred him with a stainless steel Smith and Wesson Chief's Special revolver in a presentation case. Joseph received everything with good humor and with dignified humility.

At the end of the festivities, Nancy told Joseph what a great group of people he worked with as she watched them congratulate him on his retirement. She said it really was too bad that he could not stay involved with them to some degree.

Joseph smiled, but he waited until later to tell her what a tremendous hypocrisy the police department was. He told her not to believe or take too seriously all the accolades that had been bestowed upon him, especially by the administration who did not know him from Adam.

"In fact," he said, "they probably use the same speech and a similar plaque for all outgoing officers—changing only the names and dates to accommodate the event."

Nancy did not realize the bitterness that Joseph had harbored toward his job. She could not understand why he would feel this way when his vocation resulted in such great rewards. After all, what other line of work would have allowed him to live so comfortably based upon his background, education and knowledge? There must be something of which she was unaware. She felt it would be better not to pursue that issue as he had made his decision to leave the source of his internal controversy. He would be able to spend more time with her and their new baby.

The retirement party went very well. All who attended were of good cheer. Perhaps the free-flowing booze had the most significant influence on people's attitude and character. Not too many of the party-goers would have passed a sobriety test when they left, had there been anyone running an intoxilyzer. Boston's "Finest" would have been guilty of the very same thing for which they have arrested many people over the years.

As they left, no one seemed to notice that one lone car remained in the parking lot long after everyone else was gone and the restaurant had closed for the night. The man inside was not a guest at the gathering but had been outside watching the activity. He, too, had been drunk.

* * *

Roger called Joseph in Maine Monday morning.

"Well, I didn't expect to hear from you so soon," Joseph said.

"Naw, I just called to ask if you heard the news?" Roger said.

"What news?" Joseph asked.

"Tom Martin swallowed his gun."

"No! When?"

"Saturday night. They found him in his car in the rear of the parking lot at Pier Four."

"No shit!"

"Yeah. He must've been shit-face polluted. The medical examiner did a blood alcohol on him—he registered a point-three-six. The M.E. found a note in the car. Figured he must have written it during the party cuz the handwriting got progressively worse."

"What'd the note say?" Joseph asked.

"From what I understand, he said he had nothing left to live for. His wife divorced him five years ago. His kids all moved down south with the old lady when she left—they don't even call him on the phone. Now with his job being scrutinized for possible illegalities—all of which he denied—he figured this world held nothing further for him."

"Aw fuck!" Joseph exclaimed and then went silent.

"You OK?" asked Roger.

"Yeah. Shit, I didn't think he would ever go this route. Well, mentally," Joseph rationalized, "I guess he just couldn't take pressure." Joseph paused for a second. "Hey, Roger," Joseph said in a lighter spirit, "thanks for callin' ta tell me."

"Yeah. OK," Roger responded hesitantly, "I'll talk to ya soon. Give my best to Nancy."

"Right," Joseph said and hung up the phone.

Standing alone in the living room, Joseph looked up toward the ceiling at the corner of the room by the front window. Nancy was out shopping with the baby, who was by then a few months old.

"Well, Tom," he began, talking to no one but himself, yet as though some spiritual part of Tom Martin might be present to hear him. "You don't know how much you've just helped me. Without any more of your nosy, interfering bullshit, anything you said about me in the past is gonna die. I just want ta thank you for doin' the right thing." With that he smiled, turned and went for a walk around the lake.

* * *

With summer over for this year, Joseph only saw Terrence on rare occasions at the camp. He stopped up one weekend to make a check of things and Joseph went over to visit him.

"Hi, stranger," Joseph called out as he crossed the property boundary onto Terrence's yard.

"Hey! I haven't talked to you in a while. How's it going?"

"Good. My little girl's growin' like a weed and I've found that I like bein' home, not havin' ta worry about workin' in the real world. This retirement stuff can be addictin'. Nancy's still working, but only part time. She likes her job, but doesn't like bein' away from the baby, so this is how she compromises. How've you been?"

"Couldn't be better. Roger's been keepin' me busy and so has my little extracurricular activity," Terrence said.

"Oh yeah. How's she doin'?"

"Not pregnant. Good thing she's still on the pill, though she's threatened to stop 'cause she wants to have my baby. I keep tellin' her to wait awhile, things are gonna change, but I don't think she still buys that."

"The wife hasn't caught on yet?" Joseph asked.

"Whoa! Don't even say that! By the way, Gloria and I will be up this weekend."

"I'll keep watch."

"Just don't watch too closely."

"Naw, I saw enough of you a long time ago."

"Very funny."

* * *

On Friday night, Joseph saw the lights go on in Terrence's camp. Within minutes, Terrence called to let Joseph know he and his friend had arrived for the weekend.

Around three o'clock in the morning, although no one was aware of it, a car pulled into the roadway to the camps with its lights out. It drove to the far end of the road, away from all the inhabited homes, and parked in the woods out of sight.

The car remained there, virtually unknown to anyone, until the next night. About two o'clock in the morning, when all the camps were in darkness, the car started and left in the same manner in which it had arrived.

* * *

It was noontime on October 4th. Terrence and his wife, Louise, were up for the week. They had a few relatives visiting as was becoming their habit at the end of each summer vacation. Terrence and Louise were alone in the house. Everyone else was out for the day.

At some point, there were six loud explosions originating in Terrence's house. Following that, Terrence's wife came out of the front door and walked over to Joseph's camp. She knocked at the door and waited for a response.

Nancy came to the door. She smiled widely as she greeted her friend. "Hi, Louise. Come on in. I see you have your share of company for the weekend so I really didn't expect to see you."

Louise never smiled; she simply made a statement. "I didn't come to visit, Nancy. I need your help. I think I just killed Terry."

"What? What are you talking about?" Nancy jerked her head slightly. Her smile remained but her forehead was furrowed as though trying to understand an absurd declaration.

"He and I got into a fight. Last weekend I came up in the middle of the night. I had an idea he was screwing around but I didn't want to believe it. He said he was working on a story and would be tied up after he closed the garage for the night. One of the kids wasn't feeling well, so I called the garage but no one answered. Then I called his office at the *Record* and I was told no one had seen him. I then called his daytime manager for the gas station at home and he said Terry told him he was going away for the weekend, but he didn't know where. Something at the back of my mind urged me to call the little girl that's been doing his books. Her brother answered the phone and said she'd gone away for the weekend. I decided this was the only place he might come so I drove up here and watched the house over two nights. I saw that little bitch. I went up the back outside stairs and looked in the window. I watched them fuck for an hour. I almost went in, but decided to wait to confront him and ask him why? Why? Why?

"When we came up this weekend," she continued, "and everyone was out, I went upstairs to our bedroom and I pictured that bitch in bed with Terry and I lost it. I hollered at him while he was downstairs and told him I saw everything he did this past weekend. And you know what he said? He called me a liar! He said I was seeing things! I was seeing things, all right. I saw her playing with his penis; that's what I saw. And I told him what I saw. And I told him I saw him stick it in her. He then shouted at me that I was crazy. I don't know what I said after that.

"I was just about halfway down the stairs when I saw him go into the kitchen and come out with a knife and start up the stairs toward me. I ran back up and went into the bedroom and took his gun out of the night table drawer. He was slowly nearing the top of the stairs and I've never seen him so livid. His face was bright red and both his eyes appeared almost black." She stopped speaking as she looked away from Nancy. Her mouth was still open as though she had been caught between a thought and a comment.

311

"Oh Nancy, it was like being in a horror movie. His mouth was in a . . . sinister . . . grin and his teeth were all clenched. I was scared to death of him. I told him to *stop*, that he was scaring me but he wasn't even listening to me. So, I raised his gun and pointed it at him; I thought he would stop! When he didn't, I started to back up and holler at him but he kept on coming at me and he had that knife held out in front of him. I . . . I really didn't want to do it, but what choice did I have? I squeezed the trigger and the gun exploded and jumped in my hand. I don't know if I hit him or not because he kept on coming. I pulled the trigger again and again until he finally stopped."

"Ohmigod, Louise!" said Nancy, putting her left hand up to her mouth, which was now devoid of any hint of a smile. "You mean you really did kill him?! I thought you were using that as a figure of speech."

"No," said Louise. "He fell backwards going down the top flight of stairs and ended on the middle landing just sitting there with his chin resting on his chest. I called to him but he didn't answer. For a while I was afraid to go down the stairs because that knife was still in his hand. I went down the first few steps and then ran when I got close to him but he never moved. I thought I must have killed him. That's when I thought I'd better come here."

"Let me call for an ambulance and also to the sheriff's office and tell them there's been a . . . an . . . an accident—a shooting in self defense—and I'll come over with you and take a look."

"No!" Louise screamed. "I don't want to go back there while he's still there. Let's wait 'til someone gets here."

"Where is all your company?" Nancy asked.

"They won't be back for awhile."

"Joe's gone into Skowhegan. I don't know how soon he'll be back either."

Nancy went to the phone and dialed 911 and told them there had been a shooting accident and an ambulance was needed and someone had to notify the sheriff's office.

The dispatcher said for her to stay on the line while she notified both agencies.

Nancy blurted out to the dispatcher that it was her next door neighbor and that it was self-defense; her husband had come after her with a knife. She was shaking as she spoke on the phone. The seriousness of what had taken, and was taking, place finally hit her.

It took about twenty minutes for the Delta Ambulance to arrive. They came in on the camp road just after Belgrade Rescue got on scene. The sheriff's deputy was minutes behind both, having traveled from his patrol route in Albion.

Joseph, returning home from Skowhegan, followed the sheriff's patrol car up the dirt road wondering what was happening and fearing that there might have been an accident involving his family. He never anticipated what he was about to see.

As with any accident involving a gruesome death, once the scene has been secured investigators and police administrators are called to the location. In this case, the sheriff, Frank Hackett; myself, the chief of administrative services, the patrol sergeant, Mike Poulin, and two detectives, Kevin Cookson and Gil Turcotte, arrived within minutes of the radio call from the deputy who had responded to the scene of the shooting.

Local news media were on site as state police representatives began to reach this destination, aware only that an incident had taken place in which gunfire was involved.

The sheriff's personnel secured the area with a wide yellow tape upon which was emblazoned the words: SHERIFF'S LINE—DO NOT CROSS. We, the administrative people, along with the detectives, then viewed the crime scene.

Slumped against the wall, which formed the landing for the stairway, four steps up from the bottom floor and nine steps below the second floor, was the deceased. He had been wearing a white T-shirt, which was now drenched with blood. His blue jeans were now more a shiny purple where the blood had mixed with the color of the fabric. Surprisingly, his white Reeboks remained unblemished. Terrence's head rested upon his massive chest above his enormous belly—a grotesque Buddha.

With his arms by his sides, he appeared to be sitting in anticipation of someone descending from the second floor. His right hand

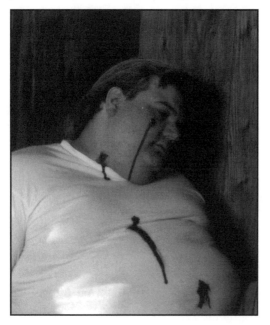

loosely clasped the kitchen knife.

There were five bullet holes in his body: one in the right cheek of his face, one in his neck, one in his chest, one in his belly and one in the area of his genitals.

The handgun was found on a small table next to the couch in the living room. It was a snub-nose, nickel-plated, Smith and Wesson .357 calibre with a six-shot capacity. There were six spent cartridges in the revolver's chamber.

I advised Louise of her constitutional rights before I asked her any questions. And, although I left most of the questioning up to the investigating detectives, Louise was quick to respond often telling me more than what was asked. It became apparent that Louise was very anxious to take the focus off of herself, as she started to implicate her now-dead husband with her next door, ex-cop neighbor.

Her adamancy increased as we discovered numerous illegal weapons in the house—she attributed the ownership to her husband.

As for herself, and according to one of her statements, she did not take much of an interest in firearms, yet the house was filled with a variety of guns—many without obvious serial numbers and several capable of being fired in an automatic, rapid-succession.

Not wanting to be implicated in the guns' ownership, Louise told us that there was a close business relationship between Joseph and Terrence involving these weapons. Of course, because this was all hearsay, there was nothing yet to substantiate Joseph's involvement.

We turned over all the notes that we took in reference to Louise's allegations to the Boston Police.

The guns were confiscated by members of the United States Department of Alcohol, Tobacco and Firearms with the exception of the handgun used in the shooting of Terrence.

* * *

Hardened by his years on the job and because he had been through so many things, mostly unpleasant, Joseph managed to cope with the shooting and the death of his friend.

Later he told Nancy that somehow he expected things to end like this. He would never have wanted this to happen but he just knew what the outcome would be if Terrence continued on his course of self-destruction because of the affair he was having with Gloria.

EPILOGUE

March 1999

A year after Terrence's death, his camp was sold to a friend of Roger's who was interested in coming to Maine.

Joseph maintained his share of the garage, while Terrence's portion was sold to the daytime manager who was able to borrow the funds he needed for the purchase, thanks to a friend of Joseph's at the First New England National Bank.

Gloria went into shock following Terrence's death and began therapy at McLean Hospital in Belmont, Massachusetts. She worked part time as a bookkeeper at the hospital to help pay for her treatments and the job put some cash in her pocket.

Louise was also in therapy with a private psychiatrist—a female. Louise lost her trust in men following her husband's infidelity. No charges were filed against her as the investigators from the Maine State Police, who took over the case from the Kennebec Sheriff's Office, believed her testimony of self-defense. In Maine, only two departments can investigate a homicide other than the state police—the Bangor Police Department and the Portland Police Department.

Roger seriously considered taking his retirement from the narcotics division even though he was still actively absorbed in its work. He continued to maintain close ties with Joseph, both by phone and by occasional visits.

Seamus and the men at the Irish Pub missed seeing Joseph on a regular basis but enjoyed the times when he drove down to Boston or when they went north to Maine. They were always welcome at his home where he has a large Gaelic sign that reads CAED MILE FAILTE—A HUNDRED-THOUSAND WELCOMES.

Joseph and Nancy moved to Webster, New York, with their two children. And for a year or so, he seemed to have escaped further investigation by the Boston Police Internal Affairs Division although a separate anticorruption unit continued to keep an active file on him. The Internal Revenue Service temporarily discontinued its audits due to intervention by Joseph's cousin, George, the attorney. However IRS investigators were not willing to close the case concerning him.

Joseph did not let the possibility of further investigation keep him from enjoying the "good life" as he called it. After all, he would not have all that he did, were it not for the one thing which has kept him going these past many years—a taste for money.

* * *

But Joseph's fortunes changed. The year is 1998. The anticorruption team of the Boston Police Department completed an intense investigation of the activities of Joseph O'Fallon. They, also, have concluded numerous interviews with people who had once been a part of Joseph's files.

Once Roger Gallagher retired from the department similarities were found among those records Joseph kept and the files found in Roger Gallagher's repository in his office in the narcotics division. It was as a result of these comparisons that detectives were able to piece together some of the materials that showed collusion in the commission of crimes perpetrated by these two men.

Both men were arrested. Roger's court appearance has been delayed. His attorneys have asked for continuances to give them more time to prepare an adequate defense. Joseph has had his day in court. He was fined one-hundred thousand dollars, was ordered to pay restitution in the same amount to the Boston Police Department and has been sentenced to four years in state prison. The reasoning for the small amount of restitution is due to the fact that it was impossible to fully determine the exact amount of money which Joseph had stolen either in cash, materials or payoffs.

Because I had been a part of the Kennebec Sheriff's investigators called to the scene of Terrence's death, I was intrigued by the unfolding story of this rogue cop. I read court and department records, personally interviewed Joseph's first wife, and other people that knew him, as well as Roger and the other's involved in various stages of his life. They were able to fill in the details of Joseph's life, before and after he became a dirty cop. I went to the places he had lived and visited so that I could see what he saw in order to trace his steps. Even with my connection to the Boston Police Department, I did not know Joseph, but knew the streets and knew the department. Joseph declined to talk with me from prison.

I have changed the names of some of the principals for obvious reasons.

Joseph will probably serve only two years in prison based upon the workings of the judicial system. When he is released from incarceration, he will have more than a million dollars left from his years of preying upon other criminals.

Who says that crime does not pay?

About the Author

Peter Mars is a native of Brookline, Massachusetts. His undergraduate studies in criminal justice and police science were accomplished at Northeastern University. He has a master's degree in public administration from Columbia where he is completing his Ph.D.

Photo by Michael Glover

Mars was a Boston-area policeman for twelve years before moving to Maine where he continued in police work as chief of administrative services for the Kennebec County Sheriff's Office.

In 1997 he took an early retirement in order to write of his experiences in law enforcement. In 1998, Commonwealth Publishing released his first book, *The Tunnel*.

He recently completed his third book, *The Key*. The story is based on actual events in the life of a police officer who believed in the criminal justice system until it failed to work for him. The adventure mystery takes the reader from Arlington, Massachusetts to Attica State Prison in New York, to Tarpon Springs, Florida and eventually to Grand Cayman Island before reaching its surprising conclusion.

Mars lives with his wife, Margery, in a small town in south central Maine.